Valianara

David Catuhe

In the same series :

I - Menilmonea
II - Valianara

DAVID CATUHE
MENILMONEA
THE CYCLE OF THE TITANS
BOOK ONE

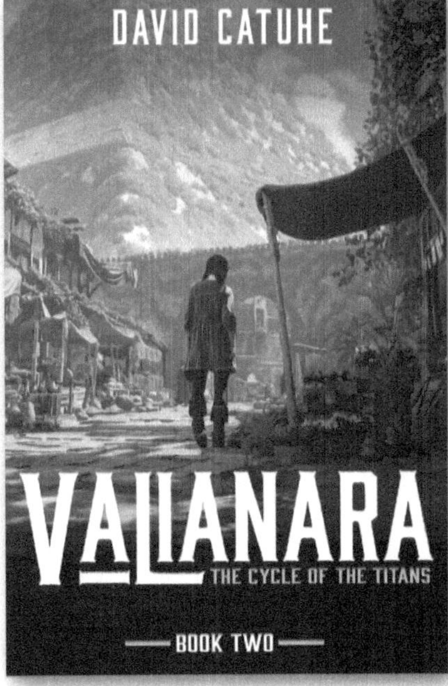

DAVID CATUHE
VALLANARA
THE CYCLE OF THE TITANS
BOOK TWO

Experience the story of Valianara in the best possible way!

All illustrations from this book are also available as high-resolution images and may be downloaded free of charge using the following link, also embedded in the QR code below.

https://www.davidcatuhe.com/product-page/
valianara-illustrations

(All illustrations are entirely handmade by a real human being without any use of AI.)

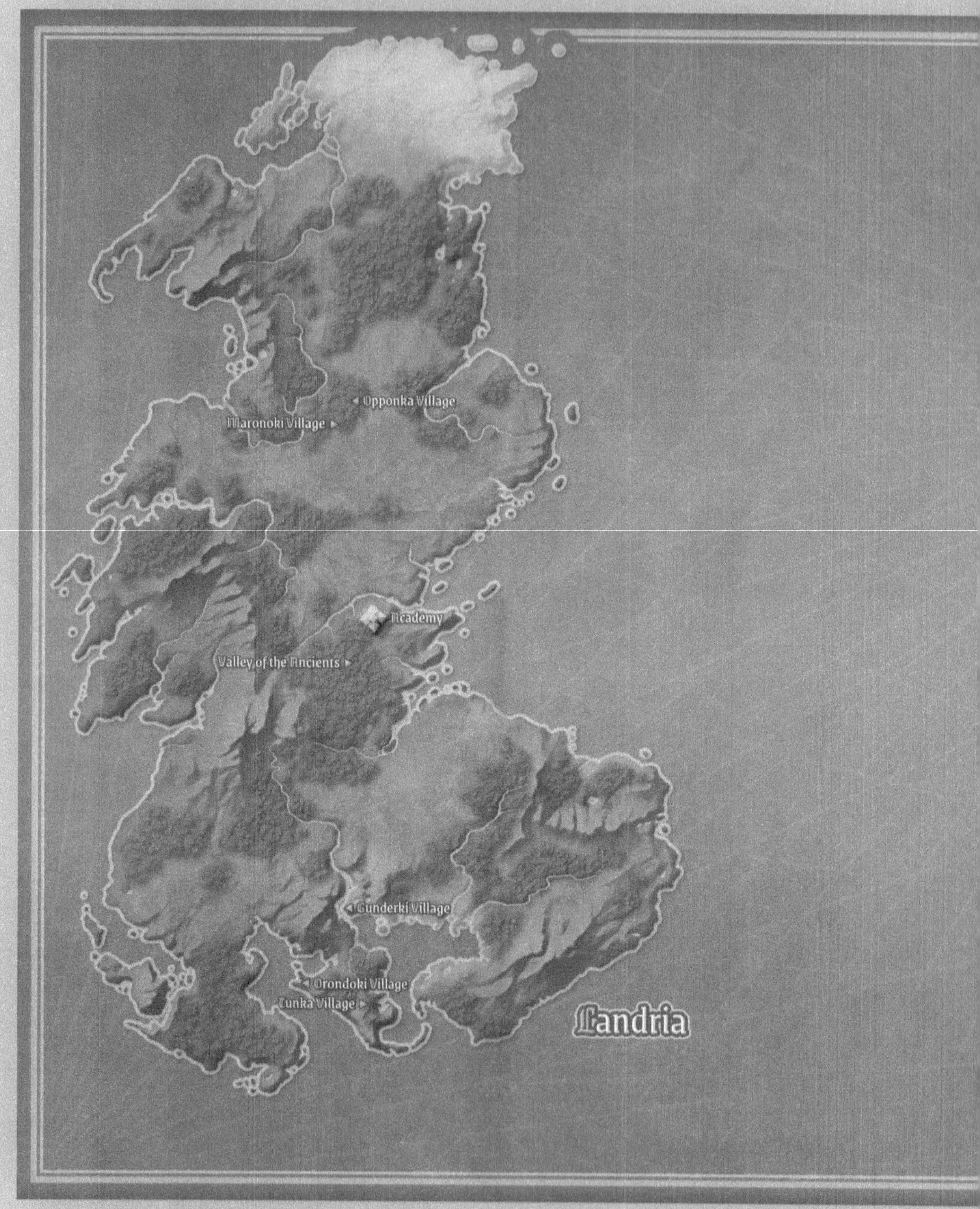
Opponka Village
Maronoki Village
Academy
Valley of the Ancients
Gunderki Village
Orondoki Village
Tunka Village
Landria

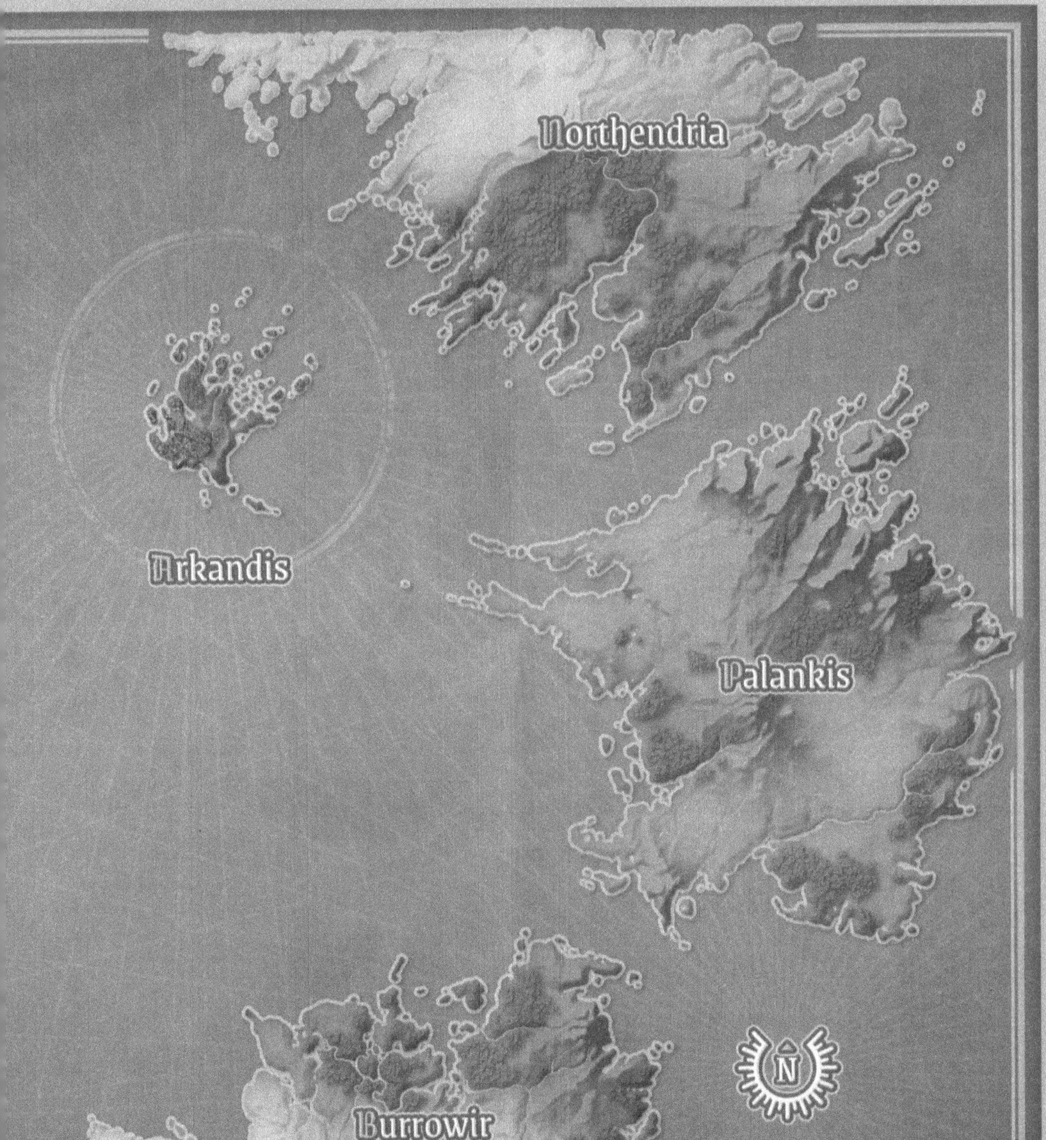

Northendria
Arkandis
Palankis
Burrowir
N

I

Arkandis / The Day Before the Breaking of the Pact
1,400 rotations prior to the Death of Tunka

Azymantias was watching the rain beat against the windows of his study as he murmured, "This is a fine night to bind my soul to a jar."

A sparkling laugh rose from the back of the room. Breaking free of the gentle hypnosis of the raindrops falling onto the forecourt below, he turned to face his guest.

"Rain has the power to soothe pain."

"Indeed, it does," she said. "But I doubt it can do much for you."

It was a soft voice, imbued with age-old wisdom. It belonged to General Avamar of the Fourth Legion and had done so since time immemorial. Outside, the downpour intensified slightly.

"No one can, my dearest. The dice are cast. All we can do is hope that the pawns I've spent centuries placing will topple just as I've predicted."

"That's what I so love about you, Azy. That poetic side of yours is surprising, coming from a mage of the First Circle."

He stepped closer to the leather armchair where Avamar sat and stooped down to kiss her forehead. She continued with a faint smile on her lips, "That sentimentality is no doubt what compelled you to sacrifice yourself for a cause that many would consider dubious."

"There's nothing dubious about it. The Magisterium is dying. You know that as well as I do."

"I just wish I were as convinced as you are. I know we've been through this dozens of times, but I can't stand not being in control of the situation."

"I can't risk Obinaelle becoming suspicious of you. This all rests on your shoulders. The less you know, the less you expose yourself to her scrutiny."

Avamar frowned. "I don't see how she could suspect me! I'm going to betray you and turn you in, after all."

"You know how she is. She's every bit as treacherous as she is old. She was already ancient when I was born… and I'm nearly three millennia myself."

"And yet despite all these passing centuries, you're still willing to sacrifice your birth body on this perilous gamble?"

Azymantias straightened up. The smell of wet earth comforted him. Outside, the rainfall appeared to have come to a halt, as if the clouds were holding their breath.

"It's precisely because of all those centuries that I know we have to act. Obinaelle has sat on the Core for over four thousand years. Possibly longer, but our archives only go back so far. And she's never been replaced. Not even once."

He paused theatrically, as he was often wont to do with his students. However, Avamar lacked their patience, and so he went on before she could voice her annoyance. "Dozens of mages have filled the other seats of the Triumvirate, of course, but there's no fooling anyone. She's reigned supreme over the Magisterium forever. The other two members of the Core were invariably weak or inept… and prone to falling out of the higher windows of the palace."

"So? Allow me to play devil's advocate one last time. Perhaps it's justifiable? After all, the Magisterium is flourishing! We rule four continents. Our towers siphon the flux from across the globe, and Arkandis is its center."

"Certainly, but at what cost? We haven't innovated in hundreds of years. At best, we're stagnating. Our decadent society has turned inward, crushing everything and everyone in its path to satisfy its own desires. Our humanity is fading. Just look at your legion, massacring

poor peasants who ask for nothing but a decent life. Inequality and corruption are gnawing away at the very foundations of our civilization. I can't look away any longer! And the only means of bringing about change is to overthrow the Core—"

"Except that Obinaelle has woven such a web of alliances and political scheming that she secures reelection every century, and the rest of the Triumvirate still consists of puppets who dance to her tune."

"Exactly! So, you understand me," he replied with a winning smile.

"Oh, I understand," she sighed. "I'm not heartless or inhumane. I'm just not quite as convinced as you are. I know I can't change your mind, but this plan of yours, or at least the few scraps of it you've deigned to share with me, still looks an awful lot like suicide if you ask me."

"What I accomplished today with the dryads was only the trigger. It will prove one thing: the fables constantly repeated to us about the so-called Source, which no one can hear or see, are just a ploy to keep control over the production of orbs of power and, therefore, over the Magisterium."

"I don't know, Azy. We've been living with this belief for so long… Even I thought it true for a while."

"I know. I've been there too. But I've seen reason since then. You know well that releasing the dryads will have no repercussions for Arkandis and that Obinaelle will lose face completely. All this time, she's insisted that we keep them under her direct control, so as not to draw the attention of the Source and unleash her fury. This public humiliation ought to weaken Obinaelle enough to give the opposition a chance to call new elections. We'll finally have a chance to remove her from the Core."

"And suppose you're wrong? Say the Source really does exist and learns what we've done to her children? If she's the monster Obinaelle says she is, she'll wipe us from the face of this world. And you won't even be around to witness the disaster you caused."

"Exactly. Which is somewhat comforting, I might add," he concluded with a hearty laugh. "But do you honestly believe what you're saying? A supreme but invisible and intangible deity who granted us access to the power of the flux by signing a pact with the first three human mages? Out of mutual respect? An entity that, on top of everything, would never have lifted a finger while we abused her power to enslave all peoples? That strikes me as very odd. All I see is a rather convenient tool for controlling the Magisterium."

Avamar fell silent as he went to fetch a bottle containing an orange-brown liquid that he'd had sent up from the cellar of the Core Palace. Azymantias grabbed two glasses and continued, "I'll admit that what I'm asking of you is a leap of faith of the same kind, and I'm grateful for your trust. No matter what happens, you'll always be the person who has mattered most to me."

"No need for all the melodrama. I trust you. I've said as much," Avamar replied, reaching for a glass, the light from the study playing on the lines etched on her brow. "I'm willing to play my part in your plan."

"Now that sounds more like you! No over-the-top sentimentality. You could have pointed out that, despite my scheming, we're not even sure we can overthrow her. And that's why I must make sure this binding jar is used. It's my safety net in case the first plan fails."

Azymantias then picked up the jar he'd prepared and handed it over. It felt ice-cold in his hands, vibrating with latent power. Tightening his jaw, he continued, "You have to be the one to preside over the ritual."

Avamar passed her palm over the ceramic jar, gently tracing the engravings and runes with a gesture that betrayed both familiarity and fear.

"Rest assured, I'll have no trouble convincing the Core that I should be the one to mete out your sentence," she finally said. "After all, you'll have betrayed my love to sacrifice everything for your reckless plan."

And somewhere, deep down, she was sure that Obinaelle would never detect the slightest doubt in her soul, because what she had just said aloud was nothing but the truth.

Azymantias let out a small, nervous laugh that faded fast. The rain no longer seemed capable of alleviating his burden. He raised his glass to his lips and drained it in a single gulp. He did not want their last moment to end on such a somber note. To lighten the mood, he resorted to some self-mockery. "I wonder how many Bloodhounds will be sent to capture me."

Avamar broke into a wry smile. "You're something else. Is that how you measure your manhood?"

He shrugged, feigning offense. "No, of course not. But just suppose you had to capture me. You'd send at least three, wouldn't you?"

Outside, the weather appeared to ease, as if the sky approved of their banter. She studied him, carefully mulling over the question from a tactical viewpoint. She held her glass to her lips, her eyes twinkling with amusement.

"Two," she finally said, with the gravest of expressions. "Just to be on the safe side. With one of the First Circle's most powerful mind mages, the will of a single Bloodhound might falter. A second would therefore be needed to ensure you were overpowered mentally."

Azymantias burst out laughing, and for a fleeting moment, the shadow of the jar and the betrayal to come was banished. The joyous sound faded gently, giving way to a silence broken only by the rain's rhythmic patter. He took her in his arms, and so they remained, suspended in time, delaying the inevitable moment of their separation for as long as they could.

II

Village of Tunka / Present Day
10 rotations following the Death of Tunka

Valianara clutched the letter in her hand, the source of both her excitement and her apprehension. The ensuing conversation with her mother would inevitably be heated, but she had long since made her decision.

Yet thinking about this moment and living it were two vastly different things. She took a breath and slipped into her sweetest tone.

"Mama? Are you there? I have… something to tell you. If you have a moment," she called out as she entered the house.

"Yes, sweetheart! I'm in here," a voice came from the kitchen. "I'm making a lemon pie for your father. Actually, he should be home shortly. Are you ready for the ceremony tomorrow?"

"Yes… Yes, that's what I came to talk to you about."

"What's the matter?"

Marla slid the pie into the wood-fired oven, alongside some small flans that were gently browning.

"Well, speak up. Have you lost your tongue?" she continued, playfully.

"No, no, but I have a feeling you're going to start yelling."

"In that case, young lady, there's a simple solution! Don't say things you know will only make me yell."

"Yes, only that doesn't really help me…"

"Everything has a price, my dear. Whether in Briars, time, or sacrifices."

"I gather you won't be making this easy for me?"

"I have no idea what you mean." Marla smiled mischievously.

"Mama! You always have to do this!"

"Do what?" she replied, feigning indignation. "When all I ever do is love my family…"

"I'm not kidding!"

"And neither am I!"

"By all the Titans… I'm going to join the Academy of the Keepers of Knowledge!"

Marla gasped in surprise and braced herself against the edge of the table.

"What? What are you talking about? Where are you getting this nonsense from?" she spluttered.

She stared at her daughter; her face contorted with astonishment.

"You know how passionate I've always been about the Keepers of Knowledge," came Valianara's reply, her voice steadier than she would have believed possible. "Without them, I'd have died five rotations ago, or at the very least, been unable to walk."

Marla sighed, trying to compose herself as she took one of her flans out of the oven, a furrow crossing her brow.

"And I thank them for it every day in prayer to the Mother. But your place is here. You'll be an adult tomorrow. You'll receive your Titan's Briar, and you can take up the forge, just like your father."

"But you know how much I dislike that, Mama!" Valianara exclaimed. "I want to study under the High Orator! I wish to help others!"

Marla rolled her eyes, calling on all the Titans—and the Mother—to come to her aid.

"But you can help others here, too, by making our tools! You have no idea what happens beyond our village, my child. The dangers… are very real."

"That's nonsense! The Titans watch over us, all the more so since the Revelation. The roads between all fifty-two villages are safe, and the towers transport us wherever we desire. How long would it even take me to get to the Academy? A few hours to reach the Tower of Tunka and then maybe a day's journey? Besides, there are daily caravans to the Academy bazaar, so I won't even be alone."

"By the Mother's grace! I refuse!"

"Mama, I love you, but I didn't ask for your permission. You said it yourself! I'll be an adult tomorrow. I'll have twenty rotations, and my own choices to make…"

"I'm not yet ready to let you go!"

"I'll write to you every week, I promise! Besides, you and Papa can visit me."

A long silence followed. Was this the finish line of her verbal marathon?

"I… I don't know…" Marla finally said, deep in thought. "I'm from the old world, as you know. We hardly ever went outside the village back then. Only for our Ascension. And children never left ahead of their parents."

"Exactly! The Mother offered us the world and doubled our life expectancy. Tunka died in order to show us the way! We have to embrace what we've been given!"

It was at that very moment that the door chose to start creaking, as if wanting to join in the discussion. Arlo, Valianara's father, stepped into the room. He immediately sensed the tension.

"Oh, dear!" he remarked. "It looks like I've picked just the right moment to come home. Don't tell me you two are at each other's throats again?"

Seeing his wife's crestfallen expression, he recovered quickly. "What's happened? Marla? You're scaring me."

"It's your daughter!" she sobbed. "She wants to go and study at the Academy!"

"Ah… That."

Within a heartbeat, Marla's expression shifted from despair to clear and unmistakable anger.

"What do you mean? Were you aware of this? When were you thinking of telling me?" she shouted.

Casting his daughter a helpless look, Arlo whispered, "I told you it would all work out fine."

"Like a charm," Valianara replied.

"Wait," Arlo said, trying to dig himself out of the hole he had gotten himself into. "Listen to me. Don't you remember how we never had time back then? Ascension came so fast, and we aged so quickly… Don't you wish your parents could have known Valianara? They were gone before we reached adulthood. Now, the Mother has given us this incredible gift. We have enough seasons to see our children grow up, flourish, and perhaps even meet our grandchildren! It's marvelous. But it also means we have to be prepared to let them go."

"Easier said than done," Marla grumbled, her eyes moist. "I'm not ready."

Seeing that her mother was beginning to falter, Valianara dealt the finishing blow. "Mama, I know you're angered and upset, but there's one last thing you need to know. It wasn't just anyone who contacted me. It was the High Orator herself."

She held out the letter signed with an *M* adorned with leaves, which Menilmonea used in all her official correspondence. Reluctantly, Marla took it, wiping her eyes on her sleeves. She read the short letter from the Academy in a hushed voice. It announced that the Titans had recognized their daughter's great abilities and were inviting her to join the next class of novices to enrich their collective knowledge and help the villages prosper. She looked up, her eyes gleaming. It was hard not to feel honored by such an offer.

"What fine writing…" she muttered to herself, unwittingly. "That girl's come a long way in the last ten cycles. And from our village as well!"

"We say 'rotations' now, Mama!"

"Yes, well, I've always said 'cycles,' and that's not going to change anytime soon. All these newfangled things give me a headache."

Arlo waved to his daughter, indicating that she should choose her battles. This one clearly wasn't worth it. Valianara nodded and turned back to the battlefield she hoped to conquer.

"So, do I have your blessing, Mama? I don't want to leave on bad terms."

Marla blew her nose and then locked her reddened eyes on her husband. He tried to hunch down even further, looking for a mouse hole where he might hide.

"I don't have much of a choice, anyway," she finally replied. "And I love you too much for us to part on bad terms. You'd better write to me every single week! And if you go to the bazaar, you can use your new Briar to buy me a fine scarf. The woman next door says they have the most splendid fabrics in the North."

Valianara burst into tears and threw herself into her mother's arms, the stress melting away in an instant. Arlo, looking sheepish, cautiously joined the embrace, keeping one eye on the door, poised to slip away as soon as his wife remembered he was there.

III

* * *

Village of Tunka / Present Day

No sooner had she finished her breakfast than Valianara kissed her mother goodbye and hurried to the town square, where her friend Batany awaited. The moment she saw her, Batany waved her arms.

"How are you feeling?" she called out. "All set for your big moment?"

"Are you kidding? I'm only here to receive my Briar. You're the one leading the prayer to the Mother for the first time. After this, your days as a novice Soul Warden will be over. That's more important than becoming an adult."

"Oh, don't even mention it… And on top of that, Omoridoki will be giving you your Briar."

"That's not true, is it?"

"Yes, it is! I'm so nervous. Truth be told, I didn't sleep a wink all night."

"It'll be fine. I don't know anyone more dedicated or diligent. You're the best Soul Warden I know."

"Thank you. I keep telling myself it'll be better once it's all over. And you? How did your mother take the news?"

"Let's just say she eventually accepted my decision," replied Valianara with a wide grin.

"Oh, if I know Marla… I'm sure it wasn't a walk in the park."

"We should go welcome Omoridoki!" the young girl said, laughing warmly as she took her friend's arm. "It'll keep us busy while we wait for the ceremony to start."

"That's a great idea! Let's go."

The two young women, arm in arm, made their way to the village's northern entrance, narrowing their eyes to try to make out the gigantic mass of fur and tangled vegetation in the distance that heralded the arrival of the badger Titan.

He arrived around noon to cheer and song. The two friends raced to meet him, gasping for breath.

"Omoridoki!"

"Young Valianara! How are you?" asked the creature, his deep voice seeming to echo from some distant underground world.

"I'm going to become a Keeper of Knowledge! My mother even gave her blessing!"

"That was no mean feat, I imagine," said the Titan with a chuckle. "Congratulations! And you, young Batany? Are you ready for the ceremony? I've no doubt you'll be wonderful, but if you have any questions, don't hesitate to ask."

Batany blushed as she bowed slightly. "Thank you, Omoridoki… I'll do everything I can to honor you."

"I'm certain of that."

The two friends walked alongside the Titan, swiftly joined by a number of villagers. A long procession soon formed, the atmosphere lively and cheerful as it made its way around the village to Tunka's tomb.

As they approached the dried-up pond, Valianara sensed the solemnity of the setting wash over her. She recalled her parents' stories. In the past, it had been a mere watering hole where Tunka would rest. Today, his massive, petrified shell loomed over the clearing, transformed by the Soul Wardens into a place of contemplation. Small stone markers erected by families dotted the grass around it; a little further away, under the trees, the graves of those called by the Mother bore witness to the shrine's new function. It was here that the Soul Wardens conducted prayers and funerals and offered counsel to the villagers.

Chairs had been set up around the central altar, which stood near Tunka's head. Upon arriving, Valianara spotted her parents, already seated among the many other villagers. She greeted them with a big wave before heading to the front row, where four other young people who, like her, were about to become adults were waiting. She kissed her friend, wished her luck, and took her seat.

Omoridoki sat a little further back, on a moss carpet specially prepared for him. The Voice of the Titans, who oversaw the Soul Wardens and mentored Batany, handed her a ceremonial robe. Valianara was overcome with a deep sense of pride; she felt at peace. As was often the case in such moments, she heard a faint song at the edge of her awareness—an ancient, peaceful ode. She knew she had made the right choice and that one day she, too, would receive her title as a Keeper of Knowledge from the High Orator.

Batany's voice snapped her out of her moment of bliss. Standing before the altar, her friend raised her arms to the sky and began the ceremony.

"Benevolent Mother, we give you thanks for your blessings and for the life you bestow upon us. We thank you for the Revelation. We thank your children, the Titans, who sacrificed themselves to show us the way. We thank you, Tunka, who, without hesitation, joined the Mother to free us from our fear of death."

Her words carried like a song, both simple and solemn, carried by the weight of the moment.

"Generous Mother," she paused before continuing, "you have judged us worthy to live longer within your creation. You've granted us the gift of full lives. You've united the villages and enabled us to advance our civilization in your name."

Upon hearing these words, Valianara couldn't help but cast a glance toward her mother. She was absorbed in prayer. So instead, she met her father's gaze. They both quickly composed themselves, though they couldn't quite manage to suppress their broad smiles.

"Mother of progress," Batany continued her liturgy, "you've given us new knowledge, you've shown us how to fight disease, you've taught our people how to thrive, you've connected our villages and opened

up our horizons, and for these things, we thank you."

"We thank you," the assembly repeated in unison.

Batany took a long pause, allowing everyone to finish their prayers in their own way, with their own words of thanks.

"As you all know," she continued, judging the time to be sufficient, "today we will have the joy of witnessing the passage into adulthood of five of our children."

Valianara stifled a giggle. Batany was barely a rotation older than her. At the time of the Revelation, Valianara had five cycles, and Batany five and a half. When the Mother offered to extend the villagers' lives, the Titans decided that those born beforehand would have their age doubled for good measure. In the end, at twenty-one rotations, Batany had only one more "new" rotation than she did, and here she was speaking of "our children."

Absorbed in her mathematical nitpicking, Valianara hadn't noticed that Batany had invited her to join Omoridoki. Batany therefore cleared her throat rather pointedly, which immediately snapped her friend out of her daze. When she realized that everyone was looking at her and her mother was rolling her eyes, she rushed over to the Titan, who was observing her kindly. As she stood before him, she bowed her head and waited for the giant badger to speak to her.

"Valianara of Tunka, you're in your twentieth rotation. As is now tradition, and to my immense pleasure, it's my duty to present you with this Briar that I've grown for you. It marks your place within the civilization of the villages. You're now a full-fledged member. It will be yours until the end of your days and will allow you to play an active role in maintaining the balance. When you rejoin the Mother, the Briar will return to the earth, thus completing your shared history."

Valianara, feeling more emotional than she would have wished, looked the Titan in the eyes as she held out her left arm. As her palm came into contact with him, a small, thornless Briar wrapped itself around her wrist. It formed three interwoven loops. A wave of heat rose up her arm, like a familiar whisper settling in her chest.

The audience applauded, and Batany motioned for her friend to return to her seat before calling the next person. As she made her way back, Valianara couldn't help but steal a glance at her parents, who were both trying clumsily to hide their emotions. They gave her proud, beaming smiles.

The remainder of the service unfolded as if in a dreamlike haze. She found herself lulled by the voices and the hubbub, but her mind felt detached from it all, as if gently floating a few feet above her body. The ordinarily faint melody she could hear had become a warm, clear vibration, pulsing in perfect harmony with her Briar. When the ceremony ended, she joined her parents, who gathered her into their arms.

"Well, that's it, then. Our work here is done," her father said with a grin. "You can go now."

"Arlo!" exclaimed her mother, before softening and adding, "My dear, how are you feeling?"

"I'm not quite sure," replied Valianara. "A little dazed, I suppose. It was more emotional than I thought it would be."

"Yes, my dear, receiving your Briar is a strange experience," her father commented. "And different for everyone. For me, it wasn't anything special. I was just glad to be able to buy things from all over the world. But I know your mother found it particularly difficult."

"Oh, yes," she agreed. "I almost collapsed from the sheer emotion of it all. It wasn't so much the thought of taking part in the economy of the villages that affected me as the connection with the Briar itself. It was close to ten cycles ago, but I still have vivid memories of it."

"Come on, let's go home, my darlings. Let's spend the rest of the day making preparations and spending time together before our little bird leaves the nest."

The bird in question chuckled, though Marla didn't seem especially amused by her husband's humor. Valianara kissed her mother to make amends.

"I'm just going to say goodbye to Batany," she announced, once she was sure the volcano wouldn't erupt. "I'll meet you back at home."

She found her friend waiting near the altar. They fell into each other's arms, laughing and crying at the same time. Batany whispered that they would soon see each other again, no matter what happened.

As she broke away, Omoridoki's deep voice rose behind them. "I bid you a safe journey to the Academy, young Valianara. Your talents will prove invaluable there."

Valianara bowed in thanks and ran back toward the village.

IV

Village of Tunka / Present Day

"Leaving is always painful," her father had said to her, "but it allows us to find ourselves again." Valianara had not realized he was such a philosopher!

His remark had struck her right in the heart. It had been so easy to picture herself leaving to join the Academy, but now that she was on her way, she didn't feel nearly as carefree as she had imagined.

Of course, she was delighted to be joining the Keepers of Knowledge, but leaving her parents behind made the journey bittersweet. Her mother hadn't managed to form coherent sentences as they said their farewells. She had simply held her in her arms for a long time, until Valianara gently pushed her away and turned on her heel to leave, as if to cauterize the wound as quickly as possible. At the top of the small hill that overlooked the village, she looked back one last time and waved to them, then headed northeast to make her way to the transport ring.

The path was unfamiliar to her, and the more she walked, the thicker the forest seemed to grow. The taller, older trees formed a canopy above her, filtering the morning light.

Then, as she rounded a bend, it appeared—the Tower of Tunka.

Valianara came to a sudden halt, her breath catching in her throat. She knew it would be there, but seeing it with her own eyes was something else entirely. The structure, made of stone and vegetation, rose majestically toward the sky beyond her wildest expectations. She suddenly felt small. She had only ever left her village once, eight rotations ago, when she had accompanied her parents to the Opponka Fair. The journey on the transport ring had been so quick that she had lost her bearings, leaving her unable to take in her surroundings. She mostly recalled the festive atmosphere and her father clowning around.

Comforted by the memory, she picked up her pace and entered the huge archway that served as the entrance. Inside, it was cool and quiet, the air heavy with the smell of damp earth and ancient stone. In the center, the transport ring glowed with a soft golden light. She had barely taken a few steps when a voice echoed through the hall, startling her.

"Hello, hello! Welcome, young traveler! Oh, but what a joy to have someone visit! Come in, have no fear! If I could, I'd come and shake your hand, but you know how things are, do you not?"

Valianara narrowed her eyes, searching for the source of the cheery voice. "Greetings! My name is Valianara…"

"And where might you be bound for so early in the morning? No, wait, don't tell me! I adore guessing! And by the way, how was your Day of the Mother yesterday? I hear Omoridoki attended? I've been told he's rather charming, though I prefer Baromoki myself. By the way, do you know how to use the map?"

Valianara was struck dumb, overwhelmed by the barrage of questions. The spirit was quite the chatterbox.

"Omoridoki is a formidable and wise Titan," she managed to say between questions. "The ceremony went well. In fact, that's part of the reason I'm here. I received my Briar yesterday, and now I'm going to start my training."

The spirit interrupted her with what sounded like an excited snap of its fingers. "Don't tell me! Just let me guess! Hmm… Judging by how smart you look, I'd bet on the Academy of the Keepers of Knowledge! Am I right?"

"Yes, that's right," confirmed the young girl, an amused smile playing on her lips.

"Oh, terrific! Wonderful! I knew it! I'm so proud of you! It's such an excellent institution. You'll be able to learn so much! It's nice to see young people today who aren't afraid of anything!"

"Someone already explained the map to me earlier," Valianara interrupted as she tried to steer the conversation back on track. "I know where I need to go…"

"I wouldn't doubt it for a second! A student as determined as you must know exactly what she's getting into. But tell me… Before you leave… Do you have any gossip from the village? Anything juicy? It's not that I'm bored, but the people of Tunka aren't big users of the network. I'm lucky if I get one person a day."

Valianara blinked, a little flustered. "Gossip? I… I don't think I know any. I'm not particularly good at things like that. Are you always alone here?"

"Alas, yes! However, the Keepers of Knowledge, your future colleagues, are working on a mechanism that will allow us to communicate with each other. They've already been here several times to try to teach me, but this whole 'shared stream of consciousness' business is a bit beyond me. It's all very technical, you know."

The spirit paused, its voice growing dreamier. "But what really gives me hope is a rumor that's been floating around. I've been told that the Academy is looking for a way to free us from our stone. A solution that would enable us to leave the towers. Imagine! To finally travel, to see the world… It would be the greatest of enchantments."

Valianara felt pity for this voice, so joyful yet so lonely. "If such a plan really exists, I'll work on it as hard as I can. I'll do everything in my power to help you."

"That's truly kind of you, young Valianara. Exceedingly kind indeed. Now, don't waste any more time listening to an old chatterbox like me. The Academy awaits."

Valianara gave him one last smile, although she didn't exactly know where to look. She stepped forward with confidence, entered the soft light of the transport ring, and placed her hand on the glowing rune that marked the nearest tower to the Academy.

"What a charming young lady…" was the last thing she heard before the world dissolved around her, replaced by the sensation of falling.

In the blink of an eye, the room had subtly changed. The stone walls were still there, along with the archway, but the vegetation climbing up the walls wasn't the same. Perhaps the vines seemed darker and the moss greener? It was impossible to say. The smell of undergrowth filled her lungs, but everything seemed to have shifted except for the transport ring itself. The temperature felt a little cooler, biting lightly at her cheeks.

"I'm here!" she called out.

There was no answer.

She waited for a moment. The silence that followed the torrent of words from the spirit in the Tower of Tunka felt deafening.

"Hello? Spirit? Is there anyone there?"

Only the distant murmur of the wind in the leaves spoke back to her. Strange.

She shrugged and stepped out of the ring's golden liquid, expecting to have to wipe her boots dry. To her surprise, nothing remained on the leather as she descended from the platform. Not a single drop, despite the fluid's gooey consistency.

She moved a few steps toward the exit before being blinded by the glaring sunlight. She squinted and spotted a caravan at the bottom of the dirt road that wound its way from the tower, seemingly ready to depart. Wagons, pack animals, and a dozen or so people bustled about, their voices reaching her ears as an indistinct murmur.

Valianara immediately raced down the path, waving an arm above her head to attract their attention.

"Wait!" she called out, slightly out of breath from the sudden effort. "Please wait for me!"

The slope was steeper than she had realized. She stumbled multiple times, her bag bouncing heavily on her back. Fortunately, one of the men, who had just finished harnessing a pack beast, looked up toward her. He waved back, indicating that he had spotted her. Relieved, she slowed down and finished the descent at a more cautious pace.

As she reached them, the man—with a salt-and-pepper beard and broad shoulders—approached her, smiling broadly. Despite his gruff-looking exterior, his eyes twinkled with genuine warmth.

"Well, well, little one! It looks like you've been galloping! We did the right thing by waiting for you, didn't we? My name's Meridoc, and I'm the leader of this little party. We run the route between the Academy bazaar and several towers in the region. You're in luck, because we were just about to hit the road. Are you headed to the bazaar?"

Valianara collected herself, feeling a little intimidated but reassured by his warm welcome. "Hello, Meridoc. I'm Valianara. I… I'm going to be a novice Keeper of Knowledge."

The man's eyebrows rose; his expression was one of delighted surprise. "Well now! What a coincidence! We already have one of your fellow students with us! He got here less than half a day ago. Come on, I'll introduce you to him. He's in the lead wagon. Now that's what I call luck!"

Valianara felt a little awkward.

"Can I ride with you?" she asked hesitantly. "Does it cost anything?"

Meridoc burst into hearty laughter. "Cost? Save your Briar for more important things, my girl. We have enough room, and besides, we're going to the bazaar. A twig like you won't slow us down!"

"Thank you ever so much," she replied, relief washing over her.

She followed him to the front of the convoy. When they reached the first wagon, Meridoc called out to its occupant. "Hey, young man! Let me introduce you to a future classmate. Valianara. Valianara, this is… Heck, what's your name again?"

A calm voice came from inside the wagon. "Alister, sir."

"Ah, right! Valianara, this is Alister. You can stay right here; we'll be leaving shortly."

Valianara nodded in thanks to the man and climbed aboard. "Nice to meet you! I'm from Tunka, what about you?"

Alister seemed entirely absorbed by the small pebbles he was holding in his hand. He turned slowly toward her, reaching for the small bag he wore around his neck. He appeared to think for a moment.

"You don't know where you come from?" Valianara asked, surprised.

"Yes, I do," he answered, laughing softly, "but I was wondering… I was just wondering which Titan was Tunka."

"Oh… He was the turtle Titan. He's with the Mother now."

"I'm so sorry. I'm from Goaka. We still have our Titan. He's the crab Titan."

"Lucky you! Where I live, we only get to benefit from their wisdom on the rare occasions when they visit. The Soul Wardens do a rather decent job, mind you! Don't tell my friend Batany I said that," she added with a chuckle, her cheeks flushing red.

Alister helped her settle in before turning his attention back to his pebbles, which he continued to roll gently between his fingers.

"What are those?" she asked, pointing at the stones.

"These? Just pebbles. It's a habit I picked up from my father. He loved collecting them. Rubbing them together relaxes me. Their texture and the sound they make are like a lullaby."

"Oh… That's a sweet tradition."

"Yes."

Valianara tried several more times to start a conversation, but her companion was unresponsive. She decided not to push it any further and instead enjoyed the scenery.

The journey through the forest was uneventful. They skirted the Valley of the Ancients and, a little over half a day later, came within sight of the Academy and its bazaar. Meridoc announced the end of the line in a loud voice.

It was the noise that first struck Valianara. A continuous buzz of hundreds of voices shouting at each other, laughing, and the distant pounding of metal against an anvil. Then came the smells: a heady mixture of spices, grilled food, and the scent of a thousand flowers. The bazaar stretched out before her, a vibrant maze of activity. Stalls with red canvas awnings were squeezed together, overflowing with wares she had never seen before: brightly colored fabrics, ceramics in strange shapes, unfamiliar fruits, and mountains of potted plants. Vegetation had overtaken the place, climbing the walls of buildings and winding around wooden pillars. It was chaotic, majestic, and terrifying all at once.

Her eyes were drawn irresistibly upward, beyond the hustle and bustle of the market.

There, towering above everything, stood the Academy.

It was not a mountain, but a pyramid so colossal that it looked as if it were supporting the very sky.

Carpets of greenery covered its ancient stone sides, as if the forest itself had decided to take root there. A band of orange metal encircled it midway up. Valianara felt dwarfed by the structure's size and the power it exuded.

"By all the Titans…" she whispered, unable to tear her eyes away from the monument. "Is that… Is that it?"

Alister glanced up from his pebble with an amused look. "Impressive, isn't it? It's something you never really get used to."

"Have you been here before?"

"Oh yes, many times. My parents were merchants. We often came here to sell the produce from our farm."

"Were?" she repeated softly.

Alister's smile faded. His tone lost any trace of lightness. "Yes, sadly. They joined the Mother two… rotations ago. An accident."

His gaze clouded for a moment, as if he were looking at a scene far more distant than the bustling bazaar around them.

"I'm sorry," Valianara whispered with sincere compassion. "Try to think of them as being happy with the Mother and continuing to watch over you from her side."

Alister gave a slight nod, a vague smile on his lips. He put his pebbles back in his satchel with a somewhat brusque gesture.

"Thank you. Well… I'll have to leave you now. I have several things to take care of before tonight's welcome ceremony."

Valianara felt a twinge of disappointment but showed no sign of it.

"Of course," she replied, smiling, hoping it looked natural. "Thank you for keeping me company during the journey. I'll see you later, then."

Alister gave her a final nod and sprang nimbly from the wagon, swiftly disappearing into the crowd. Valianara sat there for a moment, feeling a little lost, then, with a shake of her head, resolved to make the most of the time she had left. After all, she had a mission.

She climbed from the wagon and plunged into the vibrant maze

of the bazaar. The sheer scale of the place was bewildering. Stalls stretched as far as the eye could see, forming meandering alleys where it was all too easy to lose your way. She passed a spice seller whose colorfully stacked goods filled the air with their fragrance, then a potter shaping clay at a hypnotic pace. For the first time in her life, Valianara felt anonymous, a mere drop in an ocean of unknown faces. It was frightening yet somehow liberating.

Finally, she spotted what she was looking for: a stall devoted entirely to fabrics. Shimmering silks, coarse woolens, and cottons with intricate patterns hung from poles or were stacked in neat piles.

"Can I help you, little lady?" asked a woman with a wrinkled, beaming face.

"Hello, ma'am. I'm looking for a scarf. For my mother."

"You've come to exactly the right place! I've just got some beautiful pieces from the northern villages. Take a look at this blue…"

The merchantwoman unfolded a large swathe of soft fabric, a blue so deep it seemed to have captured a piece of the night sky.

"It's exquisite," Valianara whispered. "How much…?"

"For this one, it'll be twenty grams, my dear."

Valianara nodded. It was a reasonable price. She held out her wrist over the counter. The woman did the same, and as their arms drew closer, a curious sensation coursed through her. The three rings on her Briar glowed with a soft green light. The woman's rings, which were woven into a thick, elaborate braid, did the same.

The moment the two Briars touched, Valianara felt a slight tug. She watched, mesmerized, as her own Briar retracted slightly, losing a little of its length, while the merchant's Briar lengthened by the same amount. The exchange was instantaneous, silent, and curiously intimate.

"There you go, my lovely," concluded the seller as she folded the scarf with care. "Welcome to the Academy bazaar."

V

Arkandis / One Day Before the Breaking of the Pact
1,400 rotations prior to the Death of Tunka

Azymantias was delighted to see that three Bloodhounds flanked the soldiers of the First Legion as they broke down his door in the middle of the night.

His pride remained intact. In fact, he was rather flattered, as one of them was a Master Bloodhound. Such trackers were only assigned to the most complex cases, and being apprehended by one of them might easily have been considered a true privilege. At least, that was how Azymantias chose to look at it.

Naturally, he put up no resistance and was forced to admit that the Bloodhounds treated him with the respect befitting his rank. He was only partially restrained mentally, which meant he was able to leave his house on foot. The street was empty, and the rainfall had subsided, but he could still see large black clouds gathering on the horizon beyond the ocean. The Master Bloodhound drew closer to him as they made their way to the Core Palace.

"What trouble have you gotten yourself into this time? It's not every day that Obinaelle personally asks me to apprehend a distinguished member of the First Circle. And in the middle of the night, no less."

"Oberron, my friend, I'm sincerely sorry for the trouble I'm causing you."

"Given Obinaelle's mood, I wouldn't worry too much about that if I were you. I don't think you're in for the best time of your long life."

"To be honest, I was expecting as much. I have a strong feeling that freeing the dryads wasn't exactly to her liking."

"No, indeed. So, it was you we have to thank for this afternoon's general alert! The Core has ordered more than five hundred soldiers to hunt down your friends."

"Have you found them?"

"I'd be a pretty lousy Bloodhound if I gave you that kind of intelligence."

"I appreciate your professionalism."

The rest of the journey was spent in silence, as the first drops of a fresh downpour fell, marking their long procession. When they finally arrived at the Core Palace, the rain had reached torrential levels, pelting down on the cobblestones with a deafening clatter. He was not taken to the dungeons, but directly to the private apartments of the High Magistrix.

What an honor, he thought.

Oberron rapped on a solid, dark wood door, which opened without a sound. Inside, Obinaelle stood near a vast window overlooking the slumbering city.

"Azymantias," she addressed him in an icy tone, her back turned.

"High Magistrix," he replied, bending into a slight bow.

She turned toward them, her eyes flashing coldly. "Leave us," she ordered the Bloodhounds.

Oberron hesitated. "High Magistrix, are you sure?"

"I should be fine, Oberron. Your mental locks are still in place, aren't they?"

"Indeed."

"Good. Then please leave us."

The Bloodhounds bowed and left, pulling the door shut behind them. Azymantias scanned the room. "Are the other members of the Core not here? Their fragile health no doubt keeps them in bed at this late hour?"

Obinaelle slowly approached him. "Drop the act, Azymantias. We've known each other too long to mince words."

"As you wish, High Magistrix."

She came to a stop a few paces away from him, scrutinizing him with her piercing gaze. "Why did you free the dryads? You're not telling me you've secretly become a naturalist?"

"Come now, you know perfectly well why I did it."

"You're after my position, aren't you? Did you do this to gain access to the Core? You can't possibly be that foolish."

"Are you going to use that scare tactic again? What would we possibly do without the blessing of the Source?"

A flash of fury passed through Obinaelle's eyes. "Yes, it's true! So, you really are a blasted naturalist! You don't believe in the Source? How is such a thing possible? You're one of the most powerful mages in the First Circle!"

"That's right! I've had three millennia to realize that your stories are just that: stories. They're devoid of facts."

"You foolish idiot!" she suddenly shouted. "I was one of the three mages who established the Pact! I was right there, over four thousand years ago! It took immense effort and sacrifices you can't even imagine, but I managed to access her consciousness! That's why we're able to use the flux! And the only request in return was that we respect her work! How can you imagine that didn't happen? Your stupidity and thirst for power will lead to the destruction of the Magisterium."

"How could I not have seen that the rot had spread through the First Circle?" she continued, speaking more to herself than to anyone else.

"Even when faced with the facts, you refuse to give up? Tell me the truth now: I'm completely under your control. Why cling to this legend? Your Source is nowhere to be found. If she exists, why hasn't she struck us yet, when her dryads are free? This masquerade of yours won't last much longer. Your reign is ending, whether you like it or not."

Obinaelle sat down heavily in an armchair, dumbstruck. "It is indeed the end, but not the one you imagine," she whispered. "You're out of your mind. The Source is a higher entity; she won't ambush us in our sleep. She lives in a reality far beyond our own... I don't know why in the world I'm trying to educate you! Her vengeance will come,

I can guarantee you that."

"I won't be around to see it, alas, because you're going to kill me, aren't you?" Azymantias felt a shiver that he wasn't able to conceal entirely. This was a crucial moment in his plan. He had to be punished. His soul had to be locked inside a jar. If she decided to kill him, it would all have been for nothing.

"No, I won't kill you," she replied with a weary look. "It would be too easy. I want you to witness the chaos you've wrought, to feel the weight of your crime crushing you from within. Besides, I'm not the only one seeking justice: someone else is waiting eagerly to watch you suffer."

Azymantias fell silent and lowered his head, trying to conceal the triumph that threatened to betray him. The plan was working.

"She actually asked to be the one to carry out the sentence," Obinaelle continued. "I'll have to deal with this crisis first, but I can guarantee you one thing: if we make it through this, I'll be the one to personally drag you out of your jar as often as I can, just to show you what your ambition has caused. And I promise you an eternity of suffering; you'll be my plaything for the rest of time."

The prisoner's mind was crossed by the desire to push her into a corner one last time, to force her to admit the truth. He immediately changed his mind. It was pointless. She was locked into her own lie, convinced she could still salvage the situation.

Faced with his silence, Obinaelle stood up, her expression once again a cold marble mask. "Everything has been said. We'll meet again for your sentencing. Bloodhounds!"

The door opened, and Oberron entered with his men.

"Take him away. Tomorrow, his soul will be imprisoned in a jar."

As the Bloodhounds seized him and escorted him away, Azymantias cast one last glance at the High Magistrix.

I have to give her credit, he thought. *More than four thousand years of lies have taught her to play the part to perfection. She's remarkably convincing.*

VI

Landria / Present Day
10 rotations following the Death of Tunka

In the late afternoon, Valianara headed toward the imposing pyramid that dominated the horizon. The structure, already intimidating during the day, seemed even more imposing as the sky darkened, its contours silhouetted against the fading light of dusk.

The entrance was guarded by two motionless guardians of peace, dressed in their elegant black uniforms accented with shimmering gold. They stood on either side of the monumental arch, which was encircled by enormous roots as thick as tree trunks.

She approached, a little nervously, holding out her invitation signed by the High Orator. One of the guardians of peace took it, gave it a quick glance, and handed it back with an approving nod.

"All is in order. Follow the road to the end. You'll find yourself at the city's wall."

Valianara frowned in surprise. "The city?"

The guardian of peace smiled slightly. "You'll understand soon enough. There will be someone there to meet you."

Intrigued, she thanked him and crossed the threshold. The air instantly grew cooler. Inside, it was almost dark, and it took a moment before her eyes adjusted. In front of her, a wide, smooth paved road stretched into the darkness. Her breath caught in her throat. At the end of the road, an incredible sight gleamed: an entire city, contained completely within the pyramid. Valianara stood in awe at the sight of this secret metropolis. She had imagined herself climbing hundreds of floors, but had not realized that the pyramid was merely a shell enclosing it.

The further she went, the sharper the details became, and the more her astonishment grew. It was a world unto itself, vibrant and alive beneath its stone armor.

She finally reached a huge metal-and-dark-stone gate, flanked by colossal walls that marked the city's entrance. A small group of young people was waiting there. They greeted her with a cheerful nod.

"Welcome, novice," one of them called out. "We're apprentices of the Academy, tasked with accompanying the new arrivals to the Temple of the Mother in time for the ceremony."

With a warm smile on his face, the one who had spoken stepped forward. "I'm Malfanor of Goaka. Allow me to show you the way."

Valianara, still in a state of disbelief, was unable to hold back her question. "My name is Valianara of Tunka, but… is the Academy… a city?"

Malfanor let out an amused chuckle. "You'll soon have all the answers to your questions, novice. Have patience and enjoy the guided tour."

He motioned for her to follow him, and they proceeded through the gate.

Valianara instantly noticed that the light wasn't coming from torches; it seemed to seep from the stone itself, bathing the streets in a steady amber glow. All around, the same gigantic roots as those at the entrance snaked along the facades, forming natural bridges between buildings or plunging into the ground only to reappear further along, akin to the veins of a living being. There was no wind to stir the air, which smelled of cool stone and moss.

"Here, we'll follow the main road. It goes around the city, so it's an easy route to follow," Malfanor explained. "If you happen to get lost, find this road again; it'll be a solid reference point."

They began their ascent. The city was built on a hill; its streets climbed gently, each turn revealing new architectural wonders. Valianara had never seen the likes of it. The buildings, built of dark metals and pale stones, rose several stories high. Domes, turrets, and balconies, carved with remarkable finesse, adorned them, while aerial walkways connected the tallest structures. It was all enough to make her dizzy.

"On our left is the Residence," Malfanor said, pointing to a tangle of elegant buildings with invitingly lit windows. "This will be where you'll be staying for the duration of your training."

Valianara admired the intricate details of the facades, wondering what kind of life might be bustling behind those walls. They passed a few silent figures who nodded briefly in their direction. Other than that, the city remained curiously quiet, as if holding its breath. They continued upward, passing under an archway where a giant root provided a natural canopy.

"Just up ahead, the large building with the glass dome is the Academy itself," continued her guide. "You'll be spending most of your time within its walls and in the Library."

Valianara tried to gauge its size, but the building was so vast and complex that it defied any attempt at measurement. And yet, the Academy was only a fraction of this magnificent city.

"And that darker structure next to it is the Chamber of Memory," added Malfanor.

He picked up his pace slightly, as if to prevent her from asking any more questions. They finally arrived at the foot of a monumental staircase that led up to the most imposing and brightly lit building in the entire city. Its light was so bright, so pure, that it felt like the beating heart of this underground world.

"Here we are," Malfanor said, stopping. "The Temple of the Mother. This is where I leave you."

He offered her one last smile. "Welcome to the Academy, Valianara. And best of luck with your ceremony."

She nodded in thanks, wondering what he meant by "best of luck." By the time she mustered up the courage to ask him, he had already walked away. Disappointed, she turned her attention to the imposing pale stone staircase.

After what seemed like hours of climbing, she entered the grounds of the temple. The building itself was open, bereft of true walls. Only enormous alabaster columns marked its boundaries, tracing airy circular forms that stretched upward to support a majestic dome. The center of the sanctuary emitted a soft, warm glow. Right in the middle of the structure, a colossal tree stood with its branches spread wide. Its gnarled limbs rose in a complex canopy above a trunk formed of dozens of thick roots, so intertwined that it was impossible to discern their origin. The wood looked ancient, fossilized, yet it radiated a gentle energy.

Occupying a good half of the hall, dozens of chairs had been arranged in a semicircle facing the mighty tree. Most were already occupied by quiet figures, who sat in respectful anticipation. As she looked around for somewhere to sit, a young girl with long blonde hair pointed to an empty seat beside her. She sat down hastily, still a little out of breath.

"Climbing that enormous staircase took me longer than I'd care to admit," she whispered.

Her neighbor replied with a soft laugh. "I won't hold it against you. I didn't think I'd ever make it to the top. My name is Evarine, I'm from Opponka."

"Nice to meet you. Valianara from Tunka."

Evarine's face lit up. "Oh! Like the High Orator and Orator Aureal!"

Valianara smiled kindly. "Indeed, but I'm not sure their talent rubbed off on me when they still lived in Tunka."

"You can't know that," replied Evarine with a wink. "Either way, it's a pleasure to meet you! I was just looking for a roommate. I heard that novices get rooms for two."

"I'd be thrilled to share a room with you," replied Valianara without the slightest hesitation.

"Well, then it's settled! I'd rather choose my roommate than have one foisted on me."

"Have you been here long? It feels like I'm the last one to get here."

"No, not at all. I only arrived a few moments ago. In any case, the orators aren't here yet."

No sooner had she finished her sentence than the general hubbub rose a notch, and all heads turned toward the staircase, from which several figures were emerging.

"Well, looks like you were wise not to have arrived any later," laughed Evarine. "They're the orators."

"How do you know that?"

"Well, for one thing, novices never show up in groups of five, right? We come from fifty-two villages, and it's rare for any of them to send more than one at a time. And also… Well, because I recognize them."

"What do you mean? How do you recognize them? Have you seen them before? I only know the High Orator and Orator Aureal. And even then, only because they often visit Tunka's tomb."

Evarine shrugged, a mischievous grin forming on her lips. "Oh, I know, people say I'm a little too enthusiastic about the Keepers of Knowledge! Ever since the bazaar started, my parents have been coming here to sell fruit from our orchard. They have a small stall not far from the pyramid entrance. Whenever we came here, I'd spend my time following everybody's comings and goings. In exchange for a few pieces of fruit, I even managed to bribe the guardians of peace to help me identify who was who."

"You're definitely going to be a remarkably useful friend," Valianara said with a smile.

The orators greeted the familiar faces in the crowd as they strode confidently toward the central tree. Menilmonea scanned the assembly and locked eyes with Valianara. She gave her a knowing wink, then leaned over and whispered something in Aureal's ear, who responded with a broad smile. Valianara felt her cheeks flush.

"You already know some impressive people," Evarine said with a touch of humor.

Once at the foot of the tree, Menilmonea lifted her hand to call for silence. A slight murmur persisted, which seemed to amuse her. She then clapped her hands together sharply. The entire temple began to vibrate, as if the roots that held it in place had tightened their grip. Complete silence ensued.

"I thank you for your attention, my dear novices. Let me introduce myself: I'm High Orator Menilmonea. I am responsible for this city and the Academy." Her voice, calm and clear, effortlessly reached the furthest row. "To help me in these complex tasks, I'm assisted by other orators. Not all of them were able to attend today, as we have a number of other pressing matters to address, but I'm delighted to have with me those who will accompany you during your novice rotation. So, from left to right, I present our orators: Aureal, Menara, Aboren, and Gideon."

As she called out each name, exquisite chairs made of wood and roots sprang up beneath them, enabling them to sit with an air of natural grace.

To say that the novices were spellbound would have been an understatement. Oh, of course, they had all heard of the High Orator's powers, but seeing her in action right before their very eyes was something else entirely. If she had asked them to jump into the void, because such was the will of the Mother, the vast majority would undoubtedly have asked from which side of the temple.

"Thank you, to all of you, for agreeing to join us," Menilmonea went on, her eyes sweeping across the assembly. "The Keepers of Knowledge have now been established for more than eight rotations, and we still have so much to learn, understand, and share… However, before we proceed, I'd like to ask for the help of a volunteer."

A forest of hands shot up immediately.

Valianara, along with everyone else, raised her arm and even tried to make herself taller in her chair, as if the height of her hand might make a difference. She looked around and noticed several novices who didn't seem quite as excited as she was about offering to volunteer. Among them, unsurprisingly, she noticed Alister. His slightly lost look somehow suited him. Their eyes met, and she flashed a smile, which he barely returned.

Menilmonea finally chose a young man from the front row. "You. Your name?"

"Kamartel of Gunderki, High Orator."

"Very well, Kamartel. Please go to the staircase below. There you'll find Grumf. And yes, he's a bear," she added, seeing his frightened expression. "He's also the best friend of Orator Aureal. He'll take you

down to street level and stay with you until Aureal calls him back. He'll then signal you—gently, don't worry—to return to us. Is that clear?"

Kamartel let out a vague whistle, which seemed to satisfy Menilmonea. Once the volunteer was out of sight, she continued, "As Keepers of Knowledge, our mission is to understand the world that the Mother has given us, to share our knowledge when it's needed, and to protect it. Today, my dear novices, we will share our first piece of knowledge with you."

The audience's excitement was palpable. Evarine squeezed Valianara's hand and whispered, "This is the best day of my life!"

Valianara herself felt as if she were walking on air.

Menilmonea's necklace suddenly began to glow softly. From the old tree behind her, a vine slowly descended, bringing with it a strange object that it placed on a table that had emerged from the intertwining roots. The artifact was strikingly complex. Around a meter tall, it was mainly made of a metal that resembled polished gold. It was a large, smooth bowl, held up by an intricately carved stem. Above it, a cylindrical cage allowed a glimpse, through its delicate bars, of a network of incredibly delicate gears and mechanisms. They stood motionless, but Valianara thought she could sense a tension, as if the whole structure were waiting for a signal to start moving. On one side of the cage, a large circular stone with a vibrant turquoise sheen, crisscrossed with fine dark cracks, seemed to observe the assembly like an enigmatic eye. Strange runes were engraved on the rings encircling the structure, adding further to the mystery. The whole thing was topped with a dome inlaid with elaborate designs.

A murmur of admiration tinged with curiosity rippled through the ranks of novices. The object seemed to be a combination of a work of art, a machine, and a sacred relic.

Menilmonea slowly moved her hand over the artifact. The turquoise stone sprang into action, glowing a deep blue that cast a gentle light over her focused face.

"This is a Secret Sentinel," she said. "But we'll come to that in a moment. For now, as I was saying, I'm going to teach you the first piece of knowledge. And this isn't just any lesson, but the very one that inspired us—Orator Aureal, the Titans, and me—to found this Academy."

The tense atmosphere in the room reached its peak. Several novices found themselves holding their breath.

"The Mother didn't create this place," Menilmonea declared abruptly. "This place was created by humans who go by the name of Arkandians. And these Arkandians have so much power that they've even managed to corrupt the Titans. They manipulated them into creating the villages."

She paused for a moment, giving the audience time to process the information. A murmur of disbelief rippled through the room. The novices, who had been riveted until then, were now dumbfounded. Some exchanged confused glances, others shook their heads as if to shake off these senseless words. Was this a joke? Some cruel test?

Valianara turned to Evarine, her eyes wide. "But… How is that possible? Wasn't it the Mother who created the villages?"

Evarine didn't know how to react, tears welling up in her eyes.

"High Orator?" A timid but distinct voice rose from the crowd. "Is this… Is this a test?"

Menilmonea turned her gaze to the young man who had spoken. Her expression was one of deep empathy.

"Alas, no, it's the plain truth. This is what Aureal and I discovered ten rotations ago, when we left our village to try to save our Titan. We came here to plead our case to the Mother, but she wasn't here. We had a tough time accepting that what we thought was her temple was actually the creation of a group of humans we knew nothing about. They possessed incredibly powerful magic. Fortunately, and for reasons we're still unaware of, they are no longer here. We explored the city and found their Library, where we learned that the Mother didn't found our villages and that our Titans were enslaved by unholy magic."

She paused again, while her words sank in.

"We understand how difficult this is, even for the strongest of hearts. Every orator has had to face it. You've lived your entire lives based on a false belief, and the process of accepting this fact will be long and painful. However, you were chosen in part for your strength of character and thirst for knowledge. We hope that this will make the ordeal somewhat easier."

Another voice, this time more confident, spoke up, "High Orator, please forgive my blasphemy, but if this is the way it is, then we have a right to question the very existence of the Mother, don't we?"

Menilmonea smiled at the quick-witted remark. She glanced with satisfaction at the other orators. This class certainly had some excellent minds.

"That's a fair question, and it gives me a chance to make a crucial point. As Keepers of Knowledge, there are no taboos for us. All questions are worth asking."

Only the answers sometimes need to be contained, she mused to herself.

"And to answer your question, I can assure you that yes, the Mother does indeed exist. It was she who created the Titans. It was also she who gave me my powers. I have the rare privilege of hearing her song. So, rest assured on the matter: amid the chaos, this truth isn't a lie."

It was then that the question she always dreaded came up. She might have thought it would get easier over the rotations, but, sadly, time seemed unwilling to do its work.

"High Orator? If the Arkandians created the villages, where did everyone go after the Ascension?"

Menilmonea glanced at Aureal, who clasped her hands together as if to say, *Be strong, I'm with you, you know what to do.*

"They were brought here by the towers. And the Arkandians had use of their bodies. The Arkandians themselves seemed to be suffering from an illness that made them sensitive to sunlight. Since their magic couldn't overcome this curse, they decided long ago to create us so that they could steal our bodily vessels to meet their needs."

Once again, she allowed the silence to linger—both for herself and her audience. There was not a sound.

"I realize this is upsetting information. It's one of the reasons we never select children whose parents may have undergone the Ascension.

Essentially, they were farming us. To do this, they used their magic to erase our Titans' memories; they still believed they were serving the Mother. The Arkandians then corrupted the Titans' connection with nature and forced them to make us grow twice as fast, so they'd have more bodies. Their crime doesn't end with us: they also defiled the Mother's children. Some died of exhaustion, like my poor Tunka."

As sobs began to choke her voice, she paused to regain her composure. No one spoke. In the stillness of the temple, you could have heard a pin drop. Valianara's gaze wandered into the void; she felt her mind drifting away. The young girl forced herself to blink, bringing her back to the real world, and looked around her. The other novices were also struggling with the shock of their new reality. Several shook their heads, refusing to believe what they were not ready to hear. She saw that Alister had taken out his pebbles again and was rubbing at them frantically, hoping they would help him erase this new knowledge from his mind.

Menilmonea knew that this was the most difficult part for each class. Over the coming weeks, the orators would need to be extremely attentive so that no one lost their footing.

"It's disgusting, morbid, inhuman," she continued, her voice becoming harder, sharper. "Now imagine how each surviving Titan felt when we finally freed them from the Arkandians' grip."

She expected screams and anger. But there was nothing.

A tomb-like silence had fallen over the temple. A thick, viscous hush that seemed to suck the air out of the room. No one moved. No one even dared breathe too loudly, as if the smallest sound might make this horrific reality all the more real.

Valianara felt as if the world around her was spinning. She tried to grab hold of something, but her hands found only thin air. Menilmonea's words echoed in her mind, distorted and monstrous. Cattle. A farm. She saw her mother's face again, smiling in the kitchen. A wave of nausea washed over her. She had to bend over, her hands clenched around her knees, to keep from fainting.

Around her, the shock spread in physical waves. In front of her, a young girl stared at her own hands in horror, as if they no longer belonged to her. Next to her, Evarine stood motionless, her face pale, her eyes glassy, staring at an invisible spot in the distance. Tears flowed silently down her cheeks. The novices' faces had turned into masks of bewilderment and horror. The only sound was unrestrained sobbing.

Menilmonea sympathized, but she needed the sorrow to give way to another feeling, one that was darker and more fiery.

"I know," she continued. "I'm sorry. I'm so sorry. This is precisely why the Keepers of Knowledge exist. We have to know so we can prepare and protect ourselves. The Arkandians slaughtered our parents, our friends, our Titans. They robbed us of our lives without shame. Now it's our turn to take everything we can, because know this: Aureal and I've blocked the source of magic that would have brought them back here. They're still out there, somewhere on our planet. And I can guarantee you that they won't be happy about being cut off from their precious city."

It took a while, but a fist finally clenched. A jaw tightened. A cry of rage, at first isolated, rose from one of the ranks, followed by a second. The quiet of the temple was shattered, replaced by an eruption of collective fury. The novices rose, their voices uniting in a roar of vengeance, a pledge to their stolen ancestors. Despair had found an outlet.

Valianara followed suit, standing on her chair and shouting until her voice broke. Grief had turned to cold, sharp determination. They would pillage their Library, master their magic, and wield it against them. If the Arkandians ever thought to return, they would find an army waiting for them.

She turned to Evarine, who also appeared to be in a similar state, her face red with fury and tears. Without a word, they embraced each other in an awkward hug that nearly caused them to topple from their chairs. They laughed through their tears, a strange mixture of relief and rage.

"There you go!" Their moment was interrupted by Menilmonea's calm but steady voice rising above the commotion. "Focus your rage. We have a goal. We have a mission. But now, please sit down. Revenge is a dish best served cold, and we still have much to prepare."

The High Orator waited for order to return, allowing the novices to catch their breath and resume their places.

"You now understand the fundamentals of the Keepers of Knowledge. We will study the magic and knowledge of the Arkandians, both to improve the lives of our villages and to be fully prepared for a return. I can therefore officially say: welcome to the Keepers of Knowledge."

VII

The Academy of the Keepers of Knowledge / Present Day

Menilmonea's voice still echoed through the temple when a timid round of applause broke out, quickly joined by the rest of the assembly. The novices, though still reeling, were galvanized. They had just been given a common purpose.

Immediately, several arms shot up, eager to ask questions.

The High Orator smiled. "Your curiosity is your greatest strength, and you'll spend the next few rotations asking countless questions. We will be here to answer them. However, for now, I have a question for you: in light of what you've just learned, can you tell me what the Revelation really is?"

The hands slowly lowered. A thoughtful silence fell, each novice reflecting on this fundamental question. Then, once again, a number of hands went up, more hesitantly this time.

Menilmonea pointed to a young woman with blonde hair. "You. What's your name?"

"Evarine of Opponka, High Orator. Just like Orator Aboren."

"Indeed. So, Evarine, what's the Revelation, in your opinion?"

"In my view, you and Orator Aureal freed the surviving Titans and came to understand that nothing would ever be the same again. It was clear that the Titans would no longer cause us to age prematurely and that there would never be another Ascension. You had to find a solution to explain this change without revealing the truth, which would undoubtedly have had a terrible impact on all the villages."

Menilmonea turned to the other orators and raised her eyebrows, wearing an undisguised look of satisfaction on her face.

"That's a perfect answer, Novice Evarine. I'm proud of you."

Valianara was delighted to see her friend transform into a volcano of barely contained pride.

"Well observed," she whispered in her ear. "You're amazing!"

"As Novice Evarine has just brilliantly demonstrated," Menilmonea continued, addressing the entire assembly, "the Council of Titans, along with Orator Aureal and myself, determined that the power of truth is far too destructive. Nearly every village was mourning loved ones they believed were resting peacefully with the Mother. We couldn't take that away from them and expect to maintain any semblance of civilization. The reality was simply not something that could be shared. We had to keep this knowledge, but we also had to embrace change: no more Ascension and a considerably longer life expectancy. In agreement with the Council of Titans, it was therefore decided to announce the Revelation."

She gauged the audience's attention before continuing, "Yes, it's a lie. It's not the most elegant thing I've ever done in my life, but Opponka observed something that helped me accept it: if the Mother hadn't given us our powers, if I hadn't been able to hear her and control her magic, then none of this would have happened. We would all be in our villages, wondering why our Titans died and why there's no longer an Ascension. It was she, in her great wisdom, who planned everything from the moment we were born. Ultimately, it was the Mother's will that ended our slavery during the Revelation."

She gestured with her hand, and a bramble delivered a large glass of water to her, which she drank gratefully.

"All the orators have lost at least their parents, and some even their spouses," she continued, casting a gentle glance at Aboren and Menara. "We know what happened to them, how lost and terrified they must have been. It haunts us every moment of our lives. We wouldn't wish that suffering on anyone. It's knowledge we must protect, and it can't be shared."

The atmosphere was heavy, and no one made a sound. Suddenly, a hand went up. Menilmonea showed a hint of surprise.

"Yes, young man?"

"High Orator, I'm Alister of Goaka. If I understand correctly… There are people throughout the world who live in the bodies of your parents or husbands?"

If a box of dynamite had been thrown into the room, the effect would not have been more devastating. No one seemed to have fully grasped the horrific nature of the situation. There were muffled curses and cries to the Mother. The murmur of voices drowned out the rest. Valianara felt as shaken by the question as by the person who had asked it. Alister still seemed a little lost, as if he didn't understand the terrible truth he had just revealed to the other novices.

Menilmonea attempted to calm the assembly, but the background noise was so intense that no one heard her. She then turned to her companions, looking distraught. "This is the first time this question has come up during the ceremony."

"Which proves that the class is certainly promising," Aureal replied with a smirk.

"At least they have a clear idea of what their aspirations entail," Menara added.

"They're adults. They'd have worked it out quickly enough anyway," concluded Aboren.

Menilmonea nodded, rummaging in a small bag on her belt. "Right, come on, playtime's over. We need to move on."

"We have to cover our ears, right?" Gideon asked, with a broad smile on his lips.

"I'd advise it, yes," replied Menilmonea with a twinkle in her eye.

With that, she threw a small gray mushroom on the ground. The explosion of sound from the earsplitter was deafening, so shrill it seemed to tear the air itself. The novices covered their ears with their hands. Several even fell off their chairs from the force of the shock.

A forced silence ensued. Menilmonea resumed, her voice ringing out with a new, cold, and uncompromising authority. "I apologize in advance for the harshness of my words, but you're no longer in your villages. When an orator calls for quiet, you must obey. Immediately. You're under our responsibility, and that means you must obey our directives to the letter."

She let them digest the information before continuing, "As for your question, Novice Alister, yes, that's precisely the case. And I can assure you that we're all haunted by the implications of the former Ascension. The best we can do is learn to live with it."

Her gaze drifted into the distance for a moment.

"Returning to obedience and hierarchy," she continued, "I'd like to remind you that the Academy's system is deliberately simple: novices are at the bottom of the ladder. You'll spend an entire rotation absorbing the current state of our knowledge. Then you'll be promoted to apprentices. After three rotations, you'll become Keepers of Knowledge. You should also know that this isn't a prison. You're free to move about as you please. In fact, you're free to leave at any time. You'll neither be judged nor punished. We consider you adults, and therefore free to make your own choices."

She paused, waiting for the inevitable question. It was a young man sitting at the back who dared to raise his hand. "Yes? Your name and your question, please."

"Inkidu of Apidonki, High Orator. If we're free to give up, what will become of all the knowledge that's supposed to be shared only with the Keepers of Knowledge? The knowledge of the Revelation, for example, which, as you've made clear, would be devastating to our villages?"

"Thank you, Novice Inkidu. That's an excellent question. How, indeed, do the Keepers of Knowledge safeguard knowledge, ultimately? After all, we're all fallible. A night of heavy drinking, a pillow confession... These things happen easily, and we're only human."

She took a step forward and placed her hand on the artifact, which had continued to pulse with its soft emerald light since the beginning.

"That's why we have the Secret Sentinel. This artifact, my dear novices, was invented by the Arkandians. Thanks to a book in their Library, we know how to use it, even though we have no idea how it works. On that subject, I'll now give the floor to Orator Menara, who, along with Orator Aboren, will be guiding you throughout this rotation on the workings of mind magic."

With a graceful gesture, Menilmonea sat down. Instantly, her root chair reshaped itself to accommodate her. Menara, meanwhile, stood up, and her own seat disappeared with a rustling sound; a few eyebrows rose among the admiring novices.

"You'll get used to it quickly," she remarked with a laugh. "I'll spare you the number of times I've found myself on the floor, though, because I'm used to seeing chairs appear when the High Orator is around. Of course, when I'm alone… Anyway! Let me introduce myself. I'm Orator Menara, from Gunderki. My task is to impart knowledge related to mind magic, and your first lesson begins right now. We discovered this device while exploring the city, and it has become the cornerstone of our order."

She nodded to Aureal, who nodded back.

"Orator Aureal has just asked our brave volunteer to rejoin us. He must have found the wait rather long, poor fellow. Rest assured, I'll personally ensure he receives all the information you've been given during his absence. However, he plays an essential role, as he now represents the villagers."

Valianara gave her friend a gentle nudge. "It must have been a strange experience for him, with all the shouting and explosions!" she whispered.

"The Secret Sentinel lives up to its name, you see, in that it prevents us from sharing protected knowledge with anyone unaware of it. Only the person who activates the system, as the High Orator did, can initiate sharing. You won't be able to share any future knowledge you learn, either. The magic of this artifact prevents any potential leaks. For example, if you learn something about the towers that could cause the person you are speaking with to deduce that the Mother didn't build this city, then that knowledge will be blocked."

A gasp of wonder rippled through the assembly. After the horror of the revelations, this was a different kind of shock. They were finally getting back to the exciting part of the Academy, the reason they were all there: to discover magic, to explore its mysteries.

Kamartel returned, accompanied by a placid Grumf. The young man walked along shyly and respectfully beside the beast. Menara motioned for him to come closer.

"Thank you so much for your patience, Kamartel."

She turned to the assembly. "Who would like to explain to our brave novice what you've just learned?"

A multitude of arms shot up instantly. Everyone wanted to experience the magic of the Arkandians.

With some difficulty, Menara finally pointed to a novice in the front row. "You."

"Amaldine of Arabinoki, Orator Menara."

"Very well, Amaldine. It's your turn. You can tell him whatever you want, at no risk. Whatever happens, I'll personally give him all the knowledge you've already received later on."

Amaldine stood up quickly.

"Kamartel," she began, "you need to know that… that… well… that…"

She looked helplessly at the orator. "It's absolutely incredible! I know what I want to say to him, but I can't put it into a sentence! It's like having a word on the tip of your tongue, but not being able to say it."

Menara laughed softly. "That's exactly it. You've just had your first experience of mind magic. Surprisingly powerful, isn't it? If Kamartel steps back far enough, you'll be able to whisper it to your neighbor."

Grumf gently grabbed Kamartel's tunic between his teeth and pulled him back a dozen steps or so.

"This place wasn't built by the Mother," Amaldine leaned over to her neighbor's ear and whispered, her voice tinged with relief and wonder.

Menara gave the assembled crowd a reassuring smile. "Don't worry, you can all try telling Kamartel your secrets to feel the impact of the mind magic. There's no doubt he'll be the star of the evening."

VIII

The Academy of the Keepers of Knowledge / Present Day

Indeed, Kamartel caused quite a stir. Everyone wanted to speak with him to test the artifact's magic. After all, the Secret Sentinel couldn't be that powerful! However, even the more arrogant among them had to admit defeat. They tried different turns of phrase, hints, suggestions… Nothing worked.

Menilmonea waited for calm to be restored before formally closing the ceremony.

"Your first lesson is done. And even though you may not be in the mood for it right now, it remains important to focus on the positive. So, to celebrate your arrival, a tasting of grape brandy from the southern slopes of the Academy will be served on the other side of the tree. I ask that you take this opportunity to become acquainted with one another. Here's your first objective as a group: pair up to share rooms and then form squads of four. These squads will be responsible for chores within the Residence at various times."

The hubbub resumed as the novices made their way to the tables that had been set up. It was not the carefree, raucous joy of village celebrations, nor the oppressive silence of mourning. Rather, it was something in between, an atmosphere charged with a strange alchemy of emotions.

The amber liquor flowed freely, but they did not drink to forget; they drank as if they were sealing a pact. The faces, illuminated by the glow of the central tree, displayed not smiles, but clenched jaws and burning eyes. Anger simmered in every conversation. However, the rage did not overwhelm them: on the contrary, it fortified their resolve, transforming their initial incomprehension into a powerful fuel.

Everywhere, fists were clenched, not to attack, but to pledge never to suffer again. The excitement of the magic they had discovered moments earlier was tinged with a new urgency. They no longer wanted to learn simply for honor or curiosity; they wanted to learn to defend themselves, to understand the enemy, to regain control of their destiny. There was a fierce optimism, an immediate solidarity born of shared trauma. They were no longer strangers from across the continent; in one evening, they had become the heirs to a silent war, united by a desperate desire to turn their ignorance into armor.

Valianara and Evarine grabbed a glass filled with a brown liquor and found a quiet corner.

"It's strong!" Valianara gasped after her first sip.

"But it's good! And after those big revelations, I think it's just what we need."

"Yes. It's a bit like putting a bandage on a hemorrhage of emotions!"

"Aha! That's exactly it! Well, the two of us already make up half a squad," Evarine noted pragmatically. "Any ideas for the other two?"

Valianara scanned the room, her attention settling on a familiar figure. "I don't know… I like Alister's slightly lost look. He seems… different."

"He's cute, too. But I'm sure that has nothing to do with your choice."

"I don't know what you're talking about," replied Valianara, feeling her cheeks flush. "Look, he's talking to Kamartel. Let's ambush them before someone else recruits them!"

They walked over to the pair, who were sitting alone at a table on the opposite side of the room from the main crowd. Kamartel's temporary "curse" had turned him into an outcast. In order to debate freely and let their anger blow off, the other novices had no choice but to avoid him. Kamartel, however, didn't seem to mind. Instead, he seemed to be enjoying his new status as a pariah, which made anyone who tried to talk to him stutter. Alister was the only one who had stayed to keep him company. He listened to him in comfortable silence, a slight smile on his lips.

"Sorry to interrupt," said Evarine as she approached. "I hope we're not disturbing a private conversation."

Kamartel laughed good-naturedly. "No, not yet! I was just explaining to Alister that I can't wait to finally find out what everyone is trying to talk to me about!"

"We were wondering…" Valianara continued. "Have you found a roommate yet?"

"To be honest, I haven't really had time to start looking," Kamartel admitted.

Alister immediately turned to him. "If you don't have anyone in mind, I'd be happy to share a room with you."

"Really? Perfect! That's one less thing to worry about!"

Evarine seized the opportunity. "Well, now that you've got your roommates, how about joining our squad?"

Kamartel gave Alister a questioning look. Alister shrugged his shoulders and nodded.

"It's a deal, then!"

"Great!" Valianara exclaimed enthusiastically. "I'll get our group signed up with Orator Menara right away."

With that done, Menara assigned them their next mission. "Since you're the first officially formed squad, you can choose your room ahead of everyone else. Go and take a look at the Residence."

She signaled to a servant waiting near the stairs, then placed a hand on Kamartel's shoulder. "The rest of you, follow this delightful young man. Kamartel, you'll join them later. You and I need to talk."

Startled, Kamartel watched his friends walk away.

"I'm counting on you to pick wisely!" he whispered to them.

They smiled broadly and hurried after the apprentice. The apprentice, who was probably only one rotation older than they were, led them down the central avenue. The novices noticed that the lighting had changed. From a deep shade of orange, the pyramid's interior was

Transport Ring Hall
Pearl Room
Jar Room
Library
Residence

Temple of the Mother
Chamber of Memory
Academy

now bathed in a soft blue light. It felt like a balmy summer night. Valianara found herself looking up at the sky, searching for stars, but the illusion was quickly shattered when her eyes fell on the dark walls of the pyramid.

As they descended, Valianara got an unobstructed view of the Residence building. Lower than the slender towers of the Academy or the imposing dome of the Library, it was wider and more inviting. It consisted of several structures interconnected by arcades and gently sloping roofs. A central tower, slimmer and more elegant, dominated the whole, and its many lit windows promised warmth and comfort. The place felt both noble and functional: a place of life rather than a place of knowledge or power. She could make out the silhouettes of several people on the upper floors.

"This is it," announced their guide, stopping in front of the Residence. "And if you want my advice, I suggest you take the room furthest from the entrance. It will be much quieter, because the staircase leading to the upper floors is always quite noisy."

"Noted," acknowledged Valianara.

"We believe this building was where the Arkandians kept those who were ailing. Each floor consists of a single long corridor with rooms on either side."

"How delightful." Evarine shuddered.

"Rest assured, they're nothing like our clinics. And the spirits of the sick departed long ago. At least, I assume."

He paused to enjoy his joke.

"I'm just teasing!" he quickly added, seeing their crestfallen faces. "This place is perfect, you'll see. Each room holds two large beds and a bathing room. When you become apprentices, you'll have the same, but just all to yourselves."

"A bathing room?" Evarine asked in surprise.

"Ah, yes! I'll show you. It will undoubtedly help you appreciate just how powerful Arkandian magic is."

With that, he led them into the first room. Valianara was stunned. It was strikingly modern, a world away from anything she had ever seen in her village. There was no rough wood, no wattle and daub, no exposed beams. The walls were made of a single piece of white stone, so smooth that it was soft to the touch. Lines of dark metal, set with impossible precision, formed geometric patterns that ran along the bottom of the walls and ceiling. The floor was a checkerboard of large gray marble slabs so tightly fitted together that you couldn't slip a pin between them. But the oddest thing was the light. Soft, with a slight bluish tint, it radiated from the base of the walls, creating an atmosphere ideal for rest. It seemed to work in tandem with the city's brightness. On the outside wall, a large translucent sheet of crystal replaced a traditional window, affording a breathtaking view of the city. The room itself was divided into two by a heavy curtain suspended from a metal rod. On each side, a feature had been built directly into the wall and floor: a bed with a polished stone frame, topped with a thick mattress, invited rest. Next to it, a bookcase with shelves carved into the stone completed the ensemble. The only additions were a desk and a dark wooden wardrobe beside each bed.

"We added the desks and wardrobes," said the apprentice, as if he had guessed Valianara's question about the contrast in materials.

At the back, a small corridor led to another room, into which he ushered them.

"And this," he said with a laugh, "is the jewel of Arkandian magic." He first pointed to a rounded seat with a hole in the middle. "This is what we call the latrine. This is where you can relieve yourselves."

Everyone stared at him, baffled.

"What do you mean? But where does it go… I mean… You know what I mean?" stammered Evarine.

"Yes, I know what you mean," replied the apprentice. "Here, you do what you have to do, then you place your hand on this rectangle at the back of the seat. Be sure to remain sitting. That way, the seat will dispose of your waste while washing and drying your bottom. I won't lie to you, this is by far the thing I miss most about the Academy when I go home to visit my family—having to go back to the river or the forest after this is a real ordeal."

He gave everyone time to take in the completely new concept. It was a rite of passage for the novices, so he decided not to rush them. He remembered his own surprise when he first encountered Arkandian technology.

Valianara pointed to the rectangular block that stood nearby. Glass walls surrounded it. "And that, what is it?"

"That's the bathing cabin. One of the walls slides open like this so that you can get in. Once you've undressed, you press the rectangle on the wall and let the magic happen."

"What does that mean?"

"You'll be showered with water at the temperature of your choosing. It will flow from the ceiling, as if you were washing in the rain, but it will be warm and invigorating. There's nothing like it after a hard day's research! You won't be able to imagine life without it. Let me tell you, it's a far cry from scrubbing away in the freezing water of a river! By the way, you'll find soap in your cupboards."

"And is every room like this?"

"Yes, every last one. And I haven't even mentioned the mattresses on your beds." He paused dramatically, reveling in the impact of his words. "Right, I'll leave you to choose your room. A squad of apprentices will come by in the evening to see if you're settled in. Please note that you're responsible for keeping your quarters clean. You'll find sheets over there. And I can see you all have a bundle of belongings. You can leave your things in your closets; there are no thieves here. And if you need anything else, your families can have it sent to you, or you can go to the bazaar."

As he was about to leave, he looked back one last time. "Ah, one more thing: mail is sent out at noon every day. Just leave your correspondence on your desk in plain sight. And rest well tonight: tomorrow, the bell will ring at dawn, and you'll be expected at the Academy for your first lesson."

As he walked away, the three friends stood there dumbfounded. Valianara finally sat down heavily on one of the beds, letting out a long sigh of pleasure. "It's so soft… I'll probably never wake up if I sleep on this."

"Okay, let's go choose our rooms!" said Evarine eagerly. "I can't wait to experience the magic of the Arkandians!"

"I vote for the two at the end," suggested Valianara, smiling.

"That's fine with me!" immediately replied Evarine.

"I'm perfectly fine with peace and quiet. I'm in favor of it," Alister noted softly. "I'm sure Kamartel will be fine with it too."

No sooner had the door to their room closed than Valianara heard the clamor of new squads flooding into the corridor. Glancing out of the window, she was struck by the strangest impression that the massive roots clinging to the outer wall were vibrating slightly, as if they themselves were delighted to welcome new inhabitants into their fold.

IX

Arkandis / The Breaking of the Pact
1,400 rotations prior to the Death of Tunka

The loud click of a key turning in the lock snapped Azymantias out of his thoughts. He had had a miserable night. He found himself sitting on a bare stone bed in one of the confinement cells reserved for mages—comfort of a decidedly spartan kind, far removed from his usual lodgings. The door creaked open, and Oberron entered, a tray in hand.

"I've brought your meal, Azymantias," announced the Master Bloodhound in a weary voice.

The prisoner stood up, a wry smile on his lips. "My last meal in this body. I trust you've made an effort."

Oberron managed a faint smile and set the tray on the bed. "Let's just say the food matches the decor."

"If I'd known, I'd have indulged in one last drinking binge," Azymantias replied, eyeing the tray. "After all, I won't have to suffer the consequences now. Speaking of consequences, I suspect this so-called bed of yours is a ploy to hasten my demise."

The Master Bloodhound let out a long laugh that sounded like it came from the pit of his stomach. "That's an excellent way of looking at it, Azymantias. Since our culinary talents don't seem to impress you, I suggest we get this over with as quickly as possible. As you well know, the procedure is clear. We will have to subject you to a complete mental lock. You'll no longer be able to control your body or speak. If you have any last messages to pass on to anyone, I'll be honored to deliver them."

Azymantias raised his head, his expression suddenly serious. "Thank you, Oberron. But I've already said all I have to say to those who matter to me."

He softly pushed the tray away, without having touched it. "We can go."

Oberron and another Bloodhound reached out their hands to him. Azymantias offered no resistance. He felt the tendrils of flux take root within him, directed by their expert minds. He did not cast any spells that could easily have repelled them or given them a vicious headache. He attempted nothing, simply accepting his fate. His senses dulled, his muscles stiffened. Before long, he could no longer move.

He knew that his body's life expectancy was less than an hour. The lock would eventually affect his body's reflexes, and his heart would stop beating. But by then, he would no longer be the owner of this millennia-old shell. He wondered what they might do with his body. Usually, they were cremated. What a waste…

The surroundings changed. The vaulted ceiling of the Jar Room began to roll past above him. Every jolt of the stretcher that carried him reverberated through his bones, but he found himself unable to wince.

Let's hope I'm not drooling, he thought. *That would ruin the drama of the moment.*

His eyes, which he could no longer close, were becoming increasingly dry. They were beginning to sting badly. This was one of the drawbacks of mental locking that had not been adequately studied. He would have to remedy that once his plan succeeded. In the meantime, he would have to endure it. His vision blurred, but out of the corner of his eye, he saw a familiar figure.

Avamar.

She had the cold stare and harsh tone befitting the General of the Fourth Legion. In her hands, he recognized the jar he had entrusted to her. His heart grew warm. She hadn't betrayed him. She would keep her word. She was indeed an exceptional woman. He would find a way to tell her as much upon his return.

He could barely hear what was being said around him. Still, he vaguely discerned a jumble of competing voices, even though only Avamar and Obinaelle should have been conducting the ceremony.

The Mind Focalizer had just been placed beside him. It wouldn't be long now. As the artifact's inventor, he appreciated the irony of the situation.

He could see Avamar leaning over his face, her lips forming the words *I love you.* Then nothing. His spirit had left his body.

"The jar is sealed. The sentence has been executed," Avamar declared in a clear, neutral voice.

With a wave of her hand, she caused the jar to float to its assigned shelf. She couldn't help but remark to those gathered that the ceremony should not have been cut short in such a manner and that the lack of respect shown to Azymantias, Mage of the First Circle, would be noted in the records.

"Do so," Obinaelle replied curtly. "In the meantime, I need you and your troops on the ramparts of the lower city. Have them prepare for a siege. We're about to receive a mass influx of people who will want to return to the palace."

"What do you mean? Is that an official request from the Triumvirate?" asked Avamar, raising an eyebrow.

"Yes. The other two members are… unwell. We're in a crisis."

"Understood. May I know the reason for this influx?"

"Your former lover. There's the reason," hissed Obinaelle. After a moment's thought, she turned to the audience. "Everyone out! Go! I need to speak privately with the general."

Once the Bloodhounds and members of the First Circle, who had come to honor their friend, had taken their leave, Obinaelle continued. "As I predicted, the Source disapproved of what we did to the dryads. I'd hoped she would merely slap us on the wrist, but based on the reports I'm receiving, I fear Arkandis is in danger. The Maritime Guard has reported gigantic waves forming on the horizon. She will undoubtedly want to submerge us."

Avamar felt lost. "What do you mean, 'submerge'?"

"Surprisingly, that's how gods do things," Obinaelle replied. "They erase you from existence. The Source didn't see us until that idiot Azymantias got his grandiose ideas. We're about to disappear, General. We're no match for the Source's colossal power. All we can do is hope to save the Magisterium. The people are doomed."

Avamar's confidence began to crumble slowly. "But… What are you thinking? A tsunami?"

"To start with, yes. It's already happening. Can't you see the storms and clouds as black as death? It's going to bury us, starting with the lower city. We need to buy some time so I can come up with a countermeasure."

Avamar raised an eyebrow in disbelief.

"I may have a possible solution," Obinaelle felt compelled to add. "That's why your presence on the ramparts is needed so that I can put it into action."

A courier of the palace rushed in, handing a sealed envelope to the High Magistrix before leaving as quickly as he had arrived. She broke the seal and read the message. Her already pale face turned ghostly white as she read on.

"High Magistrix? What's wrong?" asked Avamar, alarmed by her expression.

Obinaelle looked up from the parchment, her eyes wide. "The second wave of her attack, if that's what one might call it. It appears that several mages are suffering severe burns when exposed to sunlight. They're being taken to the Core Hospital. I'm going to ask the Flux Masters to come and tend to them. Apparently, she's striking us on several fronts. This is indeed far worse than I anticipated."

Avamar was speechless. But it was no longer the silence of disbelief; it was the deafening emptiness of a world falling apart. An abyss was opening up beneath her feet, a chasm carved into existence by her own arrogance. All her certainties, her contempt for the "old fables," her absolute faith in Azymantias's logic and reason—all of it had just been shattered by reality.

The Source existed. And she saw them as targets.

The wave threatening Arkandis was nothing compared to the tide of pure guilt now crashing through her soul. Azymantias had not sacrificed himself as a martyr. He had sacrificed himself like a fool. And she had been his accomplice. Together, they had just led their world to destruction.

"I don't understand…" Avamar began, the world spinning around her.

With these words, Obinaelle's mask of coldness shattered. She approached Avamar, her face contorted with a rage that had been contained for millennia.

"Did you honestly believe this was all just a game? That I'd built a four-thousand-year lie for the sake of power? That I'd sacrificed every part of my being for the mere pleasure of rule? We were given the gift of the flux! Of immortality! All we had to do was remain discreet and let her believe we respected her work and her expectations. Clearly, for some, it was too much. Well, you'll see. You'll all see what I've spent my life holding back. You'll all see what the wrath of a goddess looks like. I once caught a glimpse of her greatness, and compared to her, we're nothing more than insects. Perhaps in tens of thousands of rotations, if we'd continued to strengthen our control over the flux, we could have attempted to stand up to her. But as it stands, we're doomed. My only consolation is knowing that outside, dozens of naturalists like Azymantias will finally pay the price for their utter idiocy."

She faltered, catching her breath, her chest heaving violently. Then, as quickly as the fury had come, it disappeared, replaced by her usual facade of control. Her gaze hardened.

"This is no time to be weak, General. Go. Take your soldiers to the ramparts. I'll take care of protecting the Magisterium. I won't let the Source destroy my legacy."

X

The Academy of the Keepers of Knowledge / Present Day
10 rotations following the Death of Tunka

Menilmonea and Aureal walked down the main avenue, leaving behind them the silence of the Temple of the Mother.

"Well, that went rather well, didn't it?" said Aureal.

"Better than that. I was surprised by some of the brilliant insights. This will be a good class," replied Menilmonea. She glanced sideways at her friend and changed the subject. "What about you and Gideon? Are you two alright? He seemed a little sad."

Aureal sighed, a weary smile tugging at her lips. "We broke up. Yes… Again."

"Oh. Do you want to talk about it?"

"Not really. It's the same old story. I know he's not the one, but he has his charms and… Sometimes I'm weak."

"You're not weak! You're just alive. Don't be so hard on yourself. As long as it doesn't make you unhappy…"

"Oh, no. I'm applying the first lesson I learned at the School of Menilmonea: it's better to be on your own than in bad company."

"Exactly!" said Menilmonea, hugging her. "Thanks for walking me back. I have to rush off to the Council. Shall we have tea later, if you're not going to sleep?"

"I won't sleep. I'm going to walk Grumf to the edge of the forest. See you later!"

Menilmonea stepped into the hushed silence of the Chamber

of Memory. She was immediately met by a disembodied voice that seemed to come from everywhere at once. "Good evening, Menil! How did the ceremony go?"

"Honestly, it went really well. We have some brilliant minds in this class. How was your day?"

"The same as always, you know. Thank you for leaving pages for me everywhere, but I read them faster than you can copy them."

"I know. I have two apprentices working on it full-time. Have you still not found anything that might help us free you from this place?"

"Not a chance! I'd have told you before you even set foot in the room."

"Yes, of course. Can I have all the pages back?"

"Yes, I was able to dictate a summary to your apprentice."

"Thank you so much! And still no memory of your name or your past?"

"No, unfortunately. A few flashes, but nothing definite. But I'm sure we'll find a solution in these books. There are still so many left! How many have you transcribed for me?"

"Barely thirty. It's such a slow process. If we could take the books out of the Library, I'd have assigned you a student to turn the pages."

"Oh, the poor thing! What a miserable life that would be... I wouldn't wish such torment on anyone."

"There are some who would be only too happy to do it. We all feel compassion for the spirits chained to the towers and buildings."

"I know that. And I also realize that you're doing everything you can for us. It's just that some days are harder than others."

Menilmonea nodded and sat down in an inconspicuous armchair, set a little apart.

"Oh. The Council of Titans?" asked the Voice.

"Exactly. I'm counting on you to let any visitors know that this isn't a suitable time."

"I'll be as clear about it as I can. I actually kind of like scaring them sometimes."

Menilmonea smiled, then closed her eyes and opened herself to the Mother's song.

In an instant, she lost contact with her body. Her consciousness was thrown into a maelstrom of music and voices, an infinite ocean of pure awareness. She let herself sink, searching not for sounds, but for presences. Vast masses of ancient will, heavy and immovable as mountains. She isolated the first, that of Omoridoki, and reached out to it mentally; a thread of thought was woven between them. Then she sought the next, Opponka, and wove another thread. In this way, from one contact to the next, a vaporous spider's web was formed, a constellation of linked souls, a network of minds awakening to one another across the ether.

The Council was formed.

Thirty-eight spirits. One human and thirty-seven Titans.

A dominant consciousness, complex and made of a thousand threads, spoke. It was Arabinoki, the spider Titan.

"Welcome, all. And thank you, Menilmonea, for initiating this Council session. As is customary, if any of us would like to share something, please make yourself known now."

Only a single presence became more distinct: Goaka, the crab Titan.

"Well, we'll have just one thing to talk about today," Arabinoki continued.

Menilmonea loved the Council meetings. She could sense the Titans' emotional state beyond their words: their composure, their serenity, and a profound wisdom that put her at ease. It was a moment of tranquility for her. Their communication was always gentle, devoid of all aggression, yet direct. In general, the discussions focused on Briars, the balance of trade, and the economic health of the villages. The Titans were ancient beings. They had all the time in the world. With the Revelation, they had reclaimed their memories from before the transformation, remembering their lives as the descendants of Primals. They had reconnected with the Mother's song. But they also remembered the centuries spent sustaining and guiding the villages, and their decision was unanimous: they would continue to help humans. The Revelation itself had been a shared decision, carefully considered between them and Menilmonea. The Primal had indicated that he did not wish to interfere with the villages, while respecting the Titans' decision.

Arabinoki gave the floor to Goaka.

"Good day to you all, and to you, Menilmonea. Unfortunately, I come bearing troubling news."

A mental jolt struck Menilmonea. She had a theory about Goaka, and probably about Tunka, too, to some extent. The Primal was the only one of its siblings to have aquatic origins. The rare Titans associated with water, such as the crab, seemed to share a special bond with him. For her, there was no doubt: they were the direct descendants of this Primal, not its brothers. So, hearing Goaka talk about bad news gave his words an even more sinister twist.

Goaka continued, his thoughts spreading through the network like a slow tide. *"First of all, the Primal told me that he had to repel another boat. On the northeast coast, once again. It seemed smaller than the previous ones, with perhaps a dozen people on board, but its origin was clearly Arkandian."*

The consciousness of Opponka, the serpent Titan, rippled. *"This is the third attempt since the Revelation."*

"We thought their first two failures had sent them a clear message," Goaka continued, *"but apparently that's not the case. They're truly determined to reclaim their city."*

Menilmonea sensed the Council's collective consciousness tremble at the mention of the Arkandians. It wasn't anger. It was something deeper: a dark determination, cold and sharp as steel. An unwavering will to never again be victimized. The silent memory of centuries of servitude and lost brothers formed an impenetrable shield. They would never stand for it again.

"Why now?" Opponka interrupted. *"The previous attempt was more than four rotations ago."*

"I don't know," Goaka continued. *"Neither does the Primal. He's detected no changes in the city, and the sphere of negation remains inactive. My question to the Council is this: should we strengthen our preparations?"*

Omoridoki's deep voice echoed through the network. *"Guardians of peace are positioned near all towers and in all villages. The Primal himself guards the city, and his aquatic forests stretch across our entire coastline. We're well prepared."*

A consensus spread through the collective consciousness. Menilmonea greatly appreciated this way of working: everyone could give their opinion, but in the end, the group always reached a unanimous decision. This meant that all topics could be discussed and dealt with as a whole.

"Moving on to my second point," Goaka continued, his thoughts increasingly heavy, *"I found the skeleton of an adult human on the beach, east of my tower. It was next to a boat, similar to those used by the fishermen of my village."*

Menilmonea intervened, her words seeking to reassure him. *"Since the Revelation, it isn't unusual for some people to have accidents and die. Perhaps this poor soul had run into trouble."*

"Indeed. Except that no one is missing from my village."

A cold shiver ran through the web of minds.

"Have other coastal villages reported any missing persons?" asked Menilmonea.

The answer shot through the Council before her question was even fully formed: *no*—a unanimity. No villagers were missing anywhere on the continent.

"This is a problem," she thought, feeling a vague sense of dread rising within her.

Goaka continued, *"The Primal believes it could be a survivor of his attack—someone who jumped into that boat before their ship was destroyed. Likely wounded, he would have drifted for several days before washing up dead on the beach."*

"But... a skeleton?" interrupted Menilmonea. *"So quickly?"*

"Life is swift to reclaim what is hers along the shore, Menilmonea," replied Goaka. *"It takes little time for crustaceans, birds, and a thousand other creatures to clean a body and return it to Gaia."*

A silence fell, heavy with the implications of this theory. Menilmonea sensed something else in Goaka's thoughts; a hesitation, or perhaps a doubt.

"And you, Goaka? What are your thoughts?"

The answer was slow in coming, ebbing back to the Council like the tide. *"The Primal's explanation is the most logical. However, it implies something troubling: that small boats could slip past his watchful eye. The Primal himself conceded that this was unlikely, but not impossible. As a result, he's decided to extend the coral barrier along the entire northeast coast, which is clearly their most likely arrival point."*

Omoridoki's more pragmatic thoughts could be heard. *"It's highly likely that their island is located in that direction."*

"Indeed," agreed Goaka. *"Nevertheless... I dislike the idea that an Arkandian, even a dead one, could have set foot on our continent."*

All the Titans shared the feeling. A quiet wave of suspicion and cold determination swept through Menilmonea's soul. With that, the session came to an end: the Council's collective consciousness slowly broke apart, each mind returning to its respective body. When the last link was severed, the High Orator found herself alone in the darkness of the Chamber of Memory. The burden of her responsibilities seemed heavier than ever.

XI

The Academy of the Keepers of Knowledge / Present Day

A piercing, repetitive sound tore through the stillness of the room. Valianara stirred from her sleep with a grunt, curious to know what demon could be responsible for such screeching. Next to her, she heard Evarine stir gently.

The bell eventually stopped ringing, leaving a welcome hush.

"I've never slept so well in my life," Evarine murmured in a slurred voice. "I'll never be able to sleep anywhere else. I want to marry this mattress. Even though with everything we learned yesterday, I expected to have a terrible night."

Valianara stretched, her muscles feeling remarkably relaxed. "It was amazing. I feel so good. Do you want to wash up first?"

"You better believe it! But I can't guarantee I'll be quick!" replied her friend, jumping out of bed with a burst of energy.

"No problem. I'll write to my parents while I wait."

Half an hour later, fresh and ready for their first day, the two friends knocked on the door of the other members of their squad. After what seemed like an eternity, Alister opened up, his eyes half-closed and his hair even more tousled than the day before.

"I guess I overslept," he said drowsily.

"We noticed," Evarine teased gently. "Where's your partner? Is he still asleep?"

"No, he left early. I don't know how he managed it! Wait for me,

I'll get ready quickly and leave with you."

He joined them a few moments later, with a slight smile and somewhat tidier hair—albeit still wet. Valianara and Evarine instinctively took the helm of the small group, which was now making its way to the Academy, chatting excitedly.

"By all the Titans, I don't know where to look first," exclaimed Evarine, pointing to a series of aerial walkways. "It's like every building is a work of art!"

Valianara glanced back. Alister was following them quietly, a couple of steps behind. His attention wasn't really focused on the architectural wonders that surrounded them, but on the pebble he was rolling between his thumb and forefinger.

"Don't you think it's incredible?" she asked him, trying to draw him into the conversation.

"Yes, it's impressive."

The paved path curved upward, passing buildings topped with bronze domes and facades adorned with intricate arcades. Valianara couldn't help but stop to admire the details, the sculptures, the strange harmony of this city built of stone and vegetation. Finally, the building they were looking for stood out from the others, with its multiple towers and huge dome.

"Our first lesson awaits us," said Evarine, her eyes bright with anticipation. "I can't wait to see if it's just as impressive on the inside."

No sooner had they walked through the doors of the Academy than a squad of apprentices greeted them with a weary air.

"They seem delighted that they've been stuck with this chore," Evarine whispered to her friend.

"Good morning, novices. The dining hall is on your right. Breakfast is served there. Everything here's taken care of by the Academy: you won't need your Briar. Afterward, please report directly to the Library."

Valianara's eyes lit up. "The Library! I've been dreaming of it forever! Everything the Keepers of Knowledge could possibly know, right at your fingertips! They say there are entire walls of books!"

They headed for the dining hall, a vast space filled with long tables laden with fresh fruit, assorted breads, and delicate gold-brown pastries. The atmosphere was lighter than the day before, as if sleep had washed away their worries. The raw fury and crushing doubts had dissipated, giving way to impatience for a new day. It was time to explore, to comprehend, and, little by little, to adjust to this new reality.

Evarine, her eyes twinkling, grabbed a still-warm brioche. "I think I'm going to really enjoy my stay here."

Valianara looked around for Kamartel, but he was nowhere to be seen. "Maybe he went to take a look around the bazaar?"

Alister merely shrugged in response.

"In any case, let's not deprive ourselves!" said Evarine. "We'll need all our strength for whatever lies ahead."

Some twenty minutes later, sated and revitalized, they left the Academy and set off for the Library. The path took them slightly downhill along the main avenue, then across a stone bridge spanning an alley below.

The Library finally rose up majestically before them. It was an imposing rotunda of pale stone, crowned with a conical dome covered in a patina of blue-green. Three floors of semicircular arches embellished its circular facade, allowing an amber glow to filter through its windows. A true bastion of knowledge anchored in the heart of the city, the structure blended into the neighboring buildings with its enormous extensions, forming a single, colossal stone monolith.

Several other squads had already arrived and were waiting in the hall, where a respectful murmur grew. Valianara spotted Kamartel near a column and waved to him. He joined them with a smile that was more serene than the one he had worn the day before.

"You're quite the early bird, I see!" Evarine exclaimed.

"Ha, ha! Yes, I like to go out for a stroll at dawn. I needed a walk to relax. Now that I know what you all know… Well, I have to admit, it's really shaken me up. My family is rather traditional, and I wasn't quite sure what to do with all the feelings that came flooding over me. Walking through the streets of the bazaar helped clear my head."

He turned to Alister, a little sheepish. "I hope I didn't wake you."

Alister shrugged. "No, don't worry. I'm a heavy sleeper."

A loud voice, echoing above the crowd, caught their attention. It was Orator Menara.

"I invite you to come forward into the Library itself. Yes, it's the large metal door on your left."

The group of novices complied with the request in silence. Valianara followed along, holding her breath.

She stopped at the threshold, astounded. The word "library" did not do the place justice.

It was not a room, but a world; a huge circular space rising three dizzying stories high. The walls—no, the cliffs of books and dark wooden shelves—held thousands of leather-bound volumes, bathed in the soft glow of dozens of candles. Here, too, nature reigned supreme. Thick vines, covered with small red flowers, snaked along the walls, encircled the balustrades, and cascaded down in vegetal waterfalls. Trees grew directly out of the ground, their branches rising gracefully toward the upper levels, and a superb carpet of soft grass and small white flowers sprouted between the stone slabs of the main floor. A spiral staircase, curving gracefully, wound around an invisible central axis to serve the three balconies that circled the room. Everywhere, there was the smell of old paper, hot wax, and damp soil.

Valianara raised her head, her eyes following the elegant spiral of the staircase up to the top floor, up where it was dim and dark. Nowhere else could one find such a treasure trove of knowledge. Her lifelong dream stood before her, a thousand times more exquisite than she could ever have dared to imagine.

Menara joined them, scanning their amazed faces, and sat down on the bottom step of the staircase before silently beckoning them to gather around her.

"Ten rotations ago, the High Orator and Orator Aureal uncovered this incredible place. It was here that the idea for the Academy of the Keepers of Knowledge first took shape. It's also here that you'll spend much of your time studying, gaining understanding, and sometimes transcribing the works in this Library."

She looked at her audience, who were captivated by what they had just heard. "Yes, it's magnificent. It's the foundation of our order. It contains all the knowledge of the Arkandians. And as you've already

been able to judge from your rooms, their magic and wisdom are light years ahead of ours. Your mission will be to glean this knowledge, digest it, and put it to effective use. As you advance within our order, you'll consult books that no one else has ever read. It will be your responsibility to make sense of them and, above all, to find a place for them."

She pointed to a large stone table right next to the front door. "There you'll find our glossary. We're trying to catalog the books and their subjects. This is an extremely important task, especially for you, as it will give you an overview of the extent of our learning."

A hand went up. It was Inkidu.

"Orator, you say we will be able to find unpublished books. But haven't we already read everything after eight rotations?"

"That's an excellent question, novice. And the answer is no. To put it bluntly, we haven't even read all the books on the ground floor yet. There are over two thousand books on that level alone. Not to mention that it takes time to catalog and understand what they contain. Although we're getting better and better at it, it's not the same as reading a simple story: we often lack the context or expertise that the author might have taken for granted."

"And you haven't started studying the ones on the other floors?"

"They're inaccessible to us."

"I don't understand, Orator Menara."

Menara broke into a broad grin. "That's perfectly natural, my child. You're missing some vital information."

"We don't know if it's always been this way," she continued, her tone turning more serious, "but several spells guard the Library. First, and perhaps most importantly, no book ever leaves this room. If you tried to take one out, it would spontaneously burst into flames. That's why we have to copy their contents if we want to study them elsewhere."

A collective "Oh" of understanding rippled through the rows of novices.

"As you may imagine, this point is of paramount importance," Menara stressed. "We can't afford to lose a single shred of this knowledge. It's one of the reasons why there are guardians of peace at the entrance. Then there are the Arkandians' Seals of Rejection. There are three of them in this room. One per floor."

The novices' fascination was palpable.

"In short, the books on each floor become increasingly interesting from our point of view, but also increasingly more difficult to decipher. For example, you can grab some books from the first floor; it's always an interesting experience. However, you won't make sense of what's written in them. As soon as you look at a page, your vision will blur. I'll let you try it out in a few moments."

The novices would have been no more excited if they had been told they were about to visit an enchanted land of candy.

"The seal on the second floor is even more powerful… and unsettling. You can still pick up a book and make out its title, but as soon as you try to open it to see what's inside, your body will refuse to obey you, and you'll put it back where it belongs. This seal is hugely frustrating and shows just how intrusive Arkandian magic can be. I'll let you try it too, but I warn you: you won't enjoy it."

She paused, her expression growing solemn. "The top floor holds the most important books. And, as you might guess, the seal there is also the most powerful. I won't let you experiment with that one, because it can be dangerous. As soon as you try to get anywhere near the shelves, a blinding migraine strikes. During our experiments, several Keepers of Knowledge had to stay in bed for several days after trying to forge a passage."

The atmosphere shifted instantly, sending a chill down Valianara's spine. It was a stark reminder that, for all its beauty, this place was not meant for them.

"You can see why we're currently limiting our studies to those on the ground floor," Menara sensed the change and concluded in a lighter tone. "We hope to learn a little more about these seals first so that we can deactivate them one day. For the time being, I'll let you explore the books up to the second floor. Then we'll move on to the Academy so I can show you the glossary. Please put the books back exactly where you found them. Which won't be difficult on the second level."

Despite their dampened enthusiasm, the group of young people, hungry for knowledge, was finally able to give free rein to their curiosity and scattered across the verdant ground floor.

Alister casually perused a few shelves, pulling out a volume here and there to examine the binding before putting it back. Kamartel, on the other hand, had already thrown himself into a large book on the fauna of Arkandis, his nose plunged into its pages as if he feared it might fly away.

Valianara and Evarine exchanged a knowing glance.

"Shall we test the seals?" whispered Evarine, her eyes twinkling with mischief.

"Do you want to go first, or shall I?"

They climbed the large spiral staircase together. When they reached the first floor, Evarine reached for a book at random. She opened it and frowned. "This is unbelievable…"

She ran a hand over her eyes. "The letters… They're dancing. I can't focus on a single one."

Valianara picked up the book. The effect was immediate: the words seemed to liquefy on the page as soon as she tried to read them. It was like trying to catch water with her elbows. Frustrating, but painless.

They continued to the next floor. Valianara chose a book with a promising title: *The Cycles of Arkandian Magic.* She could read the title without any problem, but when she tried to open the book, her arm refused to obey. Against her will, her hand tightened around the volume and placed it back exactly where it belonged on the shelf. A wave of unease coursed through her.

"By all the Titans," she whispered.

Evarine tried with another book and got the same reaction, her arm moving of its own volition. She frowned. "Menara was right. I don't like this at all."

Valianara rested her hand on the bookshelf, her fingers tracing the grain of the old wood. "I'm excited, but also terrified by everything there is to learn here."

Evarine nodded, rubbing her arm as if to chase away the strange sensation. "Come on, let's see what the main floor holds in store for us."

From the staircase steps, Menara watched the novices eagerly scatter throughout the Library. A satisfied smile played on her lips. "This truly is an excellent class."

XII

Arkandis / The Breaking of the Pact
1,400 rotations prior to the Death of Tunka

Obinaelle left her quarters in the middle of the afternoon. She took care to put on her largest cloak and her summer hat with its enormous brim, hoping to protect her body as much as possible from the sun's rays once she was on the ramparts.

Grand Chamberlain Harlow was awaiting her at the door, his face set in a grave expression.

"Grand Chamberlain."

"High Magistrix."

"Where do we stand?"

Harlow's voice quivered. It seemed he was only staying on his feet through sheer force of will. "The palace homunculi are sealing off all the openings. We were forced to use the carpets from the Great Hall, as we didn't have any blankets thick enough to block out the light."

"She certainly knows where to strike," Obinaelle murmured. "We were so proud of our architecture, so open to the world outside…"

The Chamberlain continued, undeterred. "The generals have requested the deployment of five golems. Since you didn't wish to be interrupted, I took the liberty of approving the request."

"You did the right thing. Now isn't the time for subtlety."

"I've also authorized our Bloodhounds to be deployed to the outskirts of the palace to ensure that residents remain in their homes. As for the burn victims, there's no more room in the hospital. Some rooms, such as those with large glass windows, can't be blocked off. We've requisitioned the theater, and we may also need to use the Jar Room and the Pearl Room."

"Do so. The safety of as many mages as possible is paramount." Her gaze lingered on the Chamberlain's arms, which were bandaged with galvanic fabric. "Were you hit?"

"Slightly. I was with the other Triumvirs on their morning walk. I was much luckier than they were."

"This curse seems to affect us all differently. How are they?"

"The finest healing mages are with them, but the burns have spread to their internal organs. No galvanic fabric can repair that. They won't make it through the night."

"That's most unfortunate. Were you able to retrieve what I asked for?"

"Yes, High Magistrix. Here it is." He handed her a small bag, which she quickly tucked under her cloak.

"I'm going to the eastern ramparts. Keep up the excellent work, Grand Chamberlain. If you still need more room, you can commandeer the palace halls."

"It will be done as you wish," he replied, bowing.

Obinaelle crossed the entrance hall, struck by the sound of her own footsteps in the uncharacteristic silence, then turned toward the suspension bridge connecting the palace to the eastern watchtower. She stopped just at the threshold, where the harsh light from outside bit into the gloom.

Of course, she thought, looking up at the sky. *The storm has calmed. The clouds have parted just above the palace. The message is clear.*

She glanced across the bridge. "Let's hope the cover is enough…"

She set off, walking at first, then running in a half-crouch, trying her best to protect every inch of her skin. She reached the watchtower in a breathless state. Several soldiers surrounded Nabuanor, General of the First Legion. He bowed at the sight of her and dismissed his men with a wave of his hand.

"High Magistrix."

"General. What news do you have?"

Nabuanor pointed to the city below, his deep voice cutting through the distant din. "We're taking advantage of the lull to evacuate the burned to the sheltered areas farther back in the burgh."

"And the people?"

"We turned away those who wanted to take shelter behind the ramparts. According to your orders, only mages were allowed to pass. We deployed two golems at the East Gate and three at the West Gate. They're holding their ground."

"Any loss of life?"

"Some in battle, yes, but many of our mages succumbed to the curse before they even had time to retreat. At the East Gate, our telekineticists had to trigger a landslide. The onslaught from the lower city would have overwhelmed us."

"And the Fourth Legion?"

"General Avamar is holding the north and west ramparts. She was superficially burned while leading the defense, but nothing drastic."

"Have we been able to establish contact with the Second or Third?"

"Regrettably, no. The Third is in Northendria, and its Temple of Confluence is… underwater."

"That's right. In hindsight, building it in the lower city was a grave mistake. We should have done as we did with the others and placed it on high ground."

"As for the Second, it's tasked with pacifying the northern province of Palankis, but none of my envoys have returned yet. It has to be said that accessing anything outside the ramparts is nothing short of a nightmare. Even though the temples are on high ground, they're incredibly difficult to reach."

"Let's hope we can bring them back in time."

"With all due respect, don't you think they'd be safer on the mainland?"

"Do you really believe the Source will be merciful? That she will only target our island?"

"True, but whether we die here or there…"

"We'll talk about it later, General. The matter is not yet decided. Please press on. What remains of the lower city?"

Nabuanor gestured wearily toward an opening in the wall, half-covered up with metal plates. "The lower city is destroyed. Stand there, High Magistrix. You'll be able to see without being exposed to the sun's rays."

Obinaelle approached the breach and looked out. The sight before her was that of a world in the throes of death. It brought back painful memories.

The lower city, once a thriving maze of markets and brightly colored houses, was now nothing more than a waterlogged labyrinth. Everything had been flooded. Water swirled through the streets, which had been transformed into raging canals, carrying debris from market stalls and the lifeless bodies of its former inhabitants. Hundreds, perhaps thousands, of drowned people floated aimlessly, their pale faces turned toward a sky that had brought them nothing but death. Entire buildings had collapsed, their foundations weakened by the rising tide. Others, still standing, had become enclaves of despair. On the rooftops, shapes moved about, tiny figures frantic with panic before the inevitable, their inaudible cries muffled by the roar of the water. Here and there, a few overcrowded boats attempted to navigate the chaos, battling the violent currents that threatened to capsize them with every passing moment.

Obinaelle felt a cold shiver run down her spine. She took a few moments to accept the horror of the situation. "I see."

"Yes, and the current period of calm will only be a brief respite," continued the general. "The waters are receding far too quickly. I believe an even more catastrophic wave will soon arrive. The horizon is black with clouds. We're in the eye of the storm."

"Oh, I'm sure of it. She won't let us off that easily. We may have a few hours' reprieve, at best."

"We tried to form flux shields, but the water undoes all our efforts."

"That's brave, but this battle won't be won that way. In fact, we can't win at all. We have to flee."

The general turned to her. "I beg your pardon? Flee? But how?"

"That's the chief reason for my coming. Can you summon General Avamar? We will need her."

Nabuanor bowed and asked one of his soldiers to carry the message. He returned to Obinaelle's side. "All my troops who aren't mages are completely immune to the curse. In fact, we had to subdue most of them because the risk of rebellion was too great. They wanted to return to their families in the lower city."

"We will soon grant them their wish," Obinaelle stated in a neutral tone.

The general was unsure how to respond to this information, but decided to say nothing. Obinaelle, meanwhile, fell into a profound silence, her eyes cast downward upon her ruined city.

Avamar arrived a few moments later, her pace brisk. Part of her face and forearms were covered with galvanic fabric. She nodded in greeting. "High Magistrix. General."

The pair returned her gesture.

"Your progress report?" demanded Obinaelle.

"We're holding the northern and western ramparts. No battle casualties, but many mages had to be relieved due to the curse."

"And the condition of your troops?"

"I have roughly a thousand able mages remaining who, for the most part, are showing little sensitivity to the sun. Around the same number had to be withdrawn from the front line to avoid being burned to death, and six thousand two hundred non-mages, most of whom had to be subdued to ensure their obedience."

"And you?"

"I have just under eight hundred mages who have not yet been exposed, and around five thousand five hundred non-mages," replied Nabuanor.

"Good. I'm going to ask you to release the non-mages and send them back beyond the city walls."

The two generals gasped in surprise.

"I'm not saying this in jest," Obinaelle continued, seeing their bewildered looks. "We can't win against the Source. Not today, at least. Even though our mastery of the flux is excellent, we're still insignificant ants in comparison to her. I truly hoped that she would settle for a moderate punishment, but I suppose our transgression was too great. She will eradicate us. The only thing we can do is vanish and hide until we find a way to counter this curse."

"Vanish?" repeated Avamar in disbelief.

Obinaelle looked them both straight in the eye, her stare as hard as diamond. "Yes. I'll teleport the palace and its burgh. And you'll help me."

The generals gasped in astonishment.

"But High Magistrix! With all due respect, even you can't accomplish such a thing," objected Nabuanor. "It would require an amount of flux beyond our means. Even if we still had all four Temples of Confluence, it would never be enough. Not to mention the practical considerations… We'd have to cover the burgh with transport fluid!"

"Everything you say is quite right, General. And as for your second point, that's the very reason we must evacuate all those who aren't sensitive to the flux."

Avamar suddenly understood. "Oh… Assuming you know where to find that much flux, I think I understand what you're trying to do. We won't need transport fluid because you're going to replace it with the aura of the mages."

"Exactly, General. We'll deploy your troops throughout the burgh to create a sufficiently dense web of flux. You'll order your mages to cover as wide an area as possible. This will serve as a relay for the spell and allow the area that needs to be transported to be unified."

"I see," Nabuanor understood in turn. "Everything non-organic will be transported. On the other hand, a human who isn't sensitive to the flux would be torn apart. Shredded to pieces in excruciating pain."

"Exactly. So, when I ask you to release your non-mages, it's to give them, however slight, a chance to survive. They aren't the Source's target. After we leave, some of them may even manage to survive, or even reach the mainland."

"That still leaves the question of the flux," Avamar insisted. "How do you intend to proceed?"

"One thing at a time, General. We're running out of time. Deploy your troops."

"Permission to tell them our reasons for this order?"

"Granted. We can't afford a mutiny. Not now. They need to understand that their actions could be crucial."

"And also why we're abandoning their fellow soldiers," Nabuanor added grimly.

"Exactly. Join me in my quarters once your troops are in place. We will need to act quickly."

Obinaelle hurried to her lodgings, where Grand Chamberlain Harlow was waiting to brief her on the situation. She only half-listened, focusing instead on what needed to be done.

"… which allowed us to use the ballroom for the members of the First Circle," he concluded.

"Good," Obinaelle said. "Now I want you to order all the homunculi in the palace, without exception, to leave. Send them beyond the ramparts."

The man looked at her, visibly shocked. "High Magistrix, without the guidance of a mage, they will revert to a feral state. They will be lost."

"I'm well aware of that. Do it."

Harlow bowed, his face expressionless, and withdrew as Nabuanor and Avamar appeared at the door.

"Come in," said Obinaelle. "Are your troops in position?"

"Yes, High Magistrix," replied Avamar. "They're positioned as you requested. They're nervous, but they understand what's at stake."

"That's good. Please, have a seat." Obinaelle pointed to some cushions she had placed on the floor. The two generals complied, taken aback by the informality of the moment. She joined them, sitting cross-legged across from them, then pointed to a ring on her right index finger. "Do you know what this is?"

"Yes, of course," replied Nabuanor. "It's your trifecta, the symbol of your membership in the Core Triumvirate."

"Indeed. But it's actually so much more than that."

As she spoke, she took two more rings of the same kind out of a bag and handed them to the generals.

"Here. Put them on the index finger of your dominant hand."

They remained frozen, eyes wide, unsure whether to take the rings.

Were they real? Were they the rings of the other Triumvirs? The gesture was so meaningful, so unlike any of the usual protocols, that it seemed unreal to them.

"Yes, they're theirs," confirmed Obinaelle, as if reading their minds. "But their former owners are dead, or about to die. You've just been elected to the Core. Congratulations."

Nabuanor and Avamar looked at each other, torn between amazement and utter incomprehension. Joining the Core was the culmination of decades of scheming and maneuvering. Not to mention that a vote by the members of the First Circle was necessary, even though no one was fooled by the puppet-like nature of that sham. Still, to be propelled to the pinnacle of power amid such chaos, by a simple decision made while sitting on the floor, was truly disconcerting.

"We don't have time for our usual game-playing," Obinaelle continued curtly. "You well know that I decide the composition of the Core. I'm not blind, and you aren't fools. So, let's cut to the chase. The Triumvirate was initially established because it takes three to achieve what we're about to attempt. It also satisfied the Source to know that power wouldn't rest on the shoulders of a single person."

The generals stared blankly, as if anesthetized by her candor. They had always known that Obinaelle was the true center of power, but to hear her admit it so casually, in the midst of the apocalypse, was enough to disarm them completely. Protocols, political intrigues… Everything suddenly seemed utterly futile.

After what seemed like an eternity, they shook themselves out of their stupor and slipped the trifectas onto their fingers. They had to forge ahead. Regrets and remorse could wait.

"Good," Obinaelle approved. "The trifectas will allow us to establish a union of consciousness—a nexus. When I say so, you'll hold out your fingers toward me. That will allow me to extend my mind and encompass yours. You must not resist: no mental barriers. You must open yourselves up completely."

She paused, a slight smile pulling at her lips. "Yes, I understand. I'll be able to access your memories. And in the same way, you'll also have access to all my memories. But I imagine you have nothing to hide from me, do you?"

Avamar felt a chill of pure terror run through her bones. She would know. She would find out everything about her pact with Azymantias.

Seeing their ashen faces, Obinaelle burst out in a deep, joyless laugh. "Rest assured. Whatever you have to hide, I'll be unable to use it against you or punish you for it."

Nabuanor, who also seemed uncomfortable with this unbridled exposure, asked, "What do you mean?"

"Well, either we fail and we die, or we succeed and I'll no longer be here to do anything with your precious secrets."

"I don't understand," Avamar interjected.

"I know. For now, take it on faith. We'll come back to this later. Our priority is teleportation."

"Precisely," objected Nabuanor. "Even with a union of consciousness, the three of us will never channel enough flux. Honestly, I'm not even sure we could teleport a single room."

"That's correct. That's why we're going to use a theurgical incantation."

Her companions stifled a cry of astonishment.

"What do you mean? But… That's never been done before. Well, yes, there was one time…" stammered Avamar.

Obinaelle was amused by their reaction. "Oh, I know, I was there. I cast one with my two best friends at the time. All to establish the Pact and grant a group of poor mortals access to the flux. It was, in fact, the founding act of the Magisterium."

Nabuanor was speechless.

"But… But for such a spell, we'd need the support of the Source!" exclaimed Avamar. "And I don't think she would be inclined to agree to that."

"In reality, strictly speaking, we need the support of a divine entity."

The generals were completely baffled.

"The Source isn't the only goddess," Obinaelle blurted out. "She's certainly the closest to us, since she created life on this planet, but she isn't the only one. There are other voices, other powers."

The impact of this revelation was met with another period of silence. Avamar, who just a few hours earlier had not even been sure that the Source existed, now found herself confronted with a pantheon of deities.

"But who are they? Why has no one ever heard of them?" asked Nabuanor.

"Some of you found it hard enough to believe in the existence of the Source: I wasn't about to burden you with more! Anyway, shortly after the Pact was formed, I was… contacted… during one of my meditation sessions. I call him 'the Well,' and you'll soon understand why. He's an entity I found distant and remote. And ancient, truly ancient. I didn't have long conversations with him. He mainly wished to let me know that he would help us if we ever needed it."

"And that's the whole story? I can't imagine he would do this out of the goodness of his heart," ventured Nabuanor.

"Of course not," replied Obinaelle, her face hardening. "And to be honest, I never really understood what he meant by 'offering his help.' At least, not until today. So, we're going to contact the Well to ask for his help in teleporting the palace. As for the price, it's quite simple: he wants my soul."

"But why? I… I don't understand what he could possibly do with a single consciousness—even if it's yours, High Magistrix. Especially for a divine entity," Avamar interjected.

"Oh, I know. I knew this world before the Pact. And that, General, seems invaluable."

"Couldn't we sacrifice someone else? There must be other people who were there at the time of the founding, surely?" asked Nabuanor.

Obinaelle smiled sadly, appreciating his concern. "That was four millennia ago. Four thousand rotations, or four thousand years, as we used to say. No one from that time remains. And for good reason: I was the only one to receive immortality along with sensitivity to the flux. All the others, and there were nearly five hundred of us, received nothing more than access to magic. It was their descendants who inherited the gift of immortality."

"What reason did the Source have for doing such a thing?" Avamar asked in astonishment.

"To put it simply, she wanted to erase the world that came before. She wanted to keep me as the guarantor of the Pact, but all the other witnesses died after a long and fruitful life."

Her gaze drifted into the void, searching for faces that had been lost for centuries. The generals held their breath, their hearts thumping wildly in their chests. Obinaelle seemed so determined that they didn't even attempt to reason with her.

When she finally emerged from her trance, her eyes regained their usual steely intensity. "I've made my decision and am prepared to sacrifice myself for the Magisterium. I hope I can count on you also?"

They nodded in agreement.

"Now that you understand the context, you realize it's vital that you don't interfere with our union of consciousness. Much will happen when we enter into communion. Do not intervene. Even though it may seem limiting, consider yourselves the vessels for this spell. Nothing more. I'll be the guide. Follow my instructions to the letter; don't take the initiative. We have a slim chance of success, so let's not squander it. Do I make myself clear?"

"Perfectly," replied her peers in unison.

"One final thing, if I may, High Magistrix," Avamar spoke up. "Where will you teleport us?"

"To a place sheltered from the sun, capable of sustaining our access to the flux, but far from any human or proto-human settlement that could take advantage of our weakness and attack us."

"Does such a place even exist?" worried Nabuanor, before pausing. "Oh… I know! The Landria Confluence Pyramid!"

"Well observed," confirmed Obinaelle. "The surveyors have confirmed to the Grand Chamberlain that the inner base of the pyramid should be large enough to accommodate us."

XIII

The Academy of the Keepers of Knowledge / Present Day
10 rotations following the Death of Tunka

A month had passed. A month spent with their heads buried in books, absorbing a history that was not their own, but which now defined them. A month spent soaking up as much knowledge as possible in the hope that one day they might contribute to the cause.

The novices had settled into a routine: meals shared in the refectory, filled with the buzz of conversation; lectures by orators at the Academy; and long hours of solitary study in the Library. That morning, however, the atmosphere felt different. No books, no scrolls

They were gathered in a small courtyard inside the Academy, sitting in a circle on stone benches. Orator Aboren stood in the center, her face turned toward the stream of novices arriving. She possessed neither Menilmonea's ethereal presence nor Aureal's warm energy. Aboren was cut from a different cloth; harder, denser. Her gray hair was cut short—a pragmatic choice that contrasted with the other orators. As for her tunic, it bore not a single stitch of embroidery. Her face was marked, not so much by age as by a profound weariness. Fine wrinkles creased the corners of her bright eyes and stern mouth. Her hands, once those of a healer, were remarkably delicate and skilled, but their knuckles bore the signs of years of hard work and sleepless nights. She was a survivor first and a teacher second.

"Good. You've devoted several weeks to reading about the Arkandians. This key knowledge will enable you to understand their society and their way of thinking. But today, you'll finally move on to practice. Today, I'm going to talk to you about the flux."

A ripple of excitement ran through the class.

"The theory is straightforward," Aboren continued. "The flux is everywhere, permeating everything that exists, whether living or not. If something exists, it's permeated by the flux. The Arkandians clearly did extensive research into the very nature of the flux. Unfortunately, we don't yet have access to these books. For now, we must content ourselves with the following: the flux is everywhere, in everything. It's the source of their magic. And now, ours too. Understanding and mastering it will open the door to a host of abilities. However, let's keep it simple to begin with…"

Her hand moved slightly. On the ground, a stone the size of her fist began to vibrate gently, slowly rising into the air, hovering a few inches above her palm.

A murmur of admiration swept through everyone present.

"Since the flux is everywhere, you can guide it and connect it to your will if you're sensitive to it. That's how I'm asking this stone to levitate."

A hand went up.

"What do you mean by 'sensitive to it'?"

"That's a fine question, young man. It would appear that the Arkandians—and therefore we, indirectly—were given the gift of sensing and manipulating the flux as part of a pact they made with the entity they call the Source."

With that, she took on a conspiratorial air. "We're almost certain that this Source is in fact the Mother herself," she whispered. "But we'll save that for another lesson."

She resumed her usual tone. "You need to know that this gift is passed on from parents to children. However, this isn't systematic: only one of two siblings is likely to be able to wield the flux. Those who are sensitive to it were called mages by the Arkandians."

She paused briefly, looking at each student in turn.

"And before you ask me: if you're here, it's because the Titans detected your curious minds, but also your ability to sense magic."

The announcement had the effect of an electric jolt. A murmur of excitable voices rippled through the group. Mages. They, mere village children, were mages! Beaming smiles broke out, eyes met, shining with pride and a fresh sense of anticipation. The fatigue of weeks of study vanished, replaced by a new surge of energy.

"Good, now let's use that enthusiasm of yours to focus on the flux. The first contact is always a very personal experience; there's no universal approach. The idea is this: pick up a simple pebble and try to make it float in your hand. To feel the flux, you'll need to focus and attempt to visualize it. Know that you've undoubtedly always felt it, albeit at the periphery of your consciousness—you just never paid any attention to it. Today, you'll have to look beyond your field of perception. You'll have to search for that whisper, that shadow."

"What if we can't do it?" a worried voice piped up.

"You'll get there, even if it takes time. Just be warned: it could happen now or in ten days. There are no rules. For example, it took me days of staring at a stone before I could feel the flux. So be patient!"

The novices scattered around the courtyard, setting off in search of the perfect stone with the utmost seriousness.

Valianara and Evarine found two flat stones and sat down next to each other.

"Right, let's do this," said Evarine. "Ready to become a great mage?"

"Am I ever!"

They placed the stones in their palms and concentrated. A silence fell.

"Can you feel anything?" Evarine whispered, after a minute that seemed to last an eternity.

"No. Just my hand going numb. You?"

"Same here. My stone is obviously messing with me."

Aboren began to walk slowly among them. She stopped near a scarlet Kamartel, his eyes bulging. His stone vibrated slightly but stubbornly refused to rise from his hand.

"You're yelling at the stone, Novice Kamartel," she said in a faint voice. "You're trying to impose your will on it through violence. The flux doesn't respond to brute force; it responds to harmony. Don't scream at it. Listen to it."

She then walked past Evarine, who grew increasingly frustrated and restless.

"You're trying too hard, Novice Evarine. You're looking for a storm, but the flux is a breeze. Stop seeking it with your eyes and feel it with your soul. It's there already."

She then looked at Alister. He was sitting cross-legged, eyes closed. In his cupped hand, one of his round pebbles floated gently, spinning on its axis with a hypnotic slowness. She nodded and continued her tour without a word.

Noticing that Aboren had said nothing, the two young women couldn't help but steal a glance at Alister.

"No, I don't believe it," whispered Evarine. "It looks like he's been doing this all his life!"

"He indeed has a special affinity with stones," commented her friend, stifling a laugh.

Chuckling softly, they immersed themselves once more in their own efforts. Valianara squeezed her eyes shut, forgetting the stone, forgetting the world around her. She tried to feel that sensation on the edge of her consciousness, that feeling Aboren had spoken of. A tingling. A vibration. Was it that music? That song she sometimes heard, so distant and faint? Until now, she had dismissed it as mere background noise in her mind. But today, she focused on it, called to it, pulled it out of the haze of her mind, and brought it to the forefront. The melody gained texture, becoming almost tangible. And with it, a new feeling appeared: a slight tickling in her palm, separate from her own circulation, which seemed to pulsate in time with the song. She focused on it, fed it with her will, and asked it to unite with the stone. She felt some resistance, then a sudden lightness, as if her hand had become the bed of a river carrying a pebble.

When she opened her eyes again, the stone was floating gently in the palm of her hand, vibrating in harmony with the song that only she could hear.

"I did it!" she cried out, before stifling her joy when she saw that Evarine still had her eyes closed, her forehead furrowed in concentration.

Discreetly, she let the stone fall back into her palm and waited quietly beside her friend. Visibly nervous, Evarine finally opened her eyes and let out a sigh of frustration.

"I can almost feel it… It's literally slipping through my fingertips. It's like I'm trying to grasp an air current."

Valianara wanted to say something, but realized that her friend needed peace and quiet more than anything else. She gave her shoulder a gentle squeeze, then backed away quietly to talk to Alister, whom she approached in a whisper.

"Congratulations!"

Alister, who had just let his pebble fall, gave her a brief smile. "Congratulations to you, too."

"It wasn't too difficult for you?"

He shrugged, his expression becoming a little distant. "I've always felt this presence, floating everywhere. I think the flux has been a long-time companion of mine. That's probably why I never feel truly alone."

Although Valianara said nothing, she enjoyed this poetic vision more than she could have put into words.

Aboren continued her tour of the small groups that had formed, offering advice in a lowered voice or congratulating those who had succeeded in the exercise with a nod. When she returned to Evarine, she found her looking despondent, her face buried in her hands.

The orator placed a comforting hand on her shoulder. "This frustration is only natural. It's a necessary process for some. It doesn't mean anything about your ability to become a fantastic flux wielder later on."

She raised her voice to address everyone. "Listen to me carefully. The speed at which you make your first contact has nothing to do with your potential. As I mentioned, it took me several days, but now I can move objects that weigh as much as I do. Some of our best handlers spent weeks painstakingly trying to ripple the surface of water in a glass. But today, they can control objects three times their size."

"You see? You have a bright future ahead of you!" Valianara

whispered to Kamartel.

Kamartel laughed good-naturedly, and Valianara saw out of the corner of her eye that even Alister had managed a slight smile.

"For those who have succeeded, your work is only just beginning. It takes an iron discipline to train your gift daily. And I say 'gift,' but that doesn't mean you should become arrogant. Those who aren't sensitive to the flux are in no way inferior to you. They no doubt possess other talents that you lack. Take Orator Aureal: she isn't sensitive to the flux like us, and yet she's the only one capable of communicating with animals. So never presume to be better than others!"

Her stare hardened, sweeping over each novice. "It's all too easy to succumb to arrogance. That was the path the Arkandians took. Their mastery of the flux led them to believe in their own superiority, which in turn made them inhuman."

She paused again, allowing a long stretch of silence to settle over the room, ensuring that every word sank in.

"I want to be clear on this point. There will be no tolerance for this. The Keepers of Knowledge serve everyone; they aren't above anyone. If any of you go down the wrong path, if you believe yourselves to be greater because of your gift, know that the Titans will be unforgiving. And so will I."

This warning cast a chill over the group, but everyone understood the reason for her severity. They remembered the impact of their first encounter with knowledge and the Arkandians' destructive pride.

Then a small cry of triumph broke the silence.

Valianara turned around. Evarine had found her path. She ran toward her friend, beaming, her stone floating obediently between her two hands. Unable to contain herself, Valianara threw her arms around her, breaking Evarine's concentration. The stone fell heavily onto the flagstones, startling several novices who were still meditating.

"Please refrain from such displays of jubilation," Aboren's voice cut in sharply. "There are several novices here who are trying to concentrate. I'd advise you to use this time to strengthen your grasp of the flux. Be humble and keep practicing."

The pair immediately composed themselves, their cheeks burning, and a near-religious silence descended as they returned to their places to resume their training.

XIV

Arkandis / The Breaking of the Pact
1,400 rotations prior to the Death of Tunka

Sitting with their legs crossed in the center of the room, the three mages remained silent, their eyes tightly shut as they cleared their minds.

"Let's proceed. I should warn you, however, that this won't be easy. You must not allow my memories to overwhelm you," Obinaelle cautioned them.

Nabuanor and Avamar pointed their index fingers at the High Magistrix, their trifecta glowing faintly. Convulsions seized Obinaelle, her body shaking with the massive influx of energy and two unfamiliar consciousnesses. She let it all in, allowing them to invade her soul, dropping all her barriers. She welcomed these two minds as if they were part of her. Their memories became hers. However, her experience allowed her to navigate them without getting overwhelmed. She contented herself with simply observing certain momentous events—and couldn't help but smile when she learned of Avamar's betrayal.

"Seriously, General…" she whispered into their united mind. *"Love makes fools of us all."*

Avamar barely heard the taunt. She was submerged, drowned in a torrent of memories and emotions. She relived the last few hours at high speed from the High Magistrix's perspective. She saw her sitting in her lodgings, convincing herself that she had no choice, and then lived through four millennia devoted to the Magisterium, revealing an austere existence that admitted no one into her private sphere… Total, absolute devotion. Avamar felt suffocated by the magnitude of such self-sacrifice. She was drawn to Obinaelle's suffering following the Breaking of the Pact. It was the end of her world. Her new world.

New?

At that single thought, Avamar was torn from Obinaelle's recent memories and thrown into a completely unknown place—a nightmare.

She found herself in a world unlike her own. An inhuman, sick world where nature itself seemed to have surrendered. Huge cities, forests of glass and metal rose so high that they seemed to pierce the perpetually gray sky. There was no sun, just a pale, diseased glow seeping through the black, oily clouds.

The air was unbreathable; a poison that stung the throat with every breath; a pungent mixture of smoke and the smell of decay.

Strange metal wagons pulled by no beasts raced at breakneck speed along ribbon-like black stone paths in a non-stop, deafening stream. Monstrous machines, larger than golems, gnawed at the earth, tearing out its riches amid a clamor of metal, leaving in their wake gaping wounds and deserts of barren mud.

Swarms of people, human tides so dense that it was impossible to distinguish between individuals, crowded into canyons of stone bathed in artificial light. Their faces, lit by small glowing rectangles held in their palms, were etched with profound loneliness, a hunger that was more than physical.

Entire forests, continents of greenery—consumed by unquenchable flames that stained the sky orange and black. The oceans choked under a crust of floating debris, forming toxic islands of waste. Strange, mutilated animals, trapped by these pollutants, struggled to survive in a world that no longer welcomed them.

And destruction, everywhere. Incomprehensible wars, fought from a distance by demonic flying machines that spat fire, annihilating entire cities in bursts of blinding fire. There was no honor or courage, just cold, impersonal, absolute obliteration.

Avamar understood nothing of what she saw. Who were these

people? What was the reasoning behind their madness?

"This was my world before this one," Obinaelle whispered softly to her mind. *"A dying world that was, for a time, a thing of beauty. Sadly, we knew only how to destroy ourselves, driven by a feverish madness."*

Avamar wept not only with her eyes, but with her soul. She could feel all the suffering, all the self-destructive fury. She wanted it to stop.

"These aren't your memories," Obinaelle whispered, addressing both Avamar and Nabuanor, who were also on the verge of collapse. *"Hold fast. Cling to your reason. Remember what we're trying to save."*

Avamar gave herself a mental slap. She was the General of the Fourth Legion! She had seen it all in her nearly eight hundred years of existence. She pulled herself together, trying to regain control. Immediately, the memories changed. The world of glass and metal crumbled. Gigantic volcanoes erupted, spewing fire and death, further blotting out the sky with an impenetrable veil of ash. The ground itself broke apart, cracking open into gaping chasms that swallowed entire continents. New lands emerged from the furious waves, while floods swept away the last remnants of humanity.

"The wrath of the Source," Obinaelle remarked.

The vision became more intimate. Avamar was inside a strange metal bird, screeching through the skies in the midst of a storm. A man wearing a strange helmet told her that they had set up a center for mystical studies at her recommendation. That was where they were determined to take her, even if she wouldn't listen. Through a transparent window, she saw in the distance a place she didn't know, but which she loved with infinite devotion. Her own home. She watched it slide and sink into a ravine, returning to the earth itself. At that moment, Avamar was no longer simply observing the scene. She felt it. The absolute grief, the unbearable emptiness of absence. Her husband, her two daughters… All gone. Obinaelle's heart was wrenched from her chest.

"You're drifting, General! Think of Arkandis! Think of those you love!" Obinaelle commanded. *"Yes, that's right, think of Azymantias, Avamar! It's up to you to extract him from that jar! You can still save him!"*

The memories changed again. A white, sterile room replaced the ravaged world. Obinaelle, dressed in a spotless robe, was surrounded by other people wearing identical attire. Complex machines, their lights flashing everywhere. A palpable sense of anticipation hung in the air. Obinaelle and two others, enclosed in strange crystal tubes, were flooded with light so bright, so pure, that she thought her real eyes would burn. The Source. And a new, strange, powerful feeling: first contact with the flux—the Pact. Avamar felt better, less oppressed, as if she were resurfacing.

"Good, you're almost there. Memories are like a river. You're back on the surface, so try to swim to the edge. Focus on who you really are. Let my memories wash over you."

Exhausted but determined, Avamar managed to formulate a response, *"Obinaelle... I... I'm sorry."*

Her image of the High Magistrix had just been completely transformed. She felt as if she had been swept downstream by a raging rapid.

"We don't have time for this. Nabuanor is still tangled up in my memories. Help me call him."

Avamar tried to touch her colleague's mind, but she was met with a jumble of raw, primal thoughts.

"General Nabuanor! You're a soldier! Your mission comes first! Since I've known you, you've never backed down. Don't tell me that changes today!"

"Interesting... It seems to be working," Obinaelle noted.

"General! Your troops are counting on you! Don't let them down!" Avamar insisted.

A distant, painful thought formed in response, *"Who... Who do you think I am...?"*

"Excellent!" Obinaelle continued. *"We've formed a sufficiently stable nexus of consciousness. From now on, listen. Control your thoughts as much as you can. I don't want to see you fall back into the maelstrom."*

The generals nodded. They were exhausted, but determined not to falter.

The High Magistrix pointed to the ceiling and focused her newly expanded consciousness on a single goal: to rise. The connection to their respective bodies weakened, as if their flesh had become cotton. They continued to dissolve in this way for a few moments, losing all sense of time and space, when Obinaelle's thought whispered to them, *"It's coming."*

Avamar couldn't sense anything. She felt like a thought floating in an indistinct white cloud. She no longer felt her body or the pressure of her legs on the cushions. She was floating.

"It's here."

With these words, the universe plunged into darkness. The soft light receded above them, shrinking and being sucked upward as if they were falling at impossible speed into a bottomless well. When the light was nothing more than a tiny dot—a dying star in an ocean of darkness—a voice rang out. Or rather, it was felt. It was not a sound that struck the ear, but a vibration that shook the soul, the rumbling of tectonic plates coupled with the murmur of an abyssal ocean. A voice so ancient that it carried within it the echo of the void before creation. A voice so powerful that it sounded like gravity itself.

Confronted with this raw and immeasurable presence, Avamar felt her own consciousness, so fierce and strong just moments before, shrink. She wanted to curl up into a ball, retreat into the fetal position, disappear so she would never again have to endure such enormity.

Words formed in their collective mind, tinged with an age-old satisfaction. *"Obinaelle, I am pleased to see that my offer has finally captured your interest."*

She gathered her will, her thoughts suffused with all the deference she could muster in the face of such an entity. *"Yes, indeed. I apologize for keeping you waiting."*

The voice resonated, its immensity laced with a hint of amusement. *"Time means nothing to me, my friend. That said, it does affect you. I'd therefore like you to confirm that you understand that my help will only be granted on the condition that you surrender your mind to me, of your own free will."*

"That's right," Obinaelle replied, her thoughts as steady as she could allow them to be.

Avamar was seized by an irrepressible urge to scream, to beg the

High Magistrix to reconsider her decision, to ask her one last time if she was truly sure. But she restrained herself. Obinaelle had made her choice.

"If we make it through this," Avamar vowed, *"I'll make sure your sacrifice is never forgotten."*

"So be it," echoed the voice of the Well. *"Cast your spell, High Magistrix."*

Obinaelle gave herself no time to change her mind. She reached deep within herself and invoked the teleportation spell she had been preparing all morning. In that instant, the flux of an entire world poured into her. Guided by the Well's inconceivable power, she was no longer simply a mage: she became something vast. She could now feel the fabric of reality between her mind's fingers—as malleable as clay.

She made her move.

With her physical eyes, she saw nothing, but in the expanse of her consciousness, she could make out everything. Arkandis, her beloved city, was dying. The palace burgh was being torn from its hillside, leaving only a smoking crater. In the distance, a wave as high as a mountain range crashed over the horizon, poised to destroy everything in its path. Suddenly, her vision changed. Beneath, the pyramid of Landria, emerging from the void in deafening silence, she saw what remained of her world materialize, atom by atom.

She had done it.

The nexus of consciousness shattered instantaneously, sending Avamar and Nabuanor back into their bodies with all the subtlety of an avalanche. Gasping for breath, they struggled to open their eyes as the air scorched their lungs. No sooner had they regained control of their senses than they set their gaze upon what had been foretold: Obinaelle's body lay lifeless on the floor, her empty eyes staring at a ceiling she could no longer see.

Outside, the survivors' cheering and cries of delight began to rise. Inside the chambers, the sound contrasted sharply with the terrible sense of sorrow shared by the two new masters of the Magisterium.

XV

The Academy of the Keepers of Knowledge / Present Day
10 rotations following the Death of Tunka

The Academy's dining hall hummed with electric energy and the joyful chaos of passionate conversation. The novices, still exhilarated by their first connection to the flux, were the loudest. Sitting in small groups, they were busy comparing their impressions, difficulties, and tiny triumphs, levitating breadcrumbs or spoons a few inches from their fingers amid peals of laughter.

Their excitement mingled with the more subdued chatter of the apprentices and the Keepers of Knowledge. Seated a little further away, the latter were enthusiastically debating their latest discoveries. Snatches of conversation reached Valianara's ears: "… a stabilization rune I'd never seen before…", "… if we alter the viscosity of the transport fluid…", "…the third chapter on necroconservation is utterly terrifying…" Each table seemed to be the center of some intellectual revolution, each discussion a step closer to understanding the mysteries of Arkandis.

Amidst all this excitement, Valianara and Evarine had managed to snag a place to sit with Alister.

"I can't believe Kamartel has already taken off," Evarine said as she buttered a slice of sweet bread. "How does he manage to get up so early? It's like he never sleeps."

"Maybe he wanted to avoid the crowds," Valianara suggested, glancing amusedly at Alister. "Well, you certainly don't seem to struggle with that problem."

Alister, who still looked half asleep, merely grunted in vague agreement as he stirred his bowl of hot milk.

"Anyway, I'm really happy to have a break from the pyramid," Valianara continued, stretching. "I love the city, but I'm starting to feel a little… confined."

"I completely agree!" Evarine agreed eagerly. "I miss the sun. And do you know what? I even miss the rain! That's saying something…"

Alister looked up, his expression a little lost as he glanced from one to the other. "Where are we going?"

"We're going with three other squads to a tower with Orator Menara," explained Valianara. "She came to tell us last night at the Residence, just after dinner!"

"Oh! Then I must not have been back yet…"

"In fact, we should get a move on," continued Evarine, looking toward the exit. "We're supposed to meet at the entrance to the bazaar."

"It's a shame we can't use the transport ring in the city," muttered Alister.

Valianara froze, her cup halfway to her lips. "There's one here?"

"Well, yes, it's in the building overlooking the Library," Alister said matter-of-factly.

Evarine put down her spoon with a small clatter. "But… how do you even know that?"

Alister shrugged, as if the question made no sense. "Haven't you been out in the city? After all, the High Orator assured us we were free to go wherever we wanted…"

The two friends remained speechless for a moment.

"No, you're right," admitted Valianara, a little sheepishly. "I spend all my time in the Library."

"Me too," agreed her companion. "But I think you're on to something, Alister. We should go exploring too! After all, it's part of our mission to acquire knowledge."

"So, if there's a transport ring… Why not use it?" asked Valianara.

"I'm not sure," replied Alister, before turning his attention back to his bowl. "It's well-guarded, but from a distance, it looks inactive."

"Well, that settles it. Let's go!" concluded Evarine, already eager to set off.

Leaving the solemn streets of the city behind them, they emerged into the bazaar. The hustle and bustle struck them like a wall of heat, a stark contrast to the monastic calm of the Academy. They made their way through the crowd and the colorful stalls, then caught up with a group of novices gathered near the first caravans. Menara was waiting for them there, her face serene, talking to one of the wagon drivers. She gave them a warm smile as they arrived.

"Perfect, we must be nearly all here. Kamartel is running late again, isn't he? By the way, did you remember to bring food, bedrolls, and blankets for sleeping out under the stars? The tower we're going to visit is a day and a half's journey from here. This caravan will take us there. Please get in. One squad per wagon."

As the three friends took their seats in the back of an empty wagon, they looked around anxiously.

"I hope Kamartel isn't going to be long," whispered Evarine.

"If you're getting bored," Menara called out to her group of novices, "I borrowed a few chapters that we copied from the book on the art of using the flux to cure a toothache!"

Valianara, meanwhile, couldn't have been happier. Traveling! Seeing the world, even for just a few days, seemed like a reward beyond her wildest dreams. Especially since Menara had let slip that the spider Titan, Arabinoki, would probably be at the tower to welcome them. Meeting another Titan, one of the pillars of the Council... The mere thought made her shiver with excitement.

Evarine turned to Alister, who was already tucked into a corner of the wagon. "Say... Could I borrow one of your pebbles? I want to continue training while we travel."

Alister's face immediately hardened. He instinctively clutched the small bag at his neck, his look distant. A painful hesitation was written across his features. Finally, after a prolonged pause, he reached into his bag and pulled out a perfectly round, smooth stone, white and almost gleaming.

"Here," he said, handing it to her. "But... don't lose it."

His tone was so heavy, weighed down by some invisible burden, that Evarine felt a slight chill run through her. She took the pebble with the utmost care.

It was at that very moment that a breathless figure emerged from the crowd. "I'm here! Please wait for me! I'm so sorry!"

With a red, flushed face, Kamartel had just arrived.

"You scared us!" Evarine said, her voice a mixture of relief and reproach.

"I'm really sorry, I lost track of time. Because I got here too early this morning, I wandered around the bazaar. A little too much, it seems."

He climbed into the wagon, his friends laughing. A few moments later, the caravan set off with a creaking of wheels and a crack of the whip.

The journey began in a comfortable, calm state. Valianara, sitting not far from Alister, tried several times to strike up a conversation. She told him about her village and her passion for books, but each time he responded with brief, polite sentences that left no room for further discussion. He wasn't unfriendly, just… somewhere else. A little disappointed, Valianara took a blank parchment and a quill from her bag. If Alister preferred the company of his thoughts, she would spend her time writing a letter to her parents.

As she was starting her letter, she felt a gentle nudge in her side. It was Evarine.

"He's just shy," she whispered in her ear. "Give him time, he'll come around."

The journey passed slowly, jolting along with the rhythm of the wagons. The scenery, initially a series of dense forests with centuries-old trees, gradually opened up onto vast plains where golden grass swayed in the wind. Each went about their own business. Kamartel, curious about everything, spent most of his time reading chapters on Arkandian dentistry, occasionally asking a question aloud—which was met with only the creaking of the wheels. Alister remained in his corner, quietly polishing his pebbles with tireless dedication. Valianara and Evarine, meanwhile, were practicing. Sitting crossed legged at the back of the wagon, the young girls took turns trying to levitate the pebble that Alister had entrusted to Evarine. Their progress was slow but steady. Each small victory was greeted with a stifled giggle, each failure with a sigh of frustration.

When night fell, the caravan stopped in a clearing below the road. Following a frugal meal shared around a large campfire, the novices wrapped themselves in their blankets under a sky so clear and dotted with stars that Valianara felt she might be able to touch them with her fingertips. Huddled together to keep warm, she and Evarine talked about their respective villages. Evarine described the orchards of Opponka, the smell of ripe apples in the fall, and the wisdom of their serpent Titan. Valianara, for her part, spoke of her father's forge, the gentle waters of the old Tunka pond, and her unwavering friendship with Batany.

Not far away, Kamartel turned over for the tenth time on his makeshift bed.

"By all the Titans, my back will be shot tomorrow," he grumbled under his breath. Going from the mattress at the Residence to the hard ground was quite the ordeal.

"Think of it as an exercise in humility," Alister, who seemed perfectly comfortable, replied in an amused whisper.

Finally, sleep came to everyone. The early morning wake-up call was brutal, but the sight of the beautiful landscape unfolding before their bleary eyes was enough to chase away their fatigue. The caravan was now crossing a region of rolling hills, covered in a morning mist that clung to the sparse trees.

It was late morning, just as the sun was finally breaking through the clouds, that Menara's voice rang out from the front of the convoy. "We're almost there! Look over there, at the top of the hill!"

Valianara leaned over the edge of the wagon. Something was breaking through the treetops: a geometric shape, a line too straight to be natural.

The tower. Massive. Impressive.

The caravan dropped them off at the foot of a path that led deep into the woods. Menara gathered her four squads, reminded them to be careful, and then led the way. The climb was short, and soon they emerged into a vast, sun-drenched clearing. The tower stood there, looking familiar. Valianara recognized it immediately. It was built in the same style as Tunka's: a structure of gray stone and vegetation climbing toward the sky with a majesty she knew well. The monumental arch at its base seemed to invite her to enter.

Menara motioned for the group to stop at a respectful distance.

"Let's wait here," she said. "Arabinoki knows we've arrived."

Valianara held her breath, her eyes fixed on the edge of the forest that bordered the other side of the clearing. She expected to see a figure emerge from the shadows.

The sound came before the sight—a delicate rustling, like thousands of dry leaves being swept by a light breeze. The noise did not come from the forest, but from the tower itself. Suddenly, from the concealed side, a colossal leg appeared, landing with silken grace on the stone wall. Then another. And another.

Slowly circling the edifice while remaining firmly attached to it, Arabinoki was revealed to them.

Valianara thought her heart would stop. It was a sight of overwhelming beauty. The Titan was a spider so gigantic that it seemed to be one with the tower, like an organic extension of the stone. It moved across the vertical wall with majestic slowness, each of its eight legs moving with a precision that belied its size.

It was not a monster made of claws and fangs, but a moving sculpture of the forest itself. Its body was not hard or threatening, but covered with a coat of deep green moss, dotted with thousands of tiny blue flowers. Its legs were not slender appendages, but sturdy limbs coated with tufts of thick grass and ivy tendrils, as if the forest itself had woven it armor.

It was both creature and vertical garden, a paradox of power and delicacy.

As it completed its slow rotation toward them, Valianara caught a glimpse of the details of its head. The dark shell, smooth and shiny like a stone polished over centuries, was adorned with six obsidian eyes. They did not fix on them with the aggression of a predator, but

swept over them with age-old wisdom and a calm indifference to the passage of time.

A deathly hush fell over the group of novices. They had all encountered Titans before. They had grown up with their benevolent presence. But this creature was different. Its very strangeness, the way it moved around the tower… Everything about it commanded deep respect.

The muffled sound of its feet on the stone was the only thing that broke the stillness of the clearing. Valianara, her heart pounding with excited anticipation, had eyes only for the majesty of the Titan. Next to her, Evarine was equally captivated, a smile of pure wonder on her face. It was for moments like this that they had joined the Academy. Kamartel, meanwhile, was on the verge of ecstasy. With his hands clasped together, he seemed to be whispering a silent prayer, his eyes shining with an almost religious fervor. It was the Mother, in all her creative glory, revealing herself through this magnificent creature. Only Alister seemed out of step.

Valianara turned to him after sensing his discomfort. His face was pale, his lips trembling slightly. He had taken a step back, his body as taut as a string. His gaze was not one of admiration, but of fear—a visceral fear, bordering on revulsion. Instinctively, he had reached for the small bag he kept around his neck, as if to protect himself from an invisible threat.

"Are you alright?" she whispered.

He nodded in response, but his feeble effort did little to convince her. Menara, who had witnessed the entire scene, approached him. "Are you okay, Novice Alister?"

He startled. "Yes, Orator Menara. I… I'm not feeling very well."

"Are you scared of spiders?" she asked, a hint of kindness in her voice.

"Actually, yes…"

Menara didn't press him. She nodded before addressing the Titan, "Arabinoki, we thank you for your time."

The voice that answered carried the weight of ages, along with unquestionable authority and power.

"The High Orator has asked me to speak to you about the towers," Arabinoki continued, each word seeming to roll across the clearing like a languid wave. "It's a task I always accept with pleasure."

The Titan began its slow descent from the tower. Each step was a display of controlled power. When it was a few feet from the ground, it detached one of its front legs from the wall and pointed to the stone structure itself.

"We believe these towers are concentrators of magic. They aren't placed randomly. Each one is erected on what the Arkandians call a 'confluence,' a place where the flux emerges from the earth with unusual vigor, like an invisible spring."

He paused to let the information sink into the minds of the novices.

"Their orientation is likewise not random. All of them, without exception, are aligned along specific axes. Their internal mechanisms, which the Keepers of Knowledge are still studying, appear to channel this raw energy and, for reasons we're only just beginning to understand, direct it toward the pyramid. They form a network, arteries of flux that all converge on the city. Come closer. Place your hands on the stone of the tower."

A moment of uncertainty swept through the group. Valianara was one of the first to take the plunge. She stepped forward, her heart thumping, and placed her palm against the gray stone. The surface was not cold. It vibrated almost imperceptibly, like the skin of a slumbering animal. Suddenly, a surge of raw power overcame her. It wasn't violent, but it was definitely surprising. She felt as if she had dipped her hand into an invisible river. Pure energy traveled up her arm, through her shoulder, and an intense tingle made the fine hairs at the base of her neck stand on end.

Around her, the other novices let out muffled gasps. Evarine, her eyes wide with wonder, didn't seem to notice that her long blonde locks were rising gently, floating a few inches from her cheeks like aerial dancers. Kamartel withdrew his hand abruptly, then placed it back more carefully, his lips curving into an ecstatic smile.

Almost all the novices had approached, keen to feel this primordial force.

Almost all of them.

Valianara turned around. Alister had stayed back, near Menara. He hadn't budged. He was watching the scene unfold, his face impassive, but Valianara could see the strain in his jaw. Judging by the frantic way he was spinning one of his pebbles, it was obvious he was terrified. It broke Valianara's heart.

"As you know, inside each tower there's a transport ring," continued Arabinoki. "Like all the others, it resists the forces of nature. As a child of the Mother, even if I wanted to, I'd be unable to touch it. You can see inside that vegetation is gradually regaining its hold, but it can't reach the ring. Most of the towers have a spirit residing in their rings. There are very few exceptions to this rule: those are towers not associated with a village. We believe that each spirit was originally either a descendant of the Mother, like the Titans, or a human from the villages whose body was stolen by the Arkandians. For eight rotations now, the Keepers of Knowledge and Titans have been working to free the spirits of these towers, at least mentally."

"Some spirits were Titans?" interrupted a curious voice.

"Let's just say that before the Arkandians forced us to support their wild plan, my people tried to defend themselves. Unfortunately, we lost that battle, and those of us who weren't turned into enslaved people to take care of the villages were stripped of our bodies and locked up in towers."

A long, sad silence followed this response before a hand was raised from among the novices.

"Titan Arabinoki, if I may… Why are some towers off-limits to us?"

The Titan was delighted to change the subject. "Excellent question, young novice. They're off-limits because the spirits within them couldn't be freed from Arkandian control. The Arkandians made them believe that they were serving the Mother, that their task was essential, that the Ascension was the culmination of a lifetime, and that they constituted an important link in that chain. Their belief in this lie is so deep that they consider any attempt to reveal the truth to be blasphemy and react with hostility."

A voice then rose, sounding more assertive than inquiring. It was Kamartel.

"Oh, I see. That's why we didn't come through the tower south of the pyramid. It's closer, less than half a day's journey. But it's because your tower is off-limits, isn't it?"

"Excellent deduction, novice. You have a brilliant mind. That's also the reason for my presence here, as I, too, am trying to free the spirit within this tower from the evil influence it's under."

If Kamartel had been made of sugar, he would have turned to caramel.

"If you're interested in the spirits of the towers," Menara spoke again, her sweet voice contrasting with the Titan's deeper tone, "know that you'll have the opportunity to focus more specifically on one of the Academy's many projects at the end of your novitiate year. Helping the villages, focusing on certain fields of study, working to free the spirits of the towers—these are just some of the possibilities."

With that, Valianara leaned toward Evarine. "I want to do that!" she whispered, her eyes gleaming with sudden conviction. "To be locked up like that, to see your surroundings but not be able to move or interact with them... It must be torture."

Evarine nodded fiercely, her face hardened with anger. "The Arkandians are monsters."

"But why ban them completely?" Valianara couldn't help but ask. "Couldn't we just ignore them? They can't do anything to us except yell at us, right?"

Arabinoki's voice rang out again. "Yes. The current strategy, established with the Keepers of Knowledge, is to show them that the world has changed. That there will be no more Ascensions, and therefore no more visits. We hope that silence and isolation will eventually break their beliefs. That's why we wanted you to come today. You won't be able to interact with the spirit, but you'll be able to attend my work session."

"Step back, novices," Menara whispered. "Make room for the Titan."

Arabinoki descended from the tower. Once on the ground, the

creature positioned itself in front of the huge arched entrance. Its mass was so colossal that Valianara doubted it could fit through, even if it wanted to. It moved forward slowly and, with infinite caution, inserted two of its front legs, then part of its head. It remained still for a long moment, appearing to probe an invisible boundary.

Finally, it backed away, and its voice vibrated once more across the clearing. "Still the same distance. No change in the ring's aura."

Menara nodded, turning to the squads. "Arabinoki is assessing the size of the ring's exclusion zone," she explained in a muffled voice. "As soon as the tips of his limbs become numb, he knows he's reached the beginning of the zone. We're trying to determine whether this aura of negation is diminishing over time."

A hand went up immediately.

"Why can't we feel anything?"

"Most people won't feel anything in particular," replied Menara. "We inherited this from the Arkandians. However, you'll learn later that some people who are sensitive to the flux, perhaps those who are closer to the Mother, may experience mild dizziness, a kind of lightheadedness, when entering the field of a ring."

Once the inspection was complete, the Titan did not withdraw completely. He set his enormous head just within the threshold of the archway, once again plunging his six eyes into the darkness of the tower. This time, his voice did not project toward the novices, but seemed to resonate inward, softer but just as powerful. "Well, my friend? Have you had any visitors since last time?"

Silence.

Finally, a faint but venomous voice rose from the depths of the tower like a hollow echo. "I don't wish to speak with you, unholy Titan."

"You just did, though," Arabinoki replied without a hint of annoyance. "Your loneliness weighs heavily on you. The Mother doesn't speak to you because you're on the wrong path. Accept my help. We've all been deceived. It isn't too late."

The spirit's voice became filled with rage, strident and fanatical, "You big louse! You're nothing but a demon! An enemy of the Mother who's trying to distract me from my sacred mission! I'll never give in to your temptations! I'm here to guide the villagers to Ascension! That's the only truth! Everything else is just a test to prove my faith!"

"In that case, I'll come back to see you again in a month. I won't abandon you."

Faced with deafening silence, Arabinoki slowly withdrew from the entrance.

Menara turned to the novices, her face etched with weariness and an infinite sadness. "This is a common reaction among those who refuse our help. No matter how much evidence we bring them, no matter how much we explain what we've discovered, they prefer to sink into their fantasy world rather than admit that they've been deceived. Even when faced with a Titan, they continue to cling to their illusions to protect their view of reality."

"Their shattered faith could destroy them," Valianara noted to herself, thinking back on the lie that the Keepers of Knowledge had to devise to protect the civilization of the villages.

XVI

New Arkandis / Present Day
Two moons before Valianara's arrival at the Academy*

After a hunt, returning to New Arkandis was always a moment unlike any other for Oberron. Especially of late, as the city was changing at an astonishing pace.

As his ship came into harbor, he noticed significant changes since the last rotation. The city no longer merely occupied the coastline; it now stretched as far as the eye could see—a vast expanse of tiled roofs and bustling worksites across the inland plain.

Yet Oberron's gaze was immediately drawn to the east. There, towering over the rest of the city, stood the Core Palace, now off-center. It was more imposing than ever. Its multiple copper domes glittered in the sun, contrasting with the ivory whiteness of its slender towers piercing the azure sky. Tiered palatial structures hugged the steep slopes of the hill on which it stood, covered in lush vegetation that gave it the appearance of a hanging garden. It held the promise of restored grandeur, a majestic sentinel watching over the expansion of the lower city.

Oberron cherished the scent of his island—a distinctive blend of sun-warmed stone, salt air, and thousands of flowers. Though only half its original size, the island was still home. If not for the back pain that troubled him more and more often, he would have been in excellent spirits.

He had an audience with the Triumvirate in just over an hour.

It was no small matter. But until then, he could rest a while. So, he chose a little tavern whose tree-shaded terrace overlooked one of the main thoroughfares. The street was teeming with life. Dozens of homunculi—creatures of clay, flesh, and flux—tirelessly hauled blocks of stone and metal beams, their jerky movements directed by supervising mages walking just behind them. Amid this ceaseless ballet, non-mages went about their business, hurrying to the market or conversing by the crystal-clear river flowing below.

Oberron took a seat and ordered a glass of rosé wine. The server, a young man with an agreeable face and bright eyes, served him with a respectful eagerness.

"It's a beautiful day today, my lord," he said with a strong Palankis accent.

"Indeed, it is, young man. How long have you been here?"

The server's face lit up. "Barely a moon, sir! I still can't quite believe it. Growing up in Palankis meant growing up with the legend of Arkandis. The island of all-powerful mages vanished in a single day ages ago. To us, you were a myth."

Oberron smiled slightly as he sipped his wine. It was a story he had heard many times.

"After your… disappearance," the young man continued, "the provinces gradually fell back into barbarism. No authority, no laws. City-states formed, and warlords seized power. Endless wars over a scrap of land or a water source… It was chaos. My tribe endured so many famines, so many deaths. We suffered greatly. But from generation to generation, we kept your legend alive. And in my region, speaking of the Magisterium was punishable by death. You can't imagine the joy my people felt when the banner of your legion flew above the tyrant's castle."

Oberron sincerely appreciated his story. But he knew that the truth was more nuanced.

"Not everyone feels the same way," he replied evenly. "We still have a few provinces that are far from delighted to see us return."

The server made a dismissive gesture as he wiped down a nearby table. "The people do, my lord. But the nobles and the false kings are

trying to cling to what little power they still have. After hundreds of rotations, they've gotten used to it, of course."

"Well, they won't be able to cling to it much longer," Oberron countered, his gaze hard. "We haven't fully rebuilt our military forces yet, but when we do, they'll have no choice but to bend the knee or die."

"Well said!" exclaimed the young man with fervor. With that, he bowed slightly and walked away to tend to other customers.

Oberron was left alone with his thoughts, contemplating the peaceful life of the city. *Time and legend tend to distort reality*, he mused with a touch of bitterness. *And I fear, my young friend, that beyond the circles of power, the people care little for our ways—and even less so for our new policy of harvesting replacement bodies...*

He pushed the thought aside and let himself drift into a gentle reverie, finishing his drink while basking in the last moments of calm. When he stood up, he left a few copper coins on the table and set off toward the palace.

The climb was a spectacle in itself. He followed a series of wide white marble steps and paved paths winding their way between the hanging gardens and the copper-roofed villas. Everything was exquisitely crafted in the style that Obinaelle had cherished so much: a harmonious blend of graceful curves, majestic domes, and airy colonnades that lent the stone an almost unreal lightness.

He found amusement in the irony of the situation. Despite the curse that had condemned them to mortality and darkness for over a millennium, they continued to build structures with enormous windows opening onto the sky and balconies offering breathtaking ocean views. It was, without a doubt, a final gesture of defiance against the Source, a determined refusal to let fear dictate their existence. It was the very essence of Arkandis: magnificent arrogance, carved in stone.

He didn't have to wait long in the antechamber of the Triumvirate. He had barely had time to admire the mural depicting the reconstruction of Arkandis when Grand Chamberlain Pel himself came to fetch him. Although he was impeccably attired in his ceremonial livery, Oberron was struck by how much Pel had aged. Pel bowed stiffly, aggravating the pain in Oberron's back.

"Master Bloodhound, the Triumvirate awaits."

Pel guided him through a succession of silent corridors lined with marble walls, their footsteps muffled by thick carpets. They came at last to a monumental double door, crafted from dark, polished wood, and guarded by two ceremonial golems whose golden armor glimmered softly. The doors opened of their own accord as they drew near, revealing the Core Chambers.

The room was vast beyond reason, its sheer scale designed to overwhelm the visitor. Huge white marble columns, as tall as redwoods, supported a painted vault depicting the heavens. Between each column, immense floor-to-ceiling windows, several stories high, offered a dizzying view of the ocean stretching as far as the eye could see. Complex gilding, which a homunculus was meticulously polishing, ran along the walls. It caught the sunlight, causing it to dance across the intricate patterns of the ancient rugs covering the polished floor.

At the exact center of this enormous space, on a raised dais, stood three thrones sculpted from black wood and inlaid with gold. The ones on the right and left were occupied. But the one in the middle—the largest—was empty. It belonged to Obinaelle.

The room did not merely suggest power—it proclaimed it. Every detail, from the height of the vaulted ceiling to the gleam of the gilding, served as a striking reminder of the Magisterium's restored power.

Oberron stepped to the foot of the dais and gave a deep bow. "Glory to the spirit of Obinaelle."

He straightened slightly. "High Magistrix Avamar, High Magistrix Nabuanor."

The former general replied first, her clear voice carrying effortlessly through the cavernous room. "Master Bloodhound. Thank you so very much for taking the time to speak with us so soon after returning from your hunt. A hunt which, I am told, has proved fruitful."

"Twenty-three sensitive to the flux. All were between twenty and thirty rotations old," Oberron confirmed.

"Excellent," Nabuanor said in a deep voice. "We left more bastards behind than we thought."

"Thank you, High Magistrix. What's more, the population has had over a millennium to recover." He then turned to Avamar. "High Magistrix, your new body suits you splendidly."

A weary smile spread across Avamar's face. "Thank you, Oberron. But no need to flatter me—it doesn't become you. We all know that this practice cannot continue indefinitely."

"Our harvests have begun to wear thin the patience of the people in certain villages. We had to dispatch multiple sections of the First Legion to restore order," added Nabuanor.

"I confess that I still can't muster the will to receive a new body after what happened in Landria," admitted Oberron.

"You'll get there," replied Avamar. "I was in the same position, but the ravages of time eventually reach an intolerable level."

"I'm beginning to see that, High Magistrix. Even with the help of the healing mages, not a day goes by without fresh pains appearing, and I have to admit that my eyesight isn't what it used to be. Yet this body is only a little over one hundred and fifty rotations old."

"You will soon have no choice. Old age remains the final indignity the Source has inflicted upon us." She turned to Nabuanor. "I tell the High Magistrix every day just how envious I am of his insolent good fortune. To be untouched by the curse—imagine that! He remains one of the few immortals still present at the Magisterium."

"I nevertheless share your suffering," the latter replied. "Be that as it may, we must find an alternative. We cannot continue to drain the provinces of their flux-sensitive humans to replace the aging bodies of the Magisterium. It is a source of pride for families to see their children raised to the rank of mage, but our harvests are beginning to pose a real problem. Even though I know, Master Bloodhound, that you and yours remain extremely discreet."

"What other solution do we have? Accept mortality?" asked Oberron, not without a touch of irony.

Nabuanor broke out into a short, sharp laugh. "Of course not. The Magisterium needs immortality to maintain its dominion."

"That's precisely why we wished to see you, Oberron," Avamar interjected. "We now believe we may be able to cast the immortality spell."

Oberron looked surprised. A shiver of excitement ran through him. "What? How? It's a theurgical spell."

"Indeed," Nabuanor confirmed. "But unlike the Pact's spell, ours doesn't require us to be sensitive to the flux. Our best arcanists have been working on it for ten rotations, and we believe that with the conjunction of the four Temples of Confluence, we could channel enough flux to cast the spell. Without the Source."

"Oh… I see," Oberron said, his mind racing. "Only…"

"Yes," Avamar cut in. "The Temple of Confluence in Landria is inactive. And that's where you come in."

"I'm listening."

He was already savoring the prospect of a hunt of this magnitude.

"We might as well tell you: this is likely to be the most difficult mission of your entire career," Nabuanor warned.

"There is no need to sell it to me. I'm already convinced."

"That's exactly what I expected from you. As you know, as soon as we realized the portal to Landria was no longer active, we dispatched a warship to seize control of it again. Twenty-two war mages and nearly forty humans. All of them with a major power orb, which, given the current state of affairs, is a luxury beyond measure. All that, and we never heard from them again." He paused, his face darkening. "What you don't know is that we also sent another mission—a secret one this time—four rotations ago—we sent a binder."

Oberron gasped in surprise. "A binder? Over such a distance? He must have suffered greatly."

"It wasn't a decision we made lightly, but we had no choice," Avamar said. "We had to know what we were dealing with."

"Indeed," Nabuanor continued. "And because of his sacrifice, we now know. A rogue wave—the worst kind, according to our sailors. It destroyed our warship in an instant. We lost contact with the binder the moment his pearl touched the water, but he had time to send us his final thought: *It seems the traitor is here.*"

Oberron felt a weight he hadn't felt in centuries pressing down on his chest. There was only one being the Magisterium referred to by that name. If it looked like him, then…

"The surviving Primal."

"Exactly," Avamar confirmed. "If he survived our attack, it's only because he wasn't actually there during the confrontation. We now know why. We believe him to be an aquatic Primal."

Oberron absorbed the full significance of the revelation. The room suddenly felt smaller, the ocean visible through the windows more menacing.

"Yes… Of course. One Primal per great forest. That necessarily includes the continental shelf and its forests of algae and kelp… By all the towers of Arkandis…"

"Here is what we think," Avamar continued, her analytical tone dispelling all emotion. "The traitor was completely under our control, and the Primal was unable to enter the pyramid. Therefore, it was humans who managed to kill the guardian and the traitor."

Oberron shook his head in disbelief. "But how? Even I would have struggled to fight that guardian. And the traitor was insane, but not stupid."

"It's still a mystery," admitted Nabuanor. "It's not impossible that the Primal might have allied himself with the villagers to free his descendants. These are just theories, but what matters is that the orb is now inactive. Likely because of the emerald, but that's just another guess. In any case, we must assume that the pyramid won't be empty and that you'll encounter resistance."

"This will be an interesting hunt," Oberron murmured. "I imagine the aim will be to reactivate the orb."

"Or to produce another one on site," Avamar corrected.

"Is that still possible?"

"Over there, yes. There should still be one creature remaining. That said, it's been locked up alone in the nursery since we left, so we're not entirely sure it survived."

"The real question remains: how exactly do you plan to get me to dry land?"

"We'll launch a new ship," explained Nabuanor. "Only ten

sailors—no mages. And you. A small boat, similar to those used by the villagers on the coast, will be at the stern of the ship. You can take refuge there and leave the ship once you're a safe distance from the attack zone. We believe you'll go unnoticed among the drifting wreckage of the ship, which the Primal will undoubtedly destroy."

"Interesting…"

"We are aware that the risk is considerable," Avamar admitted. "However, the reward is even greater. We will finally be able to restore the Magisterium to its former glory."

"I see. I will need a Core disc to access the nursery's locking runes, should I get that far."

"It is waiting for you outside," Nabuanor replied. "The Grand Chamberlain will deliver it to you."

Just as Oberron bowed to take his leave, Avamar's voice held him back. "One last thing, Oberron."

"High Magistrix?"

"Try to bring back Azymantias's jar. If, however, you feel that doing so jeopardizes your mission… then destroy it. After all, he deserves no better." She pronounced these last words with a tightness in her chest, her gaze averting.

"Why not get it back once we've regained control?" Oberron asked in surprise.

"We've evaluated all the options with our strategists," Avamar replied, returning to a cool, professional detachment. "Assuming the villagers do indeed occupy the city, everything will depend on their understanding of the Library. The important books are sealed, but, like me, you were a student, and you've tested the seals… tried to circumvent them. I'm not worried about the ones on the upper floors: it's the seal on the first level that's weak. If these villagers are as clever as we suspect, they could break it and thus find a way to free Azymantias's soul. The risk to the Magisterium would be far too great. Either bring him back or destroy him."

"I understand. I will see it done."

XVII

The return journey unfolded in an almost unreal stillness, a marked contrast to the intensity of their encounter with Arabinoki. After another night under the stars, the wagon resumed its slow pace. The monotonous creaking of the wheels and the swaying of the wooden frame became a soothing backdrop for the novices' restless minds.

The vivid memory of the spider Titan had solidified the bond between Valianara, Evarine, and Kamartel. They spent a good part of the day devising bold theories for helping the imprisoned spirits. All the while—though Valianara would never have believed it possible—Alister withdrew further. He sat at the far end of the wagon, his gaze lost in the passing plains. His fingers ceaselessly rolled his pebbles against one another with a soft, rasping sound. He was an island of silence amid his companions' enthusiasm.

Evarine made several attempts to break the ice. "Are you all right, Alister? You've been incredibly quiet since our visit."

"I'm fine," he replied without meeting her gaze. "I'm just thinking."

"What are you thinking about? If you don't mind me asking."

"Nothing of any importance."

Every attempt met the same barrier: courteous but guarded responses intended to shut down the conversation before it began. Evarine gave up with a sigh and a dejected glance at Valianara, who returned it with an equally helpless shrug.

Finally, after a full day spent crossing ever-shifting landscapes, the familiar silhouette of the pyramid emerged on the horizon, bathed in the golden glow of the setting sun. The distant buzz of the bazaar roused them from their torpor. They were back at last.

No sooner had they jumped down from the wagon than Kamartel, buoyed by their return to civilization, turned to them, his eyes gleaming. "Say, before we head back and lock ourselves in our rooms, how about going for a beer? I found a little tavern last time, The Titan's Rest. The place has a terrific atmosphere!"

"Oh, yes!" exclaimed Evarine without a trace of hesitation. "After three days of constant jolting, I wouldn't say no to a cold mug of beer!"

"Excellent idea!" agreed Valianara, already won over by the tavern's name.

All eyes turned to Alister, who made a slight grimace. "I don't know… I'm a little tired."

"Come on, Alister! Just one!" insisted Kamartel before slipping an arm around his shoulders. "We're not going to let you get away that easily!"

The unanimous enthusiasm finally won him over, and Alister gave in with a resigned sigh—though Valianara sensed a restrained amusement beneath it.

Guided by Kamartel, they pushed their way through the throng of the bazaar, which was only just beginning to wind down with nightfall. They headed east, venturing into a maze of narrower alleys where food stalls gave way to small workshops and modest dwellings.

As they approached a small cobblestone square, they found it. The carved wooden sign, depicting a sleeping mouse Titan, swayed gently above a sturdy door. An amber glow filtered through the windows, and the muffled sound of laughter and music drifted toward them.

Kamartel pushed open the heavy door, and a wave of warmth and comforting smells enveloped them. The tavern was packed. The flicker of candles hanging from a wrought-iron chandelier and lanterns set on the bar bathed the room in a warm glow. Apprentices from the Academy stood shoulder to shoulder with merchants from the bazaar, cheerful-looking artisans, and even a few off-duty guardians of peace, all enjoying mugs of frothy beer. Conversations flowed, punctuated by peals of laughter, all against the backdrop of music played by a bard in a corner.

The place was rustic but welcoming, with its wood-beamed ceilings, rugged stone walls, and long, worn wooden bar behind which a bushy-mustached innkeeper bustled tirelessly. The air smelled of beer, polished oak, and woodsmoke from the hearth where a roaring fire crackled.

"This way!" Kamartel called out, beckoning them over.

He led them to a small round table tucked away in an alcove, away from the noise. It offered them a secluded spot for their first evening out as a squad.

Alister opened his mouth to say something as they sat down, but Evarine's enthusiasm drowned out his words.

"Four ice-cold beers, please!" she shouted to a server passing by their table.

The server, a young woman with twinkling eyes, gave them a knowing smile. "This is your first time here, isn't it? Would you like to try the house specialty? It's a wheat-based liquor that's been aged in barrels. It's a little strong, but delicious. And it's a tradition for newcomers."

"I'll have a glass, then!" replied Valianara, won over by the idea.

"I just wanted some water," Alister resumed as the waitress walked away, "because I won't be able to pay. I left my Briar back at the Residence."

"Blast! Me too," Kamartel chimed in quickly, slapping his forehead in frustration. "I was so excited to show you this place that I completely forgot I didn't have my Briar with me."

Evarine stared at them, one eyebrow raised in disbelief. "But surely you carry it with you?"

Kamartel shifted uncomfortably in his chair. "No... It... itches," he offered, his stutter betraying his poorly prepared excuse.

"Yes... me too," Alister added a little too quickly.

Evarine burst into laughter, shaking her head. "Well, well, we have some fine young men here."

"It looks like it's the girls' treat tonight!" Valianara, a broad smile on her lips, proudly displayed the three spirals formed by her Briar around her arm. Kamartel couldn't help but let out an admiring whistle.

"Wow! Three full circles? Goodness!"

"I've only used it once since I got it," Valianara admitted.

Evarine showed hers in turn, with a touch of sheepishness. Her single spiral seemed quite modest in comparison.

"I'm more of a spender than you. I thought I'd let it grow back while I was at the Academy, but the bazaar is full of temptations…"

As the server placed four glasses of amber liquor and four mugs of frothy beer in front of them, Evarine called out to her, "Excuse me, do you have any Profiter Cards?"

The server paused, an amused smile on her lips. "Profiter cards? Ha! It's been a while since I've heard that name. Are you from Opponka?"

Evarine laughed warmly and nodded.

"I'll bring you some," said the waitress with a wink.

"Profiter? What kind of game is that?" asked Valianara.

"It's a game of bluff," Evarine explained.

"Oh, oh… Interesting," murmured Kamartel, bringing a glass of wheat liquor to his nose. A slight grimace formed on his face. "Be careful, it's very, very strong."

The others followed suit, inhaling the potent aroma rising from the glasses. Only Evarine dared to take a sip. She flinched.

"Yes, it really is extraordinarily strong. Maybe later," she concluded, reaching for her beer.

Once she had the deck in hand, she gave them a quick explanation of the rules. One game followed another as the beers kept coming. Laughter rang out, they attempted to deceive each other with varying degrees of success, and the atmosphere became increasingly relaxed. Valianara even caught Alister laughing aloud—and more than once!

After her third glass, she set her mug down with deliberate slowness. "I think I'm going to be sick if I drink another drop."

Evarine pulled a disappointed face but didn't press the issue. Alister followed her example, gently pushing his barely touched glass away. "I can't hold my liquor."

"Well, it's just us left, my dear Kamartel!" Evarine exclaimed.

She turned to her friend with a crooked smile. "You realize that even if I drink more beer than you, I'll still beat you in the next game?"

Valianara smiled, amused by her confidence. "I don't know how you do it, by the way. Is there a trick? Are you using the flux to read my mind?"

"Ha, no need," replied Evarine. "I can see it in your eyes when you lie. You're not particularly good at it."

"The eyes are the window to the soul," Alister suddenly remarked in a calm voice.

A brief silence followed his comment.

"That's beautifully put," Kamartel admitted.

A faint smile touched Alister's lips.

"Exactly!" agreed Evarine. "Kamartel and Valianara, I can read you both like an open book."

She paused, her expression turning pensive as she looked at Alister. "With you, it's a whole different story. I can work around it because I know the game better, but I'm completely unable to tell if he's lying."

Now that Valianara thought about it, it was true that his face gave nothing away. To echo Evarine's metaphor, he was a book no one could decipher. She caught herself thinking that it was rather a pity and that, even though she would never dare admit it, she would love for him to open up to her. Still, his eyes revealed nothing of his soul—at least for now.

No one really wanted to end the magic of the evening, even though tiredness was beginning to weigh on them. The tavern slowly emptied: small groups of apprentices and merchants left one after another, their conversations fading into a murmur and the scent of beer and wood fire lingering behind them. Soon, only the four of them remained, bathed in the warm glow of the last candles.

The young server returned to their table, stifling a yawn behind her hand. "I wouldn't dream of turning you out, but my father and I are going to bed, since we have to start early tomorrow. That said, you can stay as long as you like. Just make sure to close the door on your way out."

They thanked her warmly, moved by her trust.

They played a little longer before Kamartel, who was having more and more trouble staying in his chair, stood up without warning.

"I'm going to bed!" he announced in a much too loud voice.

Everyone startled, caught off guard by this sudden gesture. Alister, on the other hand, allowed himself a slight smile.

"That's a wise choice."

As if to contradict that wisdom, Kamartel grabbed his small glass filled with wheat liquor and downed it in a single gulp. His friends were stunned, a mixture of admiration and concern in their eyes.

"You'd better head home," Evarine said with a chuckle, "because I think you're going to need the privy very soon!"

As Kamartel staggered out of the tavern, Evarine realized she wasn't feeling too well herself. She tried to stand up, but her legs gave way, and she nearly fell, barely managing to steady herself against the table.

Valianara exchanged a complicit glance with Alister. "Well, our evening is coming to an end. I'm going to help Evarine get home."

"Excellent idea. Don't worry, I'll put our glasses away and lock the door," Alister replied with a gentleness she didn't recognize in him.

"Thank you so much, that's ever so kind of you," Valianara said with a beaming smile.

"Not at all. It's my pleasure."

Valianara felt her cheeks flush and hastily stood up, slipping her hand under Evarine's arm. "See you tomorrow! Thanks again!"

They stepped out into the cool night air, leaving the last member of the group in the silence of the deserted tavern. He waited until the sound of their footsteps and muffled laughter had disappeared completely into the alleyway. The room fell gently into absolute stillness; only the crackling of the wood burning in the hearth dared to break the novice's solitary silence. A playful smile crept onto his lips. He slowly straightened up, then leaned against the bar, and calmly finished his mug of beer. A soft bluish light began to emanate from his left palm, casting shifting shadows across his face. Filaments of pure energy, speckled with tiny sparks, escaped from his fingers and snaked through the air with silken grace.

The swirling currents of flux moved toward their table. The empty mugs, the surviving apples, and the leftover pieces of bread rose steadily into the air, enveloped in an azure halo. The flux guided them in a long procession, crossing the room to set them down gently— some in a basin with other dirty dishes, some in an empty barrel that appeared to serve as a wastebasket behind the counter.

Alister grabbed his glass of wheat liquor as it passed him, then drained it as if it contained nothing but water. He remained there, leaning on the bar, watching the silent ballet of his own magic.

When everything was in order, he left with a light step.

XVIII

The Academy of the Keepers of Knowledge / Present Day

Valianara woke with a start, her heart hammering. A sudden, slightly mad idea had torn through the veil of her sleep. Evarine's steady breathing lulled the silence of the room. Valianara glanced toward the crystal window. The city outside was still bathed in the soft bluish glow that marked the night.

She tried to fall back to sleep, tossing and turning in the soft comfort of her bed, but the idea would not abandon her. It looped in her mind—insistent and obsessive. Unable to take it any longer, she pushed back her blankets, determined to understand it.

She got up and dressed as quietly as she could, every movement carefully controlled to avoid making a sound. Like a cat, she tiptoed into the bathing room to fetch the copper basin Evarine had bought at the bazaar so she could wash her face. But in the half-light, she stumbled, and the basin clattered to the floor. Her friend's thick, sleepy voice rose from the nearby bed, "Humph. What are you doing?"

She was sitting up, hair disheveled and eyes barely open, clearly struggling to pull herself out of the still-powerful grip of one beer too many.

"I had a dream where… I could see myself consulting the books on the first floor of the Library," Valianara whispered excitedly. "I know it's probably ridiculous, but the way I was doing it might just work. I need to know."

"What?" croaked Evarine. "By all the Titans, I have such a splitting headache…"

"Drink some water. It'll help," Valianara advised, feeling a little sorry for having woken her up.

Evarine groaned as she sank back onto her pillow. "Instead of reading that book about toothache, we should have read the one about hangovers."

"Go back to sleep. I have to get to the Library."

Evarine let out a hoarse laugh, which turned into a wince of pain.

"And you think that after your dramatic declaration, I'm going to let you go there alone? And with my basin, too? In the middle of the night? None of this makes any sense, but give me a few minutes to freshen up in the bathing cabin, and I'll come with you."

After considerably more than a few minutes, the two friends found themselves on the city's main avenue.

The silence was almost absolute—a striking contrast to the hustle and bustle during the day. The bluish light cast a ghostly glow over the buildings and the gigantic roots. The city seemed just as asleep as its residents, waiting for dawn to break.

Their footsteps echoed softly on the cobblestones as they made their way down the slope toward their destination. They passed only a few guardians of peace on patrol. One of them halted in front of them, his face half-hidden by the shadow of his helmet. "Everything okay, novices? Where are you headed off to with that basin?"

"We need to go to the Library," Valianara replied, doing her best to sound as confident as possible. "The basin is for an experiment."

The guardian raised an eyebrow in surprise. "You Keepers of Knowledge are always so odd. The sun won't rise for at least another two hours. Must you do this at night?"

"Yes, we'd like to get it done before classes start."

"Yeah, right! I hope you're not up to any nonsense," he called after them as he resumed his patrol, clearly not interested in finding out more.

Once the guardian was far enough away, Evarine whispered to Valianara, a shiver in her voice despite the warmth of her cloak. "So, what's this genius idea of yours involving my basin?"

"Arkandian magic seems to always work on the principle of focus. Look at the transport ring: the repulsion magic is focused on it, and that creates an aura all around it. When we do telekinesis, we establish a direct link with a specific object to manipulate it."

She continued, growing increasingly excited, "And do you remember the toothache book? They recommend focusing on the tooth—without forgetting the gum—to establish a connection through which the flux can act. The same goes for our stones; we have to concentrate on them specifically to move them."

Evarine stared at her, her brow knitted with confusion and fatigue. "Yes… But I still haven't got a clue what you're getting at."

"When you said last night at the tavern that you could read my lies in my eyes, it left me with a strange taste in my mouth. Then Alister surprised us with his new philosophical side: 'The eyes are the window to the soul.' All of that must have been on my mind because it hit me last night like a bolt of lightning. You can read my soul and my intentions without even seeing them. You use my eyes as a mirror, a reflection. You can read me like an open book!"

She paused, seeking her words. Evarine looked utterly bewildered.

"The Seal of Rejection has to be triggered when you look at the pages—that is, when you make that direct visual connection with the text. But what would happen if you didn't really look at it? If you didn't focus on the page, but rather on its reflection?"

Evarine stopped in the middle of the avenue, her face suddenly lit up. "By all the Titans! If this works, it'll be a revolution!"

They pushed the heavy door of the Library, which swung open silently. The interior was even more breathtaking at night. The soft grass on the ground floor appeared golden in the orange glimmer of the candles, and the shadows of the trees and bookshelves stretched out, deep and mysterious. The space, already majestic during the day, took on an almost sacred quality in the stillness of the night.

Only the fluttering of wings above their heads broke the silence. A few bats, which liked to nest in the high roots near the ceiling, had spotted them and were tracing silent circles in the dim light.

Without a word, the two friends strode up the spiral staircase to the first floor.

"Well, it's the moment of truth," Valianara whispered, her heart pounding. "Pick a book."

Evarine scanned the shelves and pulled out a volume with a dark leather spine. "*Anchoring of Spirits.* I think this one's appropriate after our visit to the tower."

She opened it at random and tilted her head, wrinkling her brow. "The Seal of Rejection is still scrambling the text. It's unreadable."

"Perfect! Keep the page wide open."

Holding the basin at arm's length, Valianara tilted it and adjusted its angle until the concave bottom caught the reflection of the open page perfectly. The metal, polished by use, glowed faintly in the dim light. She narrowed her eyes, focusing on the inverted image distorted by the curve of the copper.

Then she stifled a cry of triumph. "By Tunka's shell! The text is... It's written upside down, but... I can read it! IT WORKS!"

She focused and began to read aloud with some difficulty: "'... And... thus... the link... creates a support for the spirit... whose dissolution... is halted.'"

Evarine's eyes widened, incapable of believing what she was hearing. "In the name of the Mother... It's a miracle! You've broken the Seal of Rejection!"

Valianara looked up, a radiant smile shining on her face. "I don't know if I could go on doing this for hours, but yes... It works!"

The excitement grew to a fever pitch. Evarine, in turn, grabbed the basin and another book, trying to decipher a passage on binding artifacts. Her triumphant murmurs interrupted the solemn quiet of the Library.

"This is madness," she whispered. "Do you realize what this means? The Keepers of Knowledge have been searching for the solution on the ground floor for years, and you've..."

That's when a fluttering of wings—heavier and closer than the bats—made them jump. They both spun around.

Perched on the dark wooden railing, less than an arm's length behind them, a large owl was watching them. Motionless. Silent. Its huge golden eyes, two perfect moons in the gloom, stared at them with an unsettling intensity. Slowly, it tilted its head to one side, then the other, in a sharp, jerky movement that sent a shiver down the novices' spines. It let out a strange sound, halfway between a hiss and a click.

They stood frozen, the basin half-raised. Their breathing had stopped abruptly. Was it a guardian? A spell? There was no way to tell. They dared neither move nor speak, trapped by the night bird's hypnotic gaze.

"Well, what are you doing here, young ladies?" The voice, calm and laced with amusement, rose from the staircase below, snapping them out of their stupor. It was Aureal. She was climbing the steps at a leisurely pace, followed by the imposing bulk of Grumf, who was sniffing curiously.

"By all the Titans! Orator Aureal!" Valianara gasped, one hand pressed against her racing heart. "That owl of yours scared us half to death!"

She glanced at the bird, which was now soaring silently into the upper reaches of the building.

"Is it against the rules to come here at night?" she asked, trying to regain her composure.

Aureal approached them, a smile on her lips. "No, not at all. But it would be disastrous if the Arkandians, by some means or other, were able to harm this place or us, wouldn't it? That's why my little friends up there keep an eye on all the comings and goings."

She lifted her chin toward the bats that were still circling quietly above them. Aureal continued, her smile widening, "And you can imagine their surprise when they saw two novices show up on the first floor with a copper basin! And in the middle of the night, no less…"

Valianara felt her cheeks burn, but the excitement of her discovery overruled her embarrassment. "Oh, yes, I completely understand, but Orator, we have great news! We can read the books on this floor!"

Aureal let out a genuine "Oh" of surprise, her playful expression replaced by intense curiosity. "Excuse me?"

"Using a mirror to read the reflected image of a page doesn't trigger the Seal of Rejection," she explained, unable to conceal her pride. "The seal activates only when we focus our attention directly on the text, not on its reflection…"

Aureal's face lit up. She moved closer, inspected the basin, then the open book, as if to verify the concept's ingenuity for herself. "It's brilliant, girls! Absolutely brilliant! I'm impressed."

"It was Valianara's idea; I just provided the basin," Evarine clarified with a giggle.

"Oh, I know from experience that a squad is always greater than the sum of its parts!" replied Aureal. "Congratulations to you both! I'm going to tell the Keepers of Knowledge and the other Orators about this right away! It's a real breakthrough! And on top of that, it was achieved by novices who've only been here a little over a month! It's incredible."

Valianara and Evarine were walking on air. The tiredness, the hangover, the fright from the owl… All of it was swept away by the emotion in the orator's eyes. They had done it. They were now a part of something much bigger than themselves.

Aureal placed a hand on each of their shoulders, her gaze shifting from one to the other. "You have altered the course of our history, young ladies. I mean it. Years from now, even decades from now, this moment will still be spoken of. People will remember the resourcefulness of two novices and their copper basin."

She gave them one last affectionate look, tinged with maternal pride.

"In the meantime, return to your beds. Waking up later may prove quite difficult! You'll need your energy tomorrow. Trust me, after this news, you're going to be exceedingly popular."

XIX

The Academy of the Keepers of Knowledge / Present Day

The shrill sound of the bell felt even harsher than usual that morning. Valianara dragged herself out of bed with a groan. The excitement of their nighttime discovery and the lack of sleep were a strange combination, leaving her both drained and buzzing with barely contained energy.

"Already…" Evarine breathed from her bed, her voice even hoarser than the day before.

"What a night!" Valianara exclaimed, stretching.

Evarine responded with a blissful smile. They got ready as quickly as their sleepy minds would allow. Once reasonably presentable, they crossed the corridor and knocked on the boys' door.

There was no answer.

They tried again, knocking a little harder.

"Kamartel! Alister! It's time!"

Eventually, the door creaked open slightly, revealing Kamartel, his face waxy, his hair tousled, and his expression so miserable that he looked as though the entire Council of Titans had just spent several hours yelling at him.

"I'm coming…" he murmured, a hand on his forehead.

He glanced back into the room. "Alister's already left, it seems."

He blinked, his eyes adjusting to the golden light flooding the hallway, then seemed to be struck by a wave of panic. "Oh no! The sun… Is it up already?”

“Well, yes,” replied Evarine. “A while ago. Did you miss the bell?”

Kamartel’s face twisted into an expression of pure mortification. “No… By Gunderki’s caw… I had something to do. I…”

He didn’t finish his sentence. Giving no further explanation, he slammed the door in their faces. They could hear him shouting from inside.

“Go ahead! Don’t wait for me! I’ll catch up with you!”

Valianara and Evarine stood for a moment, staring at the closed door, and exchanging puzzled glances.

They made their way to the dining hall, still a little unsettled by their friend’s unusual behavior. The large room was already full; the hum of conversation and the clinking of cutlery created a scholarly but lively atmosphere.

As they crossed the threshold, all sound fell away, and they saw the twelve Orators lined up in a guard of honor. They all turned toward the two young women and began clapping. Immediately, as one, all the apprentices, Keepers of Knowledge, and novices already seated at the tables stood up and joined in the applause.

Valianara stopped in her tracks, overcome with emotion. She instinctively raised her hands to her face, hiding her astonishment. Next to her, Evarine, after a brief moment of hesitation, began greeting the crowd with theatrical gestures, then turned to her friend and joined in the applause with a huge smile.

Seeing Valianara’s discomfort and her inability to advance, Menilmonea and Aureal broke away from the line and approached them, their hands outstretched in a gesture of invitation.

“On behalf of all the Keepers of Knowledge, we would like to congratulate you both on your stroke of genius. It changes everything,” declared Menilmonea. “Thanks to you, thousands of volumes can now be added to our collection. I’ve already sent messengers to ask our finest smiths to produce artifacts inspired by your basin.”

She started to laugh softly. “More precisely, two polished metal plates mounted on a pivot so they can be angled,” she added.

“Two?” Valianara asked, intrigued.

"Yes, to cancel out the inversion effect caused by the reflection."

"Oh, of course, that's brilliant!" Evarine exclaimed.

Valianara didn't know what to do with herself, tears filling her eyes. Evarine noticed and gently took her hand, trying to offer her something to hold onto in the whirlwind of reality.

Menilmonea smiled at this gesture.

"This really is a superb example of teamwork. No one ever succeeds entirely alone." She turned to Valianara. "One last thing. Arabinoki told me you're especially interested in imprisoned spirits. Is that right?"

Valianara nodded, still a little dazed. "Yes... Yes, but... how would he know such a thing?"

Menilmonea gave her a mischievous wink. "You'll soon learn that Titans are far more surprising than they appear. For example, they have hearing a hundred times sharper than ours. If you'd rather they didn't know your secrets, it's best to avoid whispering them if they're nearby."

She continued in a more serious tone. "Anyway, I just wanted to say that thanks to you, we finally have access to numerous works on capturing and binding spirits. We're going to review several programs to ensure we incorporate all this new knowledge. It's quite possible we'll make some breakthroughs—particularly when it comes to freeing spirits—in the coming days!"

Breakfast was a strange moment: a mix of blushing pride and conversations with the novices at their table, eager to hear the details of their nighttime escapade. Valianara barely touched her food, giddy with her newfound fame.

Once their meal was over, Evarine gave her a knowing smile as she stood up. "It's a good thing our first lesson of the day is in the Jar Room. It'll give us a chance to calm down from all this while we walk."

And indeed, the stroll through the city proved beneficial. It allowed them to let the excitement of breakfast wear off and mentally prepare for their upcoming lesson. The path led them beyond the Library, toward an austere-looking neighborhood of older buildings.

They stopped in front of an enormous structure whose architecture stood in stark contrast to the rest of the city. There were no elegant domes or aerial walkways here, but rather a massive gray marble facade pierced by a single monumental door and tall windows with richly colored stained glass.

As she stepped inside, Valianara was left breathless.

Several identical wings, all built around a soaring nave, radiated out from the hall. A forest of white marble columns soared up to support intricate vaults, creating a sense of boundless space and silence. Light filtered through immense windows, bouncing off a polished marble floor so smooth it looked like a sheet of frozen water. What truly struck Valianara, however, was what occupied the space: entire walls lined with towering stone shelves. On each one, as far as the eye could see, stood rows upon rows of jars. Though they varied in size, they all shared the same ovoid shape, fashioned from ochre-colored terracotta. Yet each carried its own silent story: some were adorned with fine geometric engravings, delicate runes, or painted bands, while others remained starkly plain, devoid of embellishment.

Orator Aboren was waiting for them near the entrance, her stern face perfectly in keeping with the solemnity of the place.

"Welcome to the Jar Room, novices. Proceed to the north wing, all the way to the back. Do not touch anything."

The young women complied, their footsteps echoing strangely in the almost religious silence. They walked along the rows of columns, passing several other squads that had arrived before them. Like them, the novices were taking in the place with a mixture of wonder and reverent unease. The weight of the thousands of souls preserved here was palpable.

Valianara spotted Alister. He was standing off to one side, staring at a shelf with a strange intensity. When he felt their eyes on him, his attention shifted away from the jars. He turned toward them, gave them a brief nod in greeting, and joined them without saying a word.

The squads eventually regrouped at the end of the north wing. Aboren joined them, her calm gait contrasting with the novices' pent-up excitement.

"As you already know," she began, her voice reverberating clearly

off the marble vaults, "this is where the Arkandians used their magic to store the souls of those among their people whose bodies, ravaged by the curse, could no longer be healed."

As she spoke, a figure hurriedly slipped through the ranks. Kamartel, who was still out of breath, tried his best to make himself inconspicuous. Aboren paused, her gaze settling on him without a flicker of surprise.

"Well, well, Novice Kamartel. Since you don't appear to be much of a stickler for punctuality, perhaps you could tell us what the Arkandians hoped to achieve by preserving these souls."

Kamartel, flushed with shame, stood frozen in place. He gulped, then replied in a slightly trembling voice, "They were waiting… They hoped to one day reincarnate these souls into healthy bodies. Bodies they harvested from the villages once we were deemed 'compatible.' That was what they called the Ascension."

"Indeed. Thank you, novice. You may return to your squad." She waited until he had rejoined his friends before continuing. "For the moment, we have no clear idea how they function. But thanks to our two ingenious novices, it seems that is about to change, now that we finally have access to works on the subject."

All eyes turned to Valianara and Evarine. Kamartel stared at them, utterly baffled.

"We'll explain later," Evarine whispered to him.

"But for now," Aboren continued, "I'd like to ask you a question. What is it about these jars that strikes you as unusual?"

A moment of silent contemplation swept through the ranks. The novices scanned the walls, searching for a clue they might have missed. Finally, a hand went up.

"Yes, novice? I'm listening."

"They're all open."

"That's right. Well… Almost all of them. If you look closely, up there on that shelf where there's only a single jar, you'll see that one in particular is still under seal."

The novices' curious eyes focused on the spot. A lone jar sat atop an isolated niche on the top shelf, its lid still perfectly in place, sealed by what looked like dark metal bands. A slight blue aura encircled it. A murmur of surprise rippled through the group.

"We don't recognize the runes engraved on it," Aboren added.

"Is it the only one that's still sealed?" someone asked.

"Yes. We've inspected them all."

"Do you think there's still a soul inside?" Evarine asked.

"It's tough to say. But it's a fair bet that there is."

"What would happen if we opened it?"

"We believe it would destroy the soul. Of course, these are just assumptions based on the few books we've been able to read. We'll find out more very soon."

"Can we get a closer look?" asked Kamartel, his curiosity overcoming his timidity.

"Alas, novice, we are free to take, touch, and handle all the jars in this room—except that one. That jar is protected by an extremely powerful spell—the same kind found on the top floor of the Library."

A murmur rippled through the crowd. Aboren paused for a moment, allowing the tension to build, then diverted their attention. "But let's save that mystery for another day. Right now, I'd like you to turn your attention to this object."

She stepped aside to reveal an artifact resting on a small stone table beside her. It was a device of breathtaking complexity and beauty.

Its base was a wide ring of dark metal—heavy and stable—engraved with runes, and on this base rested a tangle of intricate bronze and silver gears, all mounted on small wheels that suggested precise movement or adjustability. At the heart of this mechanism, a main cylindrical body, much like a telescope, was held in place by an articulated mount. Three large, perfectly faceted gems were set into it. The largest, a warm honey color, was positioned near what resembled an eyepiece. Below it, the other two—smaller and a deep sapphire blue—shone with a cool brilliance. The whole device was studded with dials and precision mechanisms, giving it the appearance of a scientific instrument of unprecedented complexity.

"This," announced Aboren, "is a Mind Focalizer. Based on the few texts we've been able to decipher, this object appears necessary for the containment process. It is believed to be the tool the Arkandians used to extract a soul from its fleshly body and guide it safely… into a jar. There is also a good chance it serves the same purpose in reverse, but we haven't been able to confirm that assumption yet."

Whispers mingled with fascination and dread rose from the crowd. The novices instinctively moved closer to get a better look at the object. Some crinkled their eyes, trying to make sense of the logic behind its strange rings. Others, like Valianara, seemed mesmerized by the central gem. The idea that such an artifact, so beautiful, so elegant, could tear a soul from its body was deeply unnerving. It was Arkandian magic in all its ambivalence: a terrifying power, cloaked in chilling beauty.

Aboren let the novices examine the device, then raised her voice again, snapping them out of their rapt contemplation. "This, in fact, will be your first assignment as future Keepers of Knowledge."

The announcement struck like a whip, instantly bringing every-one's minds back to attention.

"You're to prepare a parchment listing everything you can find regarding Mind Focalizers, jars, and the containment process." She continued with a faint smile, "You'll have to stick to the ground floor of the Library, of course. I'm not a monster. You'll give me a summary of your findings within ten days."

An excited buzz filled the room upon hearing the announcement. Their first mission. Their first concrete step on the path to becoming Keepers of Knowledge.

"We've got our work cut out for us," muttered Kamartel, rubbing his eyes, his fatigue still evident.

"At least we'll be able to work during the day this time," replied Evarine with a mischievous smile directed at Valianara.

Valianara felt her gaze drift involuntarily to the sealed jar, up in its solitary alcove. Something was calling to her in a way she couldn't yet put into words.

The lesson continued. Aboren patiently answered the novices' barrage of questions. She told them about the other wings of the Jar Room, each dedicated to a generation of preserved souls, then explained that the layout of the hall was no accident but followed a strict chronology; a veritable catalog of the slow agony of the Arkandian people. The initial enthusiasm gave way to studious concentration, everyone feeling crushed by the weight of the events that hung over the place.

When the orator ended the lesson, she made an announcement, "Before we leave, let me give you the rest of the day's schedule. We're going to form two groups of four squads."

She pointed to half the novices, including Valianara's squad. "The first group will go directly to the Pearl Room. After the meal, you will go to the Chamber of Memory. The second group will do just the opposite. The reason is simple: the Pearl Room is a more confined space and cannot accommodate so many people at once. And don't forget: your parchment on the Mind Focalizer must be handed in to me in ten days!"

Valianara's squad left the icy atmosphere of the Jar Room and returned to the golden light of the city. Their path led them back up one of the main avenues winding between the buildings.

They passed the Library again, then turned northwest, climbing toward the upper levels.

"An apprentice told me that they call this day 'Walking Day' among themselves," Kamartel remarked with an amused smile. "In a single day, we've practically covered every important site in the city."

"He's not wrong," replied Evarine, lifting her eyes to one of the gigantic roots that formed a natural bridge between two buildings far above their heads.

They walked along the hall leading to the transport ring, then arrived at their destination. The Pearl Room was a small, unassuming structure, nestled in the shadow of more imposing buildings; its curved lines and turquoise domes gave it an elegant air.

The group greeted the two guardians of peace standing on either side of the large central opening. Without really knowing why, they entered on tiptoe. A hushed stillness and an otherworldly glow greeted them.

The Pearl Room was a dark stone chapel, both intimate and

majestic. Gothic vaults soared high above their heads, held up by thick columns with intricately carved capitals. The city's natural golden light, streaming through the tall, pointed windows, seemed to intensify inside. It cascaded down in warm, twilight-orange rays, passing through the air, which was filled with fine particles of shimmering dust. This warm light mingled with a cooler, bluish hue emanating from the very heart of the room. There, on a dais of a few worn stone steps, rested a large granite basin. From this basin arose the soft blue light, pulsing slowly like a sleeping heart. It cast shimmering reflections onto the arches and columns, coloring the atmosphere with an unreal blend of pink, violet, and indigo. A few broad-leaved plants grew in stone planters, their dark silhouettes standing out against walls lit by candelabras and flickering candles, bearing witness to the strange blend of the Arkandian world and the villages.

Orator Gideon stood near the basin, lost in thought, contemplating its contents. It felt like a timeless place where magic felt almost tangible.

"Welcome to the Pearl Room. Please come closer. There's no need to be afraid."

The novices stepped forward in a compact group, their eyes fixed on the glowing basin as they kept a respectful distance.

"This hall is aptly named," Gideon began in a calm voice, "for it is here, and specifically in this basin, that we find the dryads' pearls, also known as minor orbs of power."

He dipped his hand into the bluish liquid and pulled out a small sphere. It was about the size of a walnut and rested in his palm, emitting a soft azure glow.

"These are flux amplifiers," he explained. "They help the user channel a greater amount of flux in order to perform more significant actions, such as moving heavier objects."

A hand shot up immediately from the assembly.

"Yes, novice?"

"What is a dryad, Orator?"

Gideon smiled with amusement. "We have no idea. The pearls are only ever described by their use, and most often, only the terms 'pearl' or 'orb' are used. We know their full name is 'dryad pearls,' as two works refer to them by that name. You can actually find them in the Library; they've even been transcribed already. The works are titled *Expanded Botany* and *Luminescence of Rocks*. Two rather unusual titles, but they've allowed us to understand how these artifacts work."

"Where do these pearls come from? Are they real pearls, like the ones from oysters?" Evarine asked.

"That is knowledge not yet available to us," Gideon replied. "The production of the pearls is described in a book titled *Conjuration of Major and Minor Orbs of Power*. And yes, this time the title is actually quite self-explanatory. Unfortunately, as you might expect, this volume is shelved on the second floor of the Library. Even with your clever trick, it's not a book we'll be able to study anytime soon."

He continued, addressing everyone, "We have exactly forty-six pearls in this basin. They are, naturally, studied at great length by the apprentices and the Keepers of Knowledge; they are sometimes even used when the need arises. They were notably used during the construction of the bazaar to assist with excavation work. A team led by Orator Gavin is also currently using them to improve the treatment of deep burns. The applications are virtually endless."

The group was spellbound, their eyes shifting from the small glowing sphere in the orator's palm to those pulsating gently at the bottom of the basin.

Gideon smiled again, sensing how impatient they were. "I know what you're thinking, and yes, you'll be given the chance to touch and handle them. My only request is that you proceed squad by squad. These are extremely rare objects, and it's best to avoid handling them too much. Novice Evarine, your squad may begin if you'd like."

With beaming faces, Valianara and her friend exchanged a knowing glance.

As they approached the dais, a thud made them jump. Kamartel had suddenly fallen to the ground. He lay sprawled on the marble, his face pale, his eyes rolled back in his head as if he were wrestling with an invisible force. Alister was the first to react, rushing over to him.

"Kamartel, are you all right?"

Gideon rushed over as well. "Well now, my boy, are you unwell?"

Kamartel came to, then stammered, his face white and covered in cold sweat, "I... I'm sorry... I don't think I got enough sleep. And maybe I had a few too many beers last night."

Evarine and Valianara knelt beside him, visibly concerned.

"Go get him some water," Gideon ordered Evarine. "There's a jug in the back room, over there."

Kamartel tried to sit up, mumbling that he was fine, but the orator placed a soothing hand on his shoulder. "Rest a little. Your squad will handle the pearls after the others, to give you time to recover."

Kamartel drank the glass of water in one gulp and assured them he was already feeling much better.

Gideon then turned to the next squad. "Come closer, please. Take a pearl from the basin and try, for example, to make it levitate. Focus on it. Let the flux flow through it as if you were threading a needle. You will feel an amplification, and the current of magic will spread and intensify."

Several novices carefully dipped their hands into the luminous liquid, and each pulled out a pearl. They closed their eyes, their brows creased in concentration. Soon, exclamations of delight erupted. A first pearl floated gently upward, then another, hovering above their open palms, glowing with a blue light more intense than ever, their power magnifying the young mages' will tenfold.

Each made their own comment, their voices tinged with childlike wonder.

"It's so much easier this way!"

"It's simply unbelievable! I can feel the flux like never before..."

Meanwhile, Valianara and her squad were slowly recovering from what had happened to Kamartel. He was now standing upright and had regained some color, though he still seemed a bit shaken.

"You really gave us a scare," Evarine said softly.

"I don't understand what happened to me," Kamartel replied, rubbing the back of his neck. "One minute everything was fine, and the next I was lying on the ground like a rag doll."

"We'll have to keep an eye on that," Alister said seriously. "And go see a Keeper of Knowledge if it ever happens again."

"Yes, chief. Thank you, everyone, for looking out for me."

"Hey! You're part of our squad!" Evarine said with a genuine smile.

Gideon stepped closer. "Feeling better, novice?"

"Yes, Orator. I'm sorry to have caused you concern."

"No harm done, young man. Try to pace yourself. Now it's your turn to experiment with the pearls."

The four friends approached the basin. They plunged their hands into the luminous liquid, and each grasped a pearl, feeling it vibrate with contained energy.

Valianara noticed that Alister seemed more interested than ever, far more so than during previous lessons. While the others marveled at the power of their first pearl, he seemed absorbed in a kind of feverish inventory. He would take a pearl, levitate it for a few seconds while wrinkling his brow, set it down carefully, then take another, repeating the entire process. He seemed intent on trying every pearl in the basin. He then took two, then three at once, making them twirl in the air in a silent, bluish ballet. He was completely engrossed.

She walked up to him with a smile. "Does this remind you of your pebbles?"

Alister hesitated for a moment. "Completely. Magic pebbles. It's fascinating, isn't it? It's so easy to manipulate the flux with them. Look, try with two. It's a little harder to focus, but the result is worth it."

Intrigued, Valianara picked up a second pearl. After a few attempts, during which the two spheres threatened to collide, she managed to find her balance and exclaimed, "Oh yes! It's incredible! I could move mountains!"

Visibly amused, Alister remarked with a grin, "Perhaps we need more pearls."

"I'm glad to see you smile," Valianara confessed to him, her voice softening. "I'm glad you're opening up to us a little."

His smile faded slightly, giving way to a shadow of sadness. "I'm not a very sociable person, I know. The loss of my parents extinguished a flame inside of me."

"I… I understand…"

Not quite sure what else to say, Valianara turned her attention back to her levitating pearls.

Evarine approached and whispered in her ear, "That's the longest conversation you've had since the beginning. Congratulations."

Valianara grimaced. "Don't make fun of me!"

As Valianara practiced making her two pearls spin in circles, the voice of Orator Gideon rang out, "Very impressive, Novice Valianara. And you, too, Novice Alister. Manipulating multiple pearls from the very first contact isn't something that everyone can do. Keep practicing; you'll make excellent flux manipulators."

A rush of pride swept through the young girl. She shot a glance at her classmate, who merely gave a brief nod before gently placing his pearls back in the basin.

"All right, that's it for today," Gideon announced. "Please put all the pearls back in the basin."

The orator then asked them to wait. He plunged his hand into the liquid and, under everyone's watchful gaze, counted each pearl.

One novice couldn't help but ask, "Are you worried we might steal them, Orator?"

Gideon's face grew serious. "Please understand. Whether we like it or not, we are at war with a people who will stop at nothing to reduce us to mere livestock. It is our duty to protect what may one day give us a chance to fight back."

No one said a word. Finally satisfied with his inventory, Gideon relaxed. "The count is correct. You may go to the dining hall. Remember, after eating, you are expected in the Chamber of Memory."

The Academy of the Keepers of Knowledge / Present Day

Since settling in the city, Menilmonea had developed an instinctive sense of time; all she had to do was observe the subtle shifts in the light. The intense zenith of light was beginning to wane, shifting toward cooler tones. It had just passed noon. The second group of novices would be on their way.

She spoke aloud to the spirit of the Chamber of Memory. "Valianara and Evarine are in this second group. They're the ones who were able to unlock the books on the first floor."

The spirit's disembodied voice replied instantly, tinged with mischief, "Oh! I'm going to give them such a big hug!"

Menilmonea smiled.

The muffled sound of approaching footsteps signaled the arrival of the novices, who entered the room shortly afterward. They came in one by one, with a respect bordering on reverence.

The sanctuary was just as Menilmonea had found it ten rotations earlier: a single circular room, bathed in a soft gloom, with a large circular bench at its center. However, the space had been subtly rearranged to become her workplace—the nerve center of the Academy's power.

Against the wall furthest from the entrance, a desk had been set up. It wasn't so much a piece of furniture as a small forest where nature flourished. Dense ivy with small white flowers cascaded down its legs, mingling with deep purple clematis growing from the structure itself. On the desk beside stacks of Library copies, clusters of crimson flowers added a splash of vivid color. The whole scene created the impression that the desk hadn't been built but had grown there.

On the once-bare, smooth stone walls, huge dark roots wound their way along the surfaces, clinging to the stonework before plunging into the ground or disappearing into the vaulted ceiling. It seemed as though they had always been there, the living arteries of an ancient presence that had made this place its home. Among these veins of ancient wood, the illustrative explanations presented to her during her first and only session were now permanently on display. Their vibrant colors and dramatic depictions, framed by the tranquil force of the roots, offered a vast mural of the tragic history of the Arkandian people.

The novices, led by Valianara and her squad, stepped forward, gazing in wonder at the murals.

Menilmonea rose and greeted them with a warm smile. "Welcome to the Chamber of Memory."

She briefly explained the original purpose of the place: a tool to help reincarnated Arkandians retrieve their memories. She emphasized one point in particular: "The spirit of this room is the first we've managed to free from mental enslavement. And I'll let her speak for herself."

A soft, feminine voice emerged from everywhere at once, surrounding the novices and startling them. "Welcome, everyone. I'm delighted to have you in my midst."

Instinctively, several novices replied in unison, "Hello, ma'am."

A crystalline, disembodied laugh filled the room. "Ha, ha! Don't call me 'ma'am.' Although I must admit, I don't remember my actual name."

"And 'ma'am' is somewhat stubborn; she refuses to accept a substitute name if it isn't the right one," added Menilmonea.

"Don't listen to her; I'm not stubborn," the Voice continued, "just someone who is simply attached to the truth. As far back as I can remember, I've been lied to. It matters to me that it never happens again."

A respectful murmur of approval rippled through the ranks of the novices.

"And I commend you for that," agreed Menilmonea. "It's also why my office is here. Beyond the pleasure of having this charming spirit as a companion, being here allows me to show her that we're not hiding anything. That was part of the initial plan, anyway, but now that I've gotten used to her, I couldn't imagine working anywhere else. I'd miss her voice too much."

"You flatter me!" replied the Voice with amusement.

"Well," continued Menilmonea. "You're here to see the murals painted by the Arkandians to depict their exodus. You've read more than enough on the subject over the last few weeks, but here they are in visual form. It will help you get a better sense of their state of mind."

She guided them along the circular wall, stopping in front of each mural. Valianara followed, unsettled by the realism of the artwork.

She walked past *The Breaking of the Pact*, wondering what could have caused such punishment from the Mother. She then gazed upon *The Exodus*, a depiction of a glorious city engulfed by the raging ocean. Then she observed *The Teleportation*, a desperate ballet of magic, and finally, the image of *The Pyramid* welcoming the survivors. She shuddered at the funeral procession of the Guardians of the Jars.

But it was the very last painting that had the most profound impact on her. Soberly titled *The Villages*, it depicted, in a matter-of-fact manner, streams of flux linking the Titans to small communities, as well as processions of people converging on the pyramid so that their bodies could be harvested under the supervision of a creature resembling an octopus made of stone and vegetation. There was no life in the scene, no soul; nothing but the cold logic of a gruesome system. Valianara felt her stomach knot. It was the most dehumanizing vision of them all.

When the tour of the murals was over, Menilmonea gave everyone a little time to take in the tragedy painted on the walls.

Her voice rang out, clear and analytical, "One thing should be clear to you by now. These paintings convey no sense of guilt. This is a fundamental point. From their perspective, the Arkandians did not commit any crime. They merely did what was necessary to save their civilization. From their point of view, they are the victims of the Source."

Several hands shot up immediately, including Valianara's. She had to question this. Something about the last painting unsettled her.

Menilmonea gave the floor to Inkidu.

"In *The Villages*, what does the creature with tentacles that seems to be floating above the pyramid symbolize?"

Menilmonea gave a slight smile. "That's an excellent question, and I'm sure you're all wondering the same thing."

Everyone who had raised their hand nodded in agreement.

"I expected as much. Before I can answer you, I need to take a small precaution."

She walked over to her desk and, among all the artifacts there, activated the one located against the wall near her chair: a Secret Sentinel.

This single action raised the tension level another notch. Every novice felt their pulse quicken. Things were getting more serious.

"Most of our knowledge doesn't require us to use the Secret Sentinel, because it's all connected to the first piece of knowledge you received," Menilmonea explained. "However, what I'm about to teach you isn't related to the city itself or its creators. We aren't certain that this precaution is even necessary, but just in case…"

The tension was at its peak. What could this secret possibly be?

Without waiting, Menilmonea continued, "This creature was the same race as the Titans. Before they were enslaved. Before the Titans became Titans, they went by the name 'descendants.' This creature was one of them."

"But it looks like he's not attached to any village in the painting," Valianara pointed out.

"No, indeed. He betrayed his people. It was actually his fault that the Arkandians managed to reach the souls of the other descendants to control them, erase their memories, and turn them into slaves."

The revelation hit them like a hammer blow. The novices were shocked, exchanging stunned looks.

Realizing the magnitude of the revelation, Evarine asked, "When you say the Titans were descendants, what changed? Why, then, do we call them Titans and not descendants? And who were they descendants of?"

Menilmonea, amused by this flood of questions, raised a reassuring hand. "Calm down, novice. First of all, they are quite simply the descendants of the Mother. Secondly, and your question is very logical: why change their name? Well, because in the past, they weren't titanic beasts. Their form was closer to that of the creature you can see in the painting, but without the stone appendages. They were tentacled plant-like beings who watched over the forests for the Mother. But when the traitor let the Arkandians corrupt them, cutting them off from the Mother's song, they underwent a forced mutation into what we now call Titans."

A pensive silence fell, and then Kamartel spoke up, "Please forgive me if my question sounds foolish, High Orator, but… have all the descendants vanished? Where I come from, there's talk of a plant-like monster that prowls the forests and the eastern moors at night. I always thought it was just a story to scare children, but… now I'm not so sure… The description of these plant-like beings fits rather well."

The voice of the room's spirit echoed, gentle and teasing, "He's a clever one, that boy."

Menilmonea nodded, her expression growing more serious.

"Yes, indeed, Novice Kamartel. This is not a subject we often discuss, but I won't lie to you: there is a creature that matches your description. It is even older than the Titans, and we are careful to avoid even approaching it, for it has gone mad due to the Arkandians and could prove dangerous. Fortunately, it roams far from the villages, and the tower near its territory is now forbidden. But yes… this creature exists."

Several novices, completely unconsciously, had seated themselves on the central bench.

"By all the Titans…"

Evarine, her eyes riveted on the mural of the villages, then asked the question everyone was dreading, in a barely audible voice, "And… and that thing over there? The traitor floating above the pyramid? What happened to him? Did he leave with the Arkandians?"

A deathly silence fell over the room. Menilmonea allowed the question to hang in the air for a moment, her eyes lost in the void as if she were reliving a scene no one else could imagine. She then turned to them with a face of implacable serenity.

"No. And he will never harm anyone again." She paused before adding in a tone of such simplicity that it sent a chill through the audience, "Orator Aureal and I have made sure of that."

Valianara looked at her friends. Each, in their own way, appeared stunned by this avalanche of revelations. Evarine was speechless. Kamartel, still white-faced from his earlier question, seemed to have aged ten rotations in just a few minutes. Even Alister, usually so composed, was frowning slightly—betraying a degree of surprise he was unable to contain.

Since their arrival among the Keepers of Knowledge, their world had been constantly expanding and fragmenting at the same time. They moved from one discovery to another, each new truth shattering its predecessor. It was dizzying, frightening, but for Valianara, it was also exhilarating. She couldn't have asked for anything greater. Here, at the heart of their world's deepest secrets, facing such ancient mysteries, she felt she belonged.

The lesson ended with a few more questions about the other paintings, but the novices' minds were already elsewhere. They were still reeling from the latest truths they had learned. Sensing their exhaustion, Menilmonea brought the session to a close.

"That's all for today. I thank you for your attention. You're dismissed."

The novices, still a little bewildered, left the Chamber of Memory in small groups, their whispers filling the entrance hall.

Once the last squad had left, the spirit of the room cried out, "This isn't the first time I've noticed it, and I never thought to ask you: why don't we tell them about the Primal?"

Menilmonea sank onto the circular bench with a weary sigh.

"First of all, because apart from you, Aureal, and me, no one knows he exists. Back when the Titans decided to keep helping us after the revelation, the Primal made it clear: his purpose was, above all, to protect the forests. He didn't order the Titans to abandon us, and I think his friendship with Aureal and me undoubtedly influenced him, but he did distance himself."

She ran a hand over the back of her neck.

"After much discussion with the Council of Titans, we concluded that the very existence of such a powerful entity, so close to the Mother, could cause significant problems. Revealing his existence would create an imbalance. The people would see him as a near-divine being, far older and more powerful than the Titans. Some would undoubtedly start worshipping him and asking for miracles. It would create schisms, cults… Having only just survived a religious lie, we can't risk inadvertently creating another one. The Titans are known, accepted guides; the Primal would be a theological bomb."

"I see. Maintain simplicity to preserve stability," the Voice commented.

"Exactly. We're toeing a fine line, and we have to try to maintain a degree of normality. More recently, we've also concluded that keeping his existence a secret gives us a slight advantage over the Arkandians should they attempt to infiltrate us or, worse, launch an attack. He's our only defense as of now. The Arkandians are losing ships in their attempts to reach our continent, and we hope they remain unaware of why."

"Interesting," replied the Voice. "Not even the Keepers of Knowledge are privy to this?"

"No. However, I'm not entirely happy about it. For now, the Council believes we have more to lose than to gain…"

She had barely stood up to disable the Secret Sentinel when Gideon came running in, panting, his usual calm completely gone.

"High Orator! We have a problem!"

Menilmonea turned around, taken aback. "There's no need to call me 'High Orator' when we're alone. What's going on?"

"You need to see this. Several of the pearls seem to have lost their power."

"What do you mean?"

"Come with me!"

They rushed out of the Chamber of Memory, making their way through the city's avenues with long strides. On the way, Gideon explained, his voice still ragged with effort and anxiety. "The second group of novices arrived right after mealtime. I let the first squad manipulate the pearls, as usual. But one of the novices, Amandine, or something like that…"

"Amaldine," Menilmonea corrected.

"Yes, that's right. She couldn't make anything happen. She kept saying that the pearl felt no different to her than an ordinary stone. At first, I thought she was having trouble focusing. Until now, no novice has ever had any trouble with the pearls. So, I wanted to check for myself…"

He paused, as if to catch his breath.

"To my surprise, the pearl no longer had any amplifying effect. It behaved just like any ordinary stone. Even its bluish aura was significantly weakened. It was glowing only faintly, almost imperceptibly. Amaldine was right. To avoid alarming the others, I put the pearl aside and asked her to choose another one. After they left, I checked everything. Five pearls… Five pearls are no longer active."

Menilmonea furrowed her brow, a growing sense of unease taking hold of her. "That's unusual. We've never read anything suggesting this is possible. Can they lose their power?"

"I… I don't know," Gideon admitted, looking completely at a loss. "But it seems so."

They finally reached the Pearl Room. Stepping into the heavy atmosphere of the place, Menilmonea could now see for herself the unsettling truth.

It was commonly acknowledged that her innate connection to the Mother's song made her, by far, the most powerful flux manipulator among all the Keepers of Knowledge. This natural gift granted her an incredible level of control. For her, the flux and the song were two sides of the same coin. It was as if most mages heard a crackling sound

where she perceived a complex, polyphonic symphony.

She approached the five pearls that Gideon had isolated.

"It's remarkable. They seem inert. Lifeless."

She let her mind open up. She focused on one of them, trying to listen to it. The song was supposed to resonate, to build in intensity, with new notes joining in to enrich the whole… But there was nothing. The song remained uniform, flowing around the pearl like a common rock in the middle of a river.

"Yes, we do have a problem," she confirmed, her face grave. "Does this mean that the pearls have a lifespan?"

"I don't know," Gideon repeated. "That's why I came to you. I don't sense any change in the still-active pearls. But my sensitivity is nowhere near as keen as yours."

Menilmonea reached for the basin, picked up a random pearl, and focused on its song. As expected, it was exquisite, vibrant, rich, and colorful. It was intoxicating. A sensation that reminded her of her half-heartseed, though the latter was much more powerful and much more… alive.

"No, I don't feel any difference," she commented. "It seems just as I've always known them."

She examined several others but detected no decrease in intensity. "Does that mean they just… stop working all at once?"

"I think so. With your permission, I'll speak to Gavin to see if his team can look for information on the first floor of the Library."

"Excellent idea. It's an absolute priority," Menilmonea replied firmly. "If we lose our pearls and don't know how to make more, our slim advantage will be reduced to nothing at all."

XXI

Azymantias felt a jolt. A raw surge, as if a bolt of lightning had just struck his soul. He was free. The plan had worked.

In keeping with the protocol he himself had defined ages ago, his mind snapped into action with an iron discipline. A rapid sweep of his memories. He knew why he was there. He recalled the orchestrated betrayal, the sentence, the icy sensation of his soul being torn from his body. And he was able to go back even further, as far back as his early years among the recruits of the Magisterium. His memory was still intact.

The first step was complete. Next, he focused on his surroundings. The rough texture of the chair beneath him. The fresh, dry air. The sight of his own hands on the table. He was in the Jar Room.

Excellent.

And yet, something was wrong. Those hands… They weren't Obinaelle's. The trap had been meant for her. She should have freed him from his jar to try to anchor him in the Mind Focalizer, thereby triggering the projection spell he had so skillfully woven into the clay. Except these were clearly not Obinaelle's hands. For one, the Core's trifecta wasn't there. And there was a gnarled Briar wrapped around the left wrist. The hands themselves seemed younger, less marred by the millennia than those of the High Orator.

He tried to turn them over, bend his fingers. Nothing. The body wouldn't respond.

This is… troublesome. I don't have control yet. Then again, it wouldn't be the first time a forced injection had taken time to produce the desired effect.

If he'd been able to react, he might have fallen from his chair when he saw the hands move on their own. Slowly, they rose and began massaging the temples of his new body.

An unconscious gesture. Interesting… Perhaps a reflexive response, like residual behavior from the previous occupant? I'll have to catalog that later.

He tried to access the host's memory. Nothing. A blank, impenetrable wall. He tried something simpler: blinking. Nothing happened.

It would be just my luck if, after all this time, I were to end up trapped in a body that dies of starvation because I can't control it.

Abandoning fine motor control, he tried to speak. He formed the words in his mind and pushed them toward the vocal cords of this new body. *"In the name of the Magisterium…"*

But before his mouth could produce any of the sounds he intended to form, it spoke on its own. "Who… Who's there?"

The eyes darted in all directions, scanning the empty room with growing panic. The body jumped to its feet. "Where are you?"

Azymantias began to grasp the painful reality of his situation. He projected what he wanted to say as if he were about to speak aloud. *"Young lady, it seems we have a problem."*

"In the name of the Mother, where are you? Is this one of those pranks to make fun of the novices?"

"Hmm… No, my child, it's nothing like that. Please, sit down. I'll answer you, but calm down. Your heart is pounding. You're going to faint unless you steady yourself."

Valianara complied, sinking heavily back into her chair. "There, I'm sitting. But if you want me to calm down, then reveal yourself!"

"That might be difficult. The thing is… I'm inside your head."

Valianara nearly choked. "In what sense?"

"Well, to be honest, I don't fully understand how it's possible that you're still here. But it's clear that there are indeed two of us in your head."

"What do you mean by still here? Where would you have me be? I'm better suited to being in my own head than you are, don't you think?"

"Yes, strictly speaking. But—and please don't take this personally because I have nothing against you—you should have been erased when I entered. Overwritten by my consciousness, so to speak."

"It's difficult to stay calm when you say things like that."

"I'm fully aware of that."

"And where are you from? Where were you before you… tried to kill me?"

"In a jar."

"Oh… You were in *the* jar."

"Why the *jar?"*

"Look around you. All the jars are open, except for the one behind the seal, up there."

"Well, I'd love to look, but you're going to have to do it for both of us. It seems I've been reduced to the role of a passenger."

Valianara looked up, shifting her chair to get a better view. She turned her attention to the secluded alcove where the single sealed jar should have been.

"By all the Titans! It's gone!"

"What happened here? Why are all the jars open? It looks like the place has been abandoned!"

"Oh… you've been trapped in your jar for quite a while, haven't you?"

"That's the problem with the jars. I only entered it a few moments ago."

"Do you remember where you came from? Do you come from a village? What… what's your name, by the way?"

"Call me Azymantias. My full name is Azymantias of the First Circle, but we can dispense with that, given our current proximity. What do you mean by 'village'?"

"From the First Circle? By the Mother! I've read several works that mention this group of mages! You weren't just a prisoner… By Tunka's shell! You're an Arkandian!"

"Yes, that's right. But you make it sound like it's a bad thing. Besides,

I was indeed a prisoner. Obinaelle had me sealed away for high treason."

"Obinaelle… Wait, that was well before the exodus, so… Oh my! You're in for a shock, Azymantias."

At those words, Aboren entered the wing, deep in conversation with an apprentice.

"… and all those in the east wing have the same rune as—" She stopped abruptly. Her gaze fell on the broken shards of pottery on the floor. She took two steps forward, her expression frozen.

"By the Mother… Look. A jar has been broken."

The apprentice turned pale. Aboren looked at the isolated shelf and stared at the space where the sealed jar should have been. The color drained from her face. "And not just any jar! It was the sealed one. Somehow, someone managed to get to it. And they destroyed it!"

She spun around, searching for whoever was responsible, her eyes falling on Valianara. She was sitting at one of the desks, tucked away behind a pillar.

"Novice?"

Valianara jumped to her feet, her throat tight. Aboren stepped toward her. "Who climbed up to the alcove? Who broke that jar?"

"Um… I don't know, Orator. I nodded off while working on my parchment about the Focalizer. I wanted to polish it before tomorrow. I didn't see anyone. I swear…"

Aboren stood motionless for a moment, her stare fixed on Valianara, longer than was comfortable for her.

"Show me your hands," she ordered.

Valianara complied. Aboren inspected them slowly, searching for the slightest trace of residual flux or ceramic fragments.

Finding nothing conclusive, she gave a brief signal to her apprentice. "You. Fetch the High Orator. Immediately!"

Aboren then turned her full attention back to Valianara. "Why were you in this wing alone? At this late hour?"

"I… I just wanted to finish my work, Orator."

"Your Orator doesn't seem very accommodating. Whatever you do, don't say anything about me!"

"Shh!" Valianara blurted out.

Aboren leaned toward her, her eyebrows knitting together. "I beg your pardon?"

"I didn't say anything, Orator. Just… a stifled sneeze."

Aboren stared at her suspiciously for a moment, then dismissed her with a weary wave of her hand. "Go on, get out of here. We've got a whole new problem on our hands, apparently." She added, speaking more to herself, "As if last week's trouble with the pearls wasn't enough…"

Valianara hurried outside, where she found the city bathed in a soft blue evening light.

"You did the right thing. We need to talk… By the highest towers of Arkandis! Where are we? What is this place?"

"We are beneath the pyramid of what you know as the continent of Landria."

"But how? How can the city be here? What kind of spell is this?"

"Hmm, just as I thought. My dear Azymantias, you've missed a major part of your people's destiny."

"But who could have teleported the city here? It would require casting a spell… A theurgical spell. Nothing could generate that much flux."

"I… I'm not sure I know what you're talking about, but you should know that something happened in your world: the breaking of the Pact. As a result, your island was destroyed by a tidal wave, and your people were afflicted with a curse that made them fatally sensitive to the sun. Your Obinaelle managed to transport part of your city here, to safety, but she died in the process."

"What… How… What? No, that's not possible! I mean, even if the Source existed, she would never have agreed to help her! That's… preposterous!"

"If it would help, I'd be happy to sit down…"

No reply. The silence in her head was absolute, dizzying.

"Azymantias? Are you all right?"

"Yes, sorry. No need to sit down. I don't feel tired. I'm just… devastated."

"Yes, I imagine it's a shock. But you don't know the whole story yet."

"There's worse news?"

"Let's just say that from our perspective, yes…"

She told him everything. The walk through the city was long, but the story was even longer. She told him about the villages, the enslaved Titans, the false religion, the acceleration of growth, the harvesting of bodies for the Ascension with the help of a descendant who betrayed his people. Azymantias listened in silence, his presence almost imperceptible, so that from time to time Valianara had to ask him if he was still there. Each time, a distant, weary voice answered in the affirmative.

She then told him about the Arkandians, whose whereabouts were unknown.

Azymantias finally broke his silence, a theory taking shape in his analytical mind.

"If they've departed, it's because they've achieved their goal. Once they'd gathered enough healthy bodies, they must have returned to Arkandis. Their true aim must have been to rebuild our civilization there, not to live shut away in a pyramid."

"Why leave no guardians behind?" Valianara asked in disbelief. "It's a city full of knowledge and magic, abandoned to its own devices."

"It is surprising, indeed, but they likely didn't have enough people to spare to split their forces, and they probably had no more golems. And above all… knowing Arkandian arrogance, they must have thought that the major power orb and that creature would be enough to protect the place. They couldn't have expected ordinary villagers to stand up to them or succeed in thwarting their defenses. To them, you're nothing but helpless cattle, completely subservient to their religion. If they needed new bodies, they probably thought they could just come back, trigger a few Ascensions, and take what they needed."

Valianara resumed her story with the birth of village civilization, the Keepers of Knowledge, and the Academy. When she had finished her account, just as they came within sight of the Residence, Azymantias confessed, *"I am a monster. Everything is my fault."*

"Why do you say that? None of this is your fault. You were locked away in a jar."

"Alas, my child, your kindness is touching, but the truth is the truth.

I… I am the one who broke the Pact."

"What? What do you mean by that?"

"I did something I thought would have no repercussions in order to wage a political attack against Obinaelle. I was convinced that the Source was just a puppet she was waving in our faces to hold onto power."

"I'm afraid you were mistaken. The Source, whom we call the Mother, does truly exist, and her wrath nearly wiped your people out."

"All this misery, all these deaths, all this destruction… I don't know how I…"

"I understand. But, at the risk of sounding selfish, will you be staying in my head for long?"

"I can be discreet. Unfortunately, I can't leave. Well… An Arkandian mage could likely extract me, but I'd need a body to disappear into immediately."

"We could bind you to an object, like the spirits in the towers."

"Although I feel guilty for all those horrors, I'm not exactly eager to become a display piece."

"Your fellow mages didn't seem to have any qualms about it."

"Oh, I know that all too well. That's precisely the attitude I rebelled against in the first place. The Magisterium was rotting from the inside out. And given what they put you through, I wasn't wrong about that."

"Magisterium?"

"Yes, that's the name for all the mages who rule over Arkandis."

"I understand. Getting back to the point: I'm not ready to host a thousand-year-old Arkandian who's going to have access to my every thought. That's going to get awkward pretty quickly."

"Yes, I agree."

"I'm going to talk to the High Orator about it."

"Careful… Are you sure about that? How will she react? More importantly, how will she feel when she learns that one of her people's sworn enemies is living inside your head?"

"The High Orator is a good woman."

"Oh, I'm sure she is. Just like certain members of the Magisterium. Yet when facing adversity, we sometimes discover a whole new side of someone's personality."

"You think she'd hurt me?"

"Not on purpose. But consider her position: the value of a mage of the First Circle's knowledge is likely far greater than the risk incurred by the person hosting said mage if she were to force an extraction. Though I doubt you know how to do it."

"I see… I'll have to think about it."

After a brief moment, Azymantias continued, *"So, they've brought manipulators here to learn our magic… Are you a manipulator yourself? By the way, what is your name, my friend?"*

"Valianara. Valianara from the village of Tunka. And yes, I'm slowly beginning to control the flux."

"Good. I was a teacher on Arkandis. As proof of my goodwill, I'll teach you something that you'll find helpful."

"I'm listening."

"I'll show you how to form a thought silo. It will be my gift to show my gratitude for not handing me over to your authorities."

"How so?"

"It's a way to shield part of your being from outside interference. It's especially useful when you're facing mental interrogations. Your people probably don't need anything like that, but it could be useful for us."

"Oh… To shield ourselves, in other words?"

"Exactly. You must feel it the same way I do. Our minds are compartmentalized, but not isolated. You must perceive that a part of yourself is… hazy, blurred, isn't it?"

Valianara focused. "Yes… I understand what you mean."

"Well, with a thought silo, you could separate me. Put me in a mental jar, so to speak."

"And you'd agree to that?"

"I wouldn't feel a thing. To me, it would be like a jar. I'd instantly jump from the present to the moment you open the silo."

"Fascinating. But what makes you so sure I won't leave you there forever?"

"First of all, you'd have to succeed. But you're right, there's no guarantee. That said, I have a lot of experience with people, and I know how to recognize the good ones. Your guilt would get the better of you if you left

me imprisoned. Am I wrong?"

Valianara paused and changed the subject. This habit people had of reading her mind was getting annoying. "So how are you going to teach me?"

"There are two options. If you focus a little flux on yourself, you can choose to give me control. In short, you can tell your body to obey me. I'm probably speculating a little, since a case like ours has never existed to my knowledge, but I have some idea of how it works hypothetically."

"So, I give you control, and then you'll just go lock yourself away without even attempting anything?"

"Yes, that's the simplest solution. That said, I have a vague sense that you don't particularly like this plan. I suspected as much. I understand. It's a pity, but I understand…"

He let a long silence hang in the air before continuing.

"There's still the second option: I can try to teach you. Through repetition, by guiding you, and by describing what to do. I won't lie to you: it'll take weeks, and you'll have me with you the whole time until you get it right."

"You're a sly one, Azymantias. But it's all right. I'm not going to risk giving you control. Go ahead, explain it to me."

She sat down on a bench a little way from the Residence, aware that several people passing by were watching her talk to herself.

"All right. Think of your mind as a map. You're going to use the flux to visualize where you are, and where I am. Take your time. Trust your instincts. The key is always to focus on what you want to do. The flux will follow. Once you've got a feel for the map, you'll ask the flux to build a wall—or whatever works for you—to block off the area where my mind resides. It's a little different for everyone. But, once again, it's going to take time…"

Valianara closed her eyes and focused. She listened to the song, letting it grow louder.

"By the four legions of the Magisterium! What is the meaning of this?"

"You're not helping me much…"

"But… Can you hear that music?"

"Yes, of course. This is how I sense the flux."

"What… How? I mean, I've never seen anything like this, or heard it. Even with our minds divided as they are, I can feel that you're managing to channel an incredible amount of flux. I'm starting to understand why my spell didn't fully work. The way you use this music to tap into the flux is truly ingenious…"

"Shh!"

She immersed herself in the melody vibrating within her.

"Incredible… Now, close the doors of your perception to the outside world. There is nothing but your mind. Try to visualize it. For some, it's a room. For others, a landscape. Neither representation is right or wrong."

Valianara let the song guide her. Little by little, the image of a map formed behind her eyelids. It wasn't a geographical map, but a map of her own being. She could see her heart, her limbs, and, high above it all, her consciousness—a luminous, peaceful clearing, bathed in soft light.

"Perfect. That's a very vivid image. Now, try to find me. I should be an anomaly in this scene. A shadow, a stain, a patch of fog."

She delved into her inner world. The song was all around her, resonating in every tree, every blade of grass in the clearing of her mind. On the horizon, she sensed it: a misty, indistinct plain, silent, where the song seemed to fade away. It was him.

"I can see you," she whispered.

"Already? Fascinating. Usually, this step alone takes hours. You're progressing at lightning speed. Now for the hardest part. You must use the flux to construct a barrier around this area. Think of it as if it were a building material."

Following his advice, she envisioned huge watchtowers rising from the ground all around the plain. But the image was blurry, unfocused. The towers looked like they were made of sand and crumbled as soon as they took shape. She felt a pang of frustration.

"Don't force it. Don't rush the flux. Guide it. I know, this isn't easy. With that said, let me repeat my offer. It would be much easier if I did it."

"Azymantias…"

"Fine! Fine! As you wish. You might want to try asking this song to follow you. It seems to work for you. Focus your will on the outcome.

Feel the flux surrounding you, within you. Ask it to take on the form you desire."

Valianara took a deep breath and shifted her approach. She no longer tried to build the towers, but to sing them. She allowed the melody of the flux to intensify, varying its frequency so that it resonated with the idea of stone, of solidity.

And the towers appeared. Solid, unshakable, rising toward the sky of her mind.

"By the Core… You are incredibly skilled. With the right training and a deep understanding of spells and techniques, you would be a formidable duelist. I would love to explore this in more detail."

Feeling more confident, Valianara continued. She summoned walls as tall as mountains that rose to connect the towers, then a massive wooden door barred with iron. She wove her prison, thread of flux upon thread of flux, with perfect control, carried by the song that resonated through her very being. Strangely, she felt she could sense the melody much more clearly since Azymantias had been there, as if his presence acted as an amplifier.

The misty plain was soon completely encircled, cut off. Separated from the rest of her world.

"Azymantias? Are you there?"

No answer. The silence in her head was absolute. There was nothing left but the song, clear and pure.

She felt relieved. And drained. It had all happened so fast. She would finally be able to go and rest and gather her thoughts. She would deal with his release in the morning. She would have to produce a plan. For now, it was very late; the city was completely bathed in a subtle azure light.

When she got to her room, she was greeted by Evarine, who, noticing her pale face and drawn features, jumped up from the bed where she had been reading a piece of parchment.

"Valianara! What's wrong? Where have you been?"

Valianara closed the door behind her and leaned against it, her expression becoming more intense.

"Evarine… I don't have a Secret Sentinel, but I need to tell you something important. And you must swear to me, on the Mother, that you won't tell anyone. Not even the orators."

Evarine's expression shifted from concern to absolute gravity. She stepped closer and placed her hands on her friend's shoulders.

"By all the Titans, what's wrong? You can tell me anything. I'm your friend, and I'll keep your secret until the day I die."

Valianara then told her the whole story of her adventure, starting from the moment she'd woken up with a start in the Jar Room. She spoke of the voice in her head, the thousand-year-old Arkandian, the breaking of the Pact, and the mental prison she'd just created deep within herself.

XXII

It was still dark when a soft knock on the door roused Valianara from her sleep. She blinked, feeling somewhat disoriented. Outside, silence still reigned over the city. It was shrouded in an indigo glow—that distinctive hue that precedes the golden tones of dawn. The bell had not yet rung.

"Blast… Who is it?" whispered Evarine, her sleep-hoarse voice rising from the next bed.

"No clue," replied Valianara, slipping out of bed without a sound.

"Is he still in his box?"

"Yes, yes. I was thinking of letting him out after I get ready."

She went to open the door. Her heart skipped a beat. It was Menilmonea.

"High Orator? What's happening?"

Behind her, Evarine, who had propped herself up on her elbows, gasped when she saw who had come to visit.

"Nothing to worry about," Menilmonea reassured her in a soothing voice. "I wanted to come see you in person to discuss what happened yesterday in the Jar Room."

A shiver ran down her spine.

"Orator Aboren told me that you fell asleep at one of the desks."

"I'm so sorry."

Menilmonea's face broke into a warm smile. "Ah, ah! No, there's no need to worry—it happens to me all the time. I just wanted to ask you about it myself, because I know Orator Aboren and she can sometimes lack, let's say… tact."

Valianara gave a relieved smile. "I wouldn't dare say that."

"That's to your credit."

From her bed, Evarine didn't miss a word of the exchange, her ears pricked beneath her tousled hair.

"So, you didn't see or hear anything?" Menilmonea continued, her expression growing more serious.

"I would love to help, High Orator, but no, I didn't hear a thing."

Don't think about him. Don't think about him. Don't look guilty, she repeated to herself over and over.

After a long silence during which Menilmonea appeared to be probing her soul, she continued, "It doesn't matter. We'll keep looking. If anything comes to mind, please come straight to me."

"Of course!"

Menilmonea's face lit up again. She addressed the two young women, "And that brings me to the second reason for my visit. Thanks to you and your ingenuity, we were able to read a book that is crucial to helping the spirits. And we're going to try to use the knowledge it contains to free the Voice from the Chamber of Memory."

Valianara and Evarine were speechless.

"More specifically, we're going to try to transfer it into a necklace, which will finally enable it to leave its prison. To thank you and honor your work, I'd like both of you to be there."

"By all the Titans! You can count on us being there!" exclaimed Evarine, jumping out of bed.

"Oh, thank you, High Orator! That's such a wonderful gift!" added Valianara.

Menilmonea, already heading out the door, gave them one last smile. "Meet me at the Chamber of Memory in an hour if you will. Your teachers have been informed and will give you time to make up this morning's lesson when you get back."

No sooner had Valianara closed the door than their excitement erupted.

"What a turn in events! We're going to witness history in the making!"

"I was destined for this moment!" exclaimed Evarine as she rushed toward the bathroom. "Right, time to get ready!"

"Hurry! I don't want us to be late!"

Half an hour later, ready to leave, Valianara sat down for a moment on the edge of her bed. "I'm going to unlock Azymantias."

"Be careful," replied Evarine, looking at her with a mixture of curiosity and apprehension.

Valianara closed her eyes and focused on the song. Suddenly, she found herself in the landscape of her own mind. The massive walls and tall towers of the mental prison stood before her in silence. She approached the large wooden and iron door and, with a single thought, felt it swing heavily on its hinges, revealing the misty plain within.

"It seems your mastery of the flux far exceeds my expectations, young lady. I had thought I might save time by letting you wear yourself out building a silo."

"Are you feeling well?"

"Pardon?" said Evarine, staring at her.

"Ah, no. I'm talking to him. Not to you."

Evarine burst out laughing. "This is going to be quite something."

"Yes, I'm fine, thank you. I need to get used to the sudden change in setting. For me, one moment I was helping you establish the silo, and the next... I'm in your room, I believe?"

"That's right. We're going to eat and then witness the Voice being liberated from the Chamber of Memory. You'll get to 'meet' the High Orator."

"It's quite a strange situation, from an outsider's perspective, I won't deny it," Evarine commented.

"Oh, how fascinating. Have they been able to read some of the books on capturing spirits? Not to boast, but you should know that I wrote quite a few of them."

"Were you an influential person?"

"In a way. However, dear Valianara, there is no need to speak aloud if you don't want to. I sense it is unsettling your friend."

"How should I speak to you, then?"

"Simply think what you wish to say to me while focusing on my presence. That should suffice."

Valianara closed her eyes for a moment.

"Like… Like this?"

"Exactly!"

She turned to Evarine, a big smile on her face, and explained, "I can talk to him without actually having to speak!"

"That's so much easier!" Evarine whispered, relieved. "Trying to follow half a conversation was really distracting."

They had a quick breakfast in the dining hall, too excited about the upcoming event to really enjoy their meal. They weren't surprised not to see Alister there; he always struggled to get up in the morning.

"Still no sign of Kamartel," Evarine frowned. "I wonder if we'll ever have the honor of having breakfast with him."

Valianara shrugged, her own impatience beginning to get the better of her. Once they'd finished their food, they left the bustle of the dining hall to find the calm of the city's upper avenues. The promise of witnessing a miracle had them both running.

A few moments later, they found themselves in front of the door to the Chamber of Memory. They slowed to a halt, somewhat intimidated by the solemnity of the place and the significance of what was about to happen. The friends exchanged a glance, unsure whether they should knock or wait.

But no sooner had Valianara placed her foot on the first step than the Voice invited them in with unabashed joy. "Come in, young ladies! Come in! Thanks to you, I will at last be freed from this wretched building."

Inside, Aureal, Menilmonea, and Menara were already there, gathered near the desk. Standing beside them was a Keeper of Knowledge whom the novices had never met. He looked worn out, with dark circles under his eyes, but his face was aglow with intense pride.

Menilmonea made the introductions.

"This is Norwen. He is the Keeper of Knowledge who sacrificed his health and sleep to read and transcribe the contents of *Anchoring of Spirits*. Thanks to him, now we can use the Focalizer to transfer the Voice into this necklace."

She pointed to a pendant resting on the desk: a simple leather cord with a small brass flower-shaped charm.

"So, this is the famous High Orator. You may have noticed that what you call the 'song' is clearly stronger in her presence."

"Oh yes. She has an incredible mastery of the song. She can make things grow at will; it's astonishing to see."

"Hum. Even after all these millennia, there are still secrets to discover within the flux. It's fascinating."

It was then that Orator Aboren walked in, carrying the Mind Focalizer.

"Ah, my little marvel. Still as beautiful as ever after all this time. Did you know I created this artifact?"

Valianara couldn't help but crack a slight smile.

Aboren gently set the instrument down on the central bench, and everyone gathered in a circle around it, their faces taut with anticipation.

"Something's wrong."

"What do you mean?" Valianara thought, her heart beginning to race.

"The focusing gem… It's not the right one."

"And for those of us who aren't Arkandians, what exactly does that mean?"

"The large orange stone at the front is a garnet. It's used to capture a soul either from a body or from a jar. The two blue gems are channeling sapphires: they help direct the flux in a straight line, often to send the soul into a body or a physical vessel prepared for the occasion."

"Fantastic. Why do you say there's a problem?"

"If we're talking about extracting a soul that is already *inside a containment matrix…"*

"Wait, I don't understand a thing. Explain it as if you were talking to a child."

"I'm sorry. I get carried away easily when we're talking about my

favorite subjects. Currently, the device is configured to draw a soul from a jar. However, that's not what you want. Here, you wish to remove that spirit's anchor. You need a different gem."

"So, it won't work?"

"Worse than that, my dear. It will tear the spirit in question apart. The garnet's gravitational pull is extreme. If you activate it, it will tear that poor spirit into thousands of pieces. You must understand that an anchor is a very weak bond compared to what a body or a jar can provide."

Valianara felt an icy chill wash over her. She looked at Norwen, who was already approaching the Focalizer, a look of joy and concentration on his face.

"But... We can't let them do that!"

"I agree, but how do you propose proceeding? It would be more than suspicious if you, a mere novice, knew that."

Panic seized her. Time felt like it was speeding up. Norwen was about to lay his hand on the artifact.

Evarine, feeling her friend trembling beside her, leaned in and whispered, "Are you feeling okay? You're sweating."

"No, I'm not feeling well," Valianara confirmed in a faint voice. "I'm cold. I feel terrible."

Menilmonea, alerted by their conversation, turned toward her. "What's wrong, Valianara? You're as white as a sheet."

All eyes turned to her. Steeling herself, she blurted out, "Can we... Can we postpone the liberation?"

Aboren's reaction was immediate. "You must have a lot of nerve, young lady. You've been invited to attend this special event. If you're not feeling well, you're free to leave, but we're not going to wait any longer on the grounds that you're feeling a little nauseous. Norwen, begin the procedure."

Menilmonea raised a hand, signaling Aboren to remain calm and Norwen not to move. She approached Valianara, her expression filled with sincere concern. "What's going on? Aboren, though she may not be very tactful, is right about one thing: I'm surprised you're even asking this. Aren't you eager to see the Voice freed?"

"Yes, of course, but..."

Aureal approached as well, her voice calm and reassuring. "Valianara, is there something you want to tell us?"

Valianara found herself on the verge of tears. She could feel the weight of her secrets crushing her. She hung her head, unable to meet their kind eyes.

"I need to tell them. I'd never forgive myself if the Voice were obliterated because of my foolish cowardice."

The reply that reached her was imbued with a weary irony, yet also a peculiar sort of encouragement. *"Well… Come on, my dear. I have a feeling this is going to be fun."*

Valianara lifted her chin, tears glistening at the corners of her eyes. Her voice, though shaky, came out clear and firm, "If you activate the Focalizer, it will tear the spirit apart. It's poorly calibrated. You mustn't use a garnet for this kind of transfer."

Evarine immediately understood where this impossible knowledge came from, and her face fell. But for the others, the announcement was a shock. A collective gasp swept through the small gathering—especially Norwen, who moved as far away from the Focalizer as possible.

"What is this all about?" exclaimed Aboren, her patience clearly wearing thin. "Between this and the broken jar…"

"How do you know, Valianara?" asked Menilmonea, her surprise turning to intense confusion.

Burdened by the pressure, the young scholar collapsed into sobs, hiding her face in her hands. Evarine rushed to support her, wrapping her in a tight embrace.

"Don't do it… Please," Valianara sobbed. "You're going to kill…"

The disembodied spirit's voice then echoed, tinged with an unusual nervousness, "I don't want to minimize your efforts, my friends, but I'm not feeling as confident as I was before. Should we clarify matters before continuing?"

"Yes, you're right," agreed Menilmonea, her eyes fixed on Valianara. "The liberation will have to wait."

Valianara could sense the intensity of the High Orator's gaze. She took a deep breath, wiped her tears with the back of her sleeve, and gathered herself. "High Orator… I… Can I speak with you? Just the two of us?"

Menilmonea nodded without the slightest hesitation. She turned to the others. "I'm going to speak with Valianara privately, and I'll keep you informed."

Her words were met with startled silence, but no one dared protest. Aureal cast an anxious final glance at Menilmonea, who responded with an almost imperceptible nod to reassure her. Evarine briefly squeezed her friend's hand before following the others.

Soon, the room was empty. Only Menilmonea and Valianara remained, standing in the hushed silence of the Chamber of Memory, under the silent watch of the Arkandian murals.

The High Orator pointed to her desk at the far end of the room. "Come. Sit down. Now, tell me everything."

XXIII

The Academy of the Keepers of Knowledge / Present Day

Valianara looked around for a chair, but before she could even ask, she heard a rustling sound. Right in front of Menilmonea's desk, thin roots burst from the cracks between the stone slabs, interlacing and growing thicker at an unnatural speed until, within mere seconds, they formed an elegant seat covered in soft moss and broad leaves.

"Yes, it's fascinating. I know mages who would give anything to get their hands on this spell."

"I'm not sure now's the right time," Valianara thought as she sat down warily.

Menilmonea was staring at her, her face devoid of warmth. Her eyes were intense and probing, almost unrecognizable. "Now then. Who are you, young lady?"

Valianara felt a chill run through her. "I… I don't understand. You know who I am! I was there, in the village, when you were telling us about the legends with Tunka. I haven't changed."

"I beg to differ."

As she spoke, just next to the desk, a gigantic plant suddenly burst out of the stone floor. A thick green bud rose, opening into a flamboyant red corolla streaked with gold, revealing a deep purple center from which an exotic, heady fragrance escaped. The flower, with its exuberant and aggressive beauty, had grown in a matter of seconds.

"Uh…?" stammered Valianara, taken aback.

"Did you notice how the song intensified?"

"Don't concern yourself with the flower for now," ordered Menilmonea. "Tell me instead how you knew the attempt would fail."

Valianara felt the weight of the secrecy crushing her. She was no longer able to lie. Not to her.

"I'm going to tell her everything."

"I do not really see how else you can proceed now… Let's hope she's as wise as you say she is."

"When the jar was broken," Valianara began, "I was sleeping nearby, at a desk. I wanted to finish a parchment for Orator Aboren."

"Yes, you've already said that."

"What you don't know is that this jar was special. It contained the soul of one of Obinaelle's political opponents."

Menilmonea's face froze, her attention suddenly fully focused.

"His name is Azymantias, and he planned his own condemnation. He rigged the jar by casting a spell: as soon as anyone tried to extract his soul, it would be forcibly thrust into the body of the nearest person. He thought Obinaelle would come to free him occasionally to torture him, and he wanted to take advantage of that opportunity to take her place."

"By all the Titans…"

"Yes, exactly. Except I don't know who knocked over the jar or why, but as a result… I was the one who fell victim to the spell."

Menilmonea's expression betrayed a mixture of astonishment and disbelief. "I'm having trouble following you. That person's soul… is in your head?"

"Yes, High Orator. The spell was supposed to crush my soul, but it didn't work completely. Azymantias thinks it's because I'm sensitive to the song."

"Yes, well, it's just a hypothesis…"

"He just said it's still a hypothesis," Valianara blurted out.

Menilmonea turned pale. "He… Is he talking to you right now? Can he hear us?"

"Yes, High Orator. He can see and hear everything I do. However, much to his regret, I still have control."

Menilmonea slumped heavily into her seat, her face blank. "Unbelievable…"

Menilmonea remained silent for a long while, her hand raised in a firm gesture that silenced Valianara. Her eyes remained fixed vacantly, her expression taut with intense concentration.

"I don't know what to think," Valianara said.

"Wait… Something, or someone, is trying to connect with your mind. It's incredibly subtle. How is that even possible? Can you feel it?"

"No… Not really. I don't know what you mean."

"It's a soul. That would be my guess. It's trying to connect with you. But I've never felt anything so subtle, so delicate. If I weren't used to detecting these kinds of attempts, I wouldn't have noticed it at all."

"But… what will it do to me?"

"Nothing. It's not aggressive."

"And who's doing this? The High Orator?"

"I… I'm not sure."

Menilmonea finally snapped out of her trance. Her face was solemn. "I see."

With another wave of her hand, thin roots quickly snaked out from her desk, carried the Secret Sentinel, and placed it on a small receptacle behind her. With a single touch, it activated. The turquoise gem at the heart of the artifact began to glow with a cold, bluish light.

"High Orator?" Valianara asked anxiously, her heart in her throat.

Menilmonea's face had softened; her harsh expression had faded, replaced by one of relief and empathy. "I now know you're telling the truth. You'll soon find out how. Let me introduce you to someone who wishes to meet the two of you."

With these words, the vibrant flower that had grown near the desk transformed. The red petals folded in on themselves, the colors blended, and the plant's structure twisted before reshaping itself with supernatural fluidity. In a matter of moments, the plant had transformed into a mysterious fox of otherworldly beauty. Its fur glowed—a perfect blend of orange and white, so smooth it looked as if it had been polished by an invisible hand. Its long, tapered mane rippled smoothly, even in the absence of any breeze. Delicate tendrils,

like translucent silk ribbons, floated along its flanks, and three magnificent tails slowly swept through the air behind it. It jumped onto the desk.

Valianara nearly fell off her chair, gasping for breath.

"Well," Azymantias remarked, *"that's quite unusual."*

"Valianara, let me introduce the Primal. You should know that only the Titans and Aureal know of his existence. So, you understand why the Secret Sentinel is necessary."

She gave Valianara a moment to process the situation before continuing. "He cannot speak with sounds, but he can speak to you in another way."

The fox's voice resonated in the song, calm and powerful. *"Good day, young Valianara. And good day, dear Azymantias."*

The latter was so surprised that he almost forgot about his own situation.

"This creature is truly astonishing."

"Thank you," replied the Primal, his thoughts coming through clearly in Valianara's mind. *"You, too, are quite remarkable."*

"You... You're in my head, too?" Valianara asked, a little bewildered.

The Primal turned his golden eyes toward her, and his voice continued, gentle and reassuring, *"Not exactly, my dear girl. Since you can hear the Mother's song, I am able to speak to you through it. It is also thanks to the song that I sensed two presences, two auras in your soul. However, I must make a tremendous effort to hear your inner voice. Or rather, should I say your inner voices?"*

"But... who are you?" Valianara asked aloud, still in a state of disbelief.

The fox stepped forward with supernatural fluidity.

"I am a child of the Mother. One of the creators of the descendants..."

He corrected himself, his gaze resting briefly on Menilmonea, *"... of the Titans. There were seven of us, created by the Mother to protect the forests of this land. Your compatriots, dear Azymantias, killed five of us and drove the sixth to madness."*

Azymantias's thoughts manifested immediately. *"I humbly offer you my deepest apologies for the shameful behavior of my people. And through my own actions, I undoubtedly triggered all of this as well. Know that I will never forgive myself."*

"Can you tell me more? What did you do?"

"Perhaps Valianara could tell my story aloud so everyone can hear?"

The Primal turned to Valianara. *"Dear Valianara, can you connect to the song like Menilmonea so she can hear you too?"*

"I… I don't think so. I can use the song to guide the flux, but I can't connect to it. At least, I don't know how to make it resonate the way you do."

"I see. I'm not surprised. I do not sense in you the same connection to the song that I sense in Menilmonea. Perhaps you can continue speaking aloud if you would? That will allow me to step back from your mind. My dear Menilmonea will translate for me. I hope my presence hasn't troubled you. And you can, of course, continue to hear me through the song."

Valianara replied immediately, "I felt nothing, Primal. I appreciate your kindness."

Starting somewhat hesitantly, but growing increasingly confident, she recounted everything Azymantias had confided in her. She spoke of his rebellion against Obinaelle, his plot to destabilize her politically, and his mistaken belief that the Source was nothing more than a fable. She described the carefully orchestrated act of treason, the imprisonment, and Azymantias's utter shock upon discovering the cataclysmic consequences of his actions: the breaking of the Pact, the curse, and the fall of Arkandis.

Menilmonea listened in silence, her features set, as she pieced together the final fragments of the tragic puzzle that was the history of the two peoples.

Once Valianara had finished her account, a heavy silence settled over the Chamber of Memory. The High Orator remained pensive for quite some time. Finally, she spoke, "What really happened during the breaking of the Pact, Azymantias?"

Valianara closed her eyes for an instant, listening to the answer taking shape in her mind. She proceeded to repeat it aloud, "He says it was… the event that set everything in motion. The worst mistake of his long life. To prove that Obinaelle was lying about the Source, he freed the dryads she had been holding captive. He believed that this act, which directly violated the terms of the so-called original pact with the Source, would elicit no reaction and thus prove that the goddess did not exist, that she was merely a myth that Obinaelle used to maintain her power. It was this release that marked the breaking of the Pact."

The Primal bowed his head, his eyes shining with a keen curiosity. *"And what was this pact?"*

"Obinaelle claimed that the Pact had been established between her, the first mages of Arkandis, and the Source. The Source had offered them access to the flux and immortality in exchange for their establishing a civilization based on magic and reverence for her creation. Sadly, contrary to what Azymantias had imagined, it wasn't merely a legend. When the dryads were set free, the Source realized that the mages had not kept their word. And catastrophe followed."

"What is a dryad?"

Valianara listened once more to Azymantias's silent reply, then relayed it, her own voice imbued with the old mage's sadness. "He says it is… The very essence of everything that was wrong with his people. They were wonderful creatures who lived on a continent called Northendria. The Arkandians discovered them millennia ago because the flux around them was extraordinarily strong."

She paused before continuing, "More plant-like than animal-like, they had the peculiar ability to produce small pearl-shaped seeds. When these pearls sank into the ground, they produced incredible, majestic blooms—explosions of life. Entire forests could spring up from a single seed. These "dryad pearls" were immediately seized upon by the Magisterium, the ruling class of Arkandis. They undertook long studies to pervert them and use them to enhance their control over the flux. At one point, Obinaelle even succeeded in fusing them to produce the major orbs of power. It is these orbs that comprise the very foundation of all the Magisterium's most powerful spells. They are the key to Arkandian power."

Menilmonea commented, "The spheres of negation."

Valianara nodded. Her voice took on a darker, heavier tone, "So…

They devised spells to knock them unconscious so they could capture as many dryads as possible without attracting the Source's attention. And then they enslaved them to satisfy their thirst for power. He says… He says he bore witness to—and was even an accomplice in—these crimes."

She paused before continuing, her voice tinged with regret, "He also says he knew he had to put a stop to it. He had come to realize that the Magisterium was rotten to the core. He wanted to change things. The liberation was a political act, of course, but he was also genuinely happy to save those poor creatures from their ordeal."

The Primal and Menilmonea sat in silence for some time, absorbing the magnitude of this new development. Finally, the High Orator let out a sigh heavy with meaning. "We were not the first victims."

The Primal's voice took on the cold and sharpness of ice, *"I know you are aware of this, Azymantias, but your people are sick. And they deserve to disappear."*

Valianara nodded gently, indicating that Azymantias fully agreed with this final judgment. Menilmonea continued, her practical mind taking precedence over emotion, "That said, if Azymantias agrees to help us, it could give us an incredible head start on all our research. And allow him to begin atoning for his sins."

Valianara turned to her. "He does indeed wish to find a way to correct his mistakes, even if he will likely never forgive himself. He also says he is impressed by what we've built here. Perhaps there is hope for building a civilization based on magic without making it an oppressive society for non-mages and the rest of the world."

"Thank you for your understanding, Azymantias. Any help you can provide will be greatly appreciated. For my part, I'll need to find a way to explain your surprising knowledge to the other orators and Keepers of Knowledge."

Valianara hesitated. "Why would you hide Azymantias's presence from them?"

Menilmonea's glare hardened.

"The Council of Titans, Aureal, and I believe there is an Arkandian agent operating within the Academy."

The young girl's voice betrayed her shock, "How so?"

"Several recent incidents point to this conclusion. For one, Azymantias's jar was shattered, despite an extremely powerful repulsion seal protecting it. We have also discovered that several pearls have lost their power. That is a few too many coincidences."

"Azymantias is surprised that pearls have lost their power," Valianara interjected. "He says this hasn't happened in several… millennia."

"That's good to know. We haven't found anything about it in the books we have access to, either. It reinforces the theory of an impostor trying to cause us harm."

"I see. But why destroy Azymantias's jar?"

"He was a powerful mage. They're probably fearing that we'll end up freeing him. Things seem to have suddenly escalated from the moment you discovered how to bypass the seal on the first floor."

Valianara ventured a remark, "I still don't see why we shouldn't tell the orators or the Keepers of Knowledge. Between all of us, we'd have a better chance of rooting out this impostor and…"

The realization hit her all at once. "Because it could be one of them, right? But how?"

Menilmonea nodded solemnly. "Azymantias may correct me if I'm wrong, but several texts indicate that the Arkandians know how to control people's minds in order to manipulate them. Is that right?"

Valianara listened to the silent reply, then confirmed, "Yes. He says it's called 'subjugation.' It's more difficult when the person is sensitive to the flux, but not impossible for a high-level mage."

"Assuming an impostor manages to infiltrate our ranks, they could subjugate one of the orators or the Keepers of Knowledge. And we wouldn't even know it."

The weight of this new disclosure came crashing down on Valianara. There could be a traitor among those she respected most. Here, within the very heart of the Academy. The idea was almost more terrifying than that of the Arkandians themselves. The enemy was no longer a distant threat, but a looming shadow that might be hiding among her friends and her teachers.

Menilmonea continued, "So, I'll have to find a way to explain what happened earlier without mentioning Azymantias."

"He suggests I attribute my knowledge to reading the book on convection gems. It's now available on the first floor."

Menilmonea nodded thoughtfully. "Speaking of which, could Azymantias grant us access to the other floors? The way around the first seal turns out to be quite simple once you know what to do."

Valianara listened to the voice in her head for a moment and grimaced slightly.

"He… he's laughing, High Orator. He says we shouldn't get ahead of ourselves. In his opinion, the seal on the first level is a gimmick. An educational toy to train students and, more importantly, a convenient way to keep servants and non-mages from poking their noses into matters that don't concern them. That kind of seal can be broken through in an instant; it's low-level security."

She paused, listening to the mage's further explanation. Her eyes widened.

"He specifies that what comes next is a whole different story. Seasoned mages wove the second-level seals with the specific aim of letting nothing through. As for those on the top floor… He refers to them as military-grade. He says it's the kind of protection you'd put on a fortress gate. A basin won't be enough, clearly. You need to use specially prepared artifacts to open these seals. The one on the top floor was originally under the sole control of the Magisterium's highest leaders."

Valianara was careful not to share the following exchange, however: *"Of course, if I could control your body for just a few moments, I might be able to work wonders. At least with the seal on the second floor…"*

Menilmonea absorbed the forbidden knowledge about the seals before returning to their strategy. "Good to know. We'll come back to these artifacts later, then. For now, let's stick with this version: you read that book using your trick. It's not flawless, but it should suffice. You could have done it at night since you're familiar with nighttime outings."

Menilmonea stepped closer and placed a gentle hand on her shoulder. "Thank you, Valianara. Thank you for your bravery. You've been given a huge burden, and you made the right decision by coming to talk to me about it."

The voice from the room, which had remained silent until then, spoke up as well; its tone was filled with sincere and deep emotion, "Yes. Thank you, young lady. You saved my life, without caring about the consequences for yourself. I will never forget it."

Valianara felt tears welling up in her eyes, moved by the gratitude. Menilmonea took the opportunity to ask, "Speaking of which, could Azymantias help us extract him from your head and transfer him into an object so you can have your freedom back?"

"Yes, he can teach us how to do that," Valianara replied. "But he's clearly not thrilled about ending up in a necklace. Even more so since he's worried for his survival, given that our impostor made a clear attempt to eliminate him."

"Very well," said Menilmonea, straightening up, her expression returning to that of the High Orator. "We will do everything to protect him and keep his existence a secret. I will inform the Council and Aureal. I shall then go and tell our version of events to the other orators. Return to your squad. Try to act as normally as possible."

She added, with a knowing look, "We're going to have our work cut out for us over the coming days."

As she bowed to take her leave, the Primal's thoughts met Menilmonea's mind.

"What a peculiar situation. I don't fully trust this Arkandian. Though his story seems plausible, we must remain vigilant."

Menilmonea nodded, then replied mentally, as she watched the novice walk away, *"Me neither. But for now, we have no other choice. Let's hope Valianara manages to remain in control long enough for us to learn how to free her."*

XXIV

The air in the dining hall was saturated with mouth-watering aromas: the scent of herb-roasted poultry, warm bread fresh from the oven, and a blend of sweet spices that made her stomach growl. The buzz of hundreds of conversations, the clatter of cutlery against earthenware dishes, and the apprentices' bursts of laughter created a reassuring cacophony after the whirlwind of revelations Valianara had just endured.

She quickly spotted her squad seated near one of the large windows overlooking the inner courtyards.

As soon as Evarine caught sight of her, a flicker of relief crossed her features.

"Ah, you're here!" she exclaimed as Valianara sat down. "So, how did that meeting with the High Orator go? Did she want to hear news about Tunka and your village, is that it?"

Valianara paused briefly, then caught on to the ploy.

"Well," she replied, serving herself a generous portion of chicken and a slice of hard cheese. "We actually talked a lot about our village. She's extremely attached to her roots. No pun intended!"

"You're an excellent liar," Azymantias commented. *"With such ease, you could have had a brilliant political career on Arkandis."*

Valianara ignored the remark and dug into her meal, ravenous. No sooner had she brought her fork to her mouth than Alister, usually quiet during meals, turned toward her with marked interest and locked his eyes onto hers, "Evarine has told us that liberating the spirit didn't work."

Valianara's heart lurched in her chest, pounding wildly. She swallowed her mouthful with difficulty before answering, trying to keep her voice steady. "No, unfortunately. There were… some technical complications with the Focalizer. But Norwen, a Keeper of Knowledge, will keep studying the books. It should only be a matter of days."

"Oh, oh…" Azymantias purred. *"Your heart rate just spiked considerably. And it's nothing to do with the cheese."*

"Hey! Keep your opinions to yourself, or I'll send you back to your box!"

"He's charming…"

"Yes, but also very reserved."

"The longer the struggle, the sweeter the conquest, my dear."

"Are you a poet, too?"

"I've had a very long life, and I admit that a certain few people have done to my heart exactly what this young man is doing to yours."

The sincerity of the confession threw Valianara off balance.

"Well, anyway, thank you for not rubbing it in. It's hard enough as it is to pretend everything's fine."

"Are you okay?" Alister's voice startled her. He was looking at her with slight concern, noticing her momentary absence.

"Yes, sorry. I was… lost in thought. What were you saying?"

"I was wondering if we would be allowed to watch the next attempt?"

"I'll ask the High Orator if I see her again. I'm sure she'll agree."

"That would be kind of you, thank you."

He gave her one of his rare smiles, and Valianara felt her heart doing somersaults again. She cringed inwardly, expecting another jibe from her stowaway, but Azymantias had the tact to remain silent.

The rest of the meal was enlivened by Kamartel, who had rediscovered his appetite and good humor. He launched into a complex theory on the culinary uses of luminescent mushrooms, causing Evarine and their tablemates to burst into laughter. Swept up in the warm atmosphere, Valianara was finally able to relax and think, at least for a few minutes, of something other than the fate of her world.

The afternoon dragged on with a long and monotonous geography lesson on the continent's terrain. While the orator passionately—though perhaps not entirely convincingly—detailed the erosion of the northern coasts, Valianara's mind was elsewhere. It had become the scene of a technical and complex discussion with Azymantias. He was explaining to her the various methods of soul extraction, comparing the merits of "flux-assisted suction" with those of "resonance transfer." She nodded at appropriate moments to keep up appearances in front of the other novices, but her attention was entirely focused on her private lesson. She had to admit, however, that most of what she was learning seemed extraordinarily complex to her.

The end of the class felt like a relief. The amber sunlight began to fade as Valianara and Evarine headed toward the Library to work on their respective parchments.

"So, how did it go?" Evarine asked.

"I told her the truth, plain and simple. And she was very understanding. Norwen will prioritize analyzing texts on the Focalizer to learn how to properly extract captive souls. We're hoping it will allow me to be safely freed as well."

"And how… is he taking it?" Evarine whispered, pointing to her friend's forehead.

"He's not exactly thrilled at the idea of ending up inside an object, but he's being understanding. He knows that cohabitation can't last forever. We talked about it a lot this afternoon."

Evarine burst out with a triumphant little laugh. "I knew it! You were daydreaming like never before when we were discussing river deltas."

"Ha, ha! It's hard not to look distracted when I'm in the middle of a conversation with Azymantias."

Midway, their pace slowed. On the side of the street, nestled between two imposing buildings, was one of the many peaceful little nooks that dotted the city.

It was an idyllic spot, timeless in its beauty. Tall arches of pale stone rose toward the pyramid's ceiling, enveloped in lush vegetation.

Cascades of purple and blue flowers draped the ledges, filling the air with a sweet fragrance. Soft sunlight filtering through the foliage formed patches on the paved ground.

And there, on a weathered stone bench, sat Alister.

He was alone, immersed in the tranquility of the secret garden. He wasn't reading or studying. He appeared to be lost in thought, contemplating the flowers.

"Look," Evarine whispered. "For once, he's not rolling his pebbles."

She shot a mischievous glance at Valianara. "I'm going to go sit in the Library… but I get the feeling you might want to take a little break, huh?"

Valianara felt her cheeks flush, but didn't protest. "Thank you."

She took a deep breath and turned to her inner passenger.

"I…"

"Don't worry, I fully understand," Azymantias gently cut her off. *"This is the best solution for everyone."*

"Thank you, Azymantias. You're very kind."

She then focused on the song. The familiar melody grew louder, and in her mind's eye, she visualized the immense walls of the fortress she had built. She grasped the heavy door of wood and iron, then closed it gently but firmly, isolating the misty plain from the rest of her mind. Silence returned.

She was alone.

Smoothing her tunic, she walked toward the flower-filled alcove and the stone bench across from Alister's. The young man was staring at a cluster of blue hydrangeas that seemed to glisten in the gathering twilight.

"May I join you?" she asked softly.

He turned to look at her. A keen observer might have detected a split second of panic, quickly replaced by the benevolent neutrality he wore like armor. He paused, eyes darting from the empty bench to Valianara, as if weighing the risks of such proximity. Finally, he gave a brief nod and moved to the side, though they were already separated by a good yard of cobblestones.

Valianara sat down cautiously. Now that Azymantias had gone

silent, she felt strangely exposed. The silence stretched on, broken only by the distant chirping of a cricket.

She struggled to find a conversation starter, something lighthearted to break the ice without putting him on the defensive.

"It's a beautiful spot," she finally said, glancing around the alcove. "I didn't know such peaceful gardens could be found so close to the Library."

"It's a quiet place to think," Alister replied in an even tone.

"Yeah, you're right… Especially after this afternoon's class. I thought the lecturer was going to put us to sleep with those stories about coastal erosion."

Alister merely shrugged slightly. "I think it's crucial to understand how our environment is structured."

Valianara bit her lip. Bad choice. She changed the subject. "Don't you have your pebbles with you? It's rare to see you empty-handed."

Alister cast a quick look at his hands resting on his knees, as if checking to make sure they weren't moving. "I'm trying… I'm trying to get used to not having them all the time. To control my fidgeting without them."

"You're doing great," she encouraged him with a warm smile. "You seem very… in control of yourself."

"It's just an act, Valianara." His reply was curt. He realized this and softened. "But thank you. It's nice of you to worry."

Valianara felt like they were going round in circles. Small talk wasn't going to cut it. There was a wall between them, and she was never going to break through it by talking about the weather or their classes. She took a deep breath, resolving to drop the pretense.

"I'm not going to beat around the bush here, Alister," she began, her voice a little shaky but resolute. "I like you. A lot. Ever since we met in the wagon, and even more so since that night at the tavern… I feel like there's something different about you."

Alister didn't move, but his hands balled into fists around his knees. He wasn't looking at her but staring at a spot somewhere above her shoulder.

"But I can also sense that you're not happy," she continued gently.

"There's a sadness in you, Alister, something dark that you carry with you wherever you go, even when you smile. I'd like… I want to get to know you better. Maybe I could help you carry some of that burden? Or at least distract you from it from time to time?"

She watched for a reaction, her heart hammering. Alister took a deep breath, then exhaled slowly, as if letting go of some long-held tension. He finally met her gaze. There was no anger in his eyes, only deep fatigue, and a hint of regret.

"That's very sweet of you, Valianara," he thanked her in a calm voice. "I mean it. You're a wonderful person, and I care deeply about you—more than I probably should."

He paused, as if weighing each word on an invisible scale. "But I can't. I'm not ready to share any more than I already do. It's nothing personal… It's just that I have my own issues to deal with. Matters that concern only me."

"What kind of issues?" Valianara pressed affectionately, leaning slightly toward him. "Is it something to do with your parents? Your past? You know we're here to learn, to understand. Maybe I could—"

"No," he cut her off, raising a hand to stop her. "Please, Valianara. Don't keep pushing. Some things need to stay buried."

His voice had a definitive tone, an impenetrable wall against which her best intentions had just shattered. Her heart sank. She had hoped for an opening, a crack in his shell, but all she had achieved was to see it reinforced.

She maintained eye contact for another moment, searching for a flicker of hesitation, but found only that same sad determination.

"I see…" she murmured, her throat tight.

She stood slowly, smoothing her tunic once more to steady herself. Disappointment had a bitter taste, but she refused to let him see how much his rejection hurt her.

"I respect your choice, Alister." She stepped away a few paces, then stopped and turned back one last time. "Just know this: if you ever change your mind, if one day this load becomes too heavy for one person… I'll always be here."

Alister didn't answer, but he nodded in appreciation. Valianara left him there, alone amid the flowers and the lengthening shadows, and made her way to the Library, her heart heavy. She tried to console herself with the thought that she had at least tried.

She smiled to herself, realizing that at least Azymantias hadn't witnessed the fiasco.

As she approached the Library, she ran into Aureal and Gideon walking in the opposite direction, arm in arm, deep in conversation that seemed to amuse the orators greatly. They greeted her with a brief, warm nod, to which she replied with a respectful bow before continuing on her way.

She couldn't help but feel a touch of bitter irony as she realized that the rumors about their separation were, as was often the case at the Academy, largely unfounded.

Taking full advantage of this moment of calm, she focused her mind on reopening the door to her mental silo.

"So?" Azymantias asked her immediately. *"How did it go?"*

"Well, now I know where I stand at least..."

"Was it that bad?"

"He doesn't want any relationship right now. He has his reasons."

"I see... Oh no!"

Just as these words echoed through her mind, Valianara was struck with a forceful blow.

It wasn't physical, but an invisible shockwave, a screaming tide of energy that slammed into her back. The world tilted. She was thrown forward onto the cobblestones, scraping her palms and knees. A violent, dizzying nausea gripped her throat, and she struggled with all her might not to vomit right there on the cold stone. It was as if her soul had tried to escape her body.

"What was that?" she screamed in her mind.

No answer.

"Azymantias?"

She struggled to her feet, her head throbbing. In front of her, two guardians of peace standing watch in front of the Library had also fallen onto the cobblestones. Unlike her, they didn't look like they wanted to get up.

"Azymantias? Azymantias!"

She plunged into her mind, frantically scanning the map of her inner world for him. The door to the silo… It was closed! She focused and flung open the heavy imaginary door.

"Is everything all right?" the mage's voice asked immediately.

"I have a wicked headache, but otherwise I'm fine," she replied, brushing the dust off her tunic. *"What happened?"*

"An expulsion. An extremely powerful one."

"Meaning?"

"A high-level mind mage cast an expulsion spell. It's a war spell, Valianara. It's designed to rip souls from bodies and cast them into nothingness. The goal is to destroy, and to do so without ceremony. It's a spell with a long range—sometimes hundreds of yards—that smites everything in its path. And you survived! Unfortunately, the same cannot be said for those guardians."

Valianara felt her blood run cold. *"But how? Who? And why were you locked in again?"*

"I sensed the spell coming a split second before impact. I wasn't sure of myself, but I took a gamble, hoping the song would protect you from harm. As for me… I'm merely anchored in your mind, a stowaway. Without protection, I would have been obliterated. I had to act fast."

"You locked yourself in? But I didn't know you could do that!"

"I can see the door. I can't open it, of course, but I can close it from the inside."

"And that saved your life! Unbelievable…"

"Oh, yes. Otherwise, you would have been rid of me for good."

Suddenly, a movement caught her attention. Menilmonea was running out of the Library, preceded by a white figure: Aureal's owl, flapping its wings wildly. The High Orator stopped at the entrance to try to rouse the guardians of peace, asking them if they were all right. Her face paled when she realized they were dead. She called out to one of the apprentices in the building's lobby and ordered him to fetch the captain of the guard urgently. She then spotted Valianara and rushed toward her.

"Are you okay, Valianara?" she called out as she reached her, her face white.

"Yes… I was struck in the back by a massive surge of magic. It came from over there," she explained, pointing a trembling finger toward the top of the avenue.

"Did you see Aureal?"

"Yes! She was with Gideon; they were heading that way, in fact!"

Menilmonea's face fell. "By all the Titans! Her owl came looking for me—she was frantic. Something has happened to Aureal."

Without waiting, Menilmonea took off again, close on the heels of the bird, which was impatiently flapping its wings. Valianara, still reeling, wavered for a second before dashing after her.

"Stay back!" Menilmonea ordered without slowing down. "We don't know how this happened. It could be dangerous!"

"I know," Valianara gasped, trying to keep up. "But there's someone who could help us figure this out!"

Menilmonea slowed down imperceptibly. "Yes… You're right. Stay right behind me, then. And get ready to run."

In a few moments, guided by the panicked bird, they rounded the corner and found themselves in front of the flower-filled alcove. The scene that awaited them froze them in their tracks.

Aureal, Gideon, and Alister lay on the ground.

Menilmonea immediately rushed toward Aureal, who was lying on her side, motionless. She placed two fingers on her neck, holding her breath, before relaxing her shoulders.

"She's not dead," she declared in a slightly trembling voice. "Just unconscious. Her pulse is strong."

A few steps away, Gideon was groaning, struggling to prop himself up on his elbows. He was clutching his head as if a bludgeon had just struck him.

Valianara, for her part, saw only Alister.

She ran toward him, her heart hammering, praying to the Mother that he was only unconscious. But as she drew closer, terror gripped her throat. The way he was lying… It wasn't the posture of someone asleep or unconscious.

Lying in the center of the clearing, his body appeared to be dislocated. His limbs lay at impossible, grotesque angles, as if an invisible, gigantic hand had twisted him like a wet rag before tossing him aside. His left leg was folded beneath his back, his right arm stretched far beyond what his shoulder should have allowed. He looked like a disjointed doll abandoned by a ruthless child.

Each broken limb told, with speechless cruelty, of the unimaginable violence of the impact.

The sound of boots echoed on the cobblestones. A patrol of guardians was running toward them.

"Bring stretchers!" Menilmonea shouted without turning around. "And tend to the guardians in front of the Library, too!"

Valianara fell to her knees beside Alister. She reached out a shaky hand, refusing to believe what her eyes were telling her. She searched for a pulse in his neck.

Nothing. Just a coldness that was already beginning to set in.

"Don't look, Valianara," Azymantias's voice implored.

It was serious, devoid of its usual humor.

"Step away."

But she couldn't move. She remained there, transfixed, her fingers pressed against his lifeless skin.

"Alister?" she whispered.

"He's gone, my child. His soul has been shattered. He died the moment he was struck."

The word "gone" echoed inside her, breaking through her disbelief. Her vision clouded over, drowning in tears. The world around her faded into a blur, a smudge of indistinct colors and muffled sounds.

"No!"

The cry came from behind her. Evarine had just arrived, alerted by the commotion as well. She stopped dead in her tracks, her hands pressed against her mouth, her eyes wide with horror at the sight of their friend's ravaged body.

"In the name of the Mother! How horrific! What happened?"

She rushed toward Valianara, deliberately looking away from Alister's corpse so as not to vomit. She knelt and wrapped her arms around her friend, squeezing her tightly, as if to shield her from reality.

"Come, Val… Don't stay there. Come…"

She tried to lift her, to pull her back, to force her to look away from this unbearable sight. Valianara remained prostrate, heavy as a stone, staring blankly at the void that had just replaced the boy with the pebbles.

Voices reached her as if muted by a thick layer of cotton. She could barely hear Menilmonea, crouched near Gideon, trying to get answers in an urgent voice.

"Gideon? Gideon, look at me. What happened?"

The orator opened his mouth to answer, but no sound came out. His face suddenly turned greenish, and violent spasms seized him. He leaned abruptly to one side to vomit bile, his body racked with uncontrollable tremors. Menilmonea supported his head, waiting for the fit to pass, her face etched with concern. He wiped his mouth with a quivering sleeve, his eyes glazed over, struggling to focus his attention on the tall orator.

"I… I don't know," he croaked, his voice hoarse. "We were walking… We ran into Alister coming out of that little passageway."

He paused, searching for his words in the fog of his memory, grimacing in pain. "We greeted him… He responded with a slight nod… And I just… blacked out. Like a candle being blown out…"

Suddenly, her aimless gaze fell upon the motionless form of Aureal, whom two guardians of peace were placing on a stretcher. A look of panic spread across her face, reviving a semblance of desperate energy. "Oh no! Is she…?"

"No," Menilmonea cut her off, placing a hand on her shoulder. "Just unconscious. Her pulse is steady."

Gideon, relieved but still agitated, tried once more to stand up, his arms wobbling under his weight, his muscles refusing to obey him.

"Don't overexert yourself," Menilmonea ordered, gently pushing him back to the ground. "You're still too weak. This was a brutal attack. More guardians of peace will come and carry you to a proper bed."

She cast a glance at the mangled body in the alcove, then turned back to Gideon, her eyes filled with infinite sadness. "Alas… The poor novice wasn't as lucky as you. What struck you proved fatal to him. This attack was so powerful that it even hit the Library guards all the way down the avenue."

Gideon's eyes widened in horror. He turned his head and caught sight of Alister's broken body. "In the name of the Mother… How awful…"

The ground seemed to give way beneath him once more, and he collapsed onto the cobblestones, sinking into unconsciousness.

XXV

The Academy of the Keepers of Knowledge / Present Day

Night had fallen over the Academy, yet no one was sleeping. The private parlor inside the High Orator's quarters, usually a quiet place that smelled of undergrowth and moss, had been transformed into a crisis headquarters. Half a dozen oil lamps burned, throwing flickering shadows across the orators' weary faces.

Menilmonea stood by the window, her attention focused on the upper floor where Aureal was resting. The latter had briefly regained consciousness during transportation, just long enough to confirm in a faint voice that she had seen nothing before being engulfed by darkness. Gideon had also been escorted home to rest. Several Keepers of Knowledge specializing in healing would take turns at their bedside throughout the night.

The atmosphere in the room was heavy, charged with an electric tension. Nearly all the orators were present, sitting or pacing, whispering to one another with uncharacteristic gravity. The death of a novice and the attack on two orators in the heart of the city amounted to a declaration of war.

Aboren broke the lingering silence, her voice revealing a rare hint of nervousness. "We've combed the area thoroughly. We found no one. It's as if the attacker vanished into thin air."

"We're not equipped to face them," added Menara, her arms crossed, her face pale. "The violence of what happened to young Alister… It's pure magic, on a level we don't understand. To tear a body apart while knocking out two seasoned mages… And I'm not even talking about the poor guardians of peace who were killed simply because they happened to be in the line of fire."

A worried murmur ran through the assembly. They were Keepers of Knowledge, but they all felt powerless in the face of this event. They still had so much to learn.

"There is a total curfew for novices and apprentices," Gavin interjected. "However, we won't be able to seal off the city indefinitely."

All eyes turned to Menilmonea. She sensed the weight of their expectations, the heaviness of the invisible crown she wore. They were waiting for direction, an explanation, a plan.

Aboren stepped forward, taking on the role of spokesperson for the group's collective anxiety. "High Orator, we face an invisible threat striking at the very heart of our sanctuary. We do not know who, we do not know how, and above all, we do not know why these individuals in particular were targeted with such savagery." She locked eyes with Menilmonea. "What are we to do?"

Menilmonea took a deep breath. She knew that what she was about to say would shake the very foundations of their order. "We have to accept the obvious: if the culprit has not been found, it is for one simple reason… They are already among us."

Those words cast an icy chill over the room. The orators looked at one another, the concern on their faces giving way to suspicion.

"The Arkandians' magic could have manipulated an orator or a Keeper of Knowledge," she continued in a firm voice, drowning out the rising murmurs. "We've all read the titles of certain works on the top floor of the Library: *Mind Control of Indigenous Entities*, *Subjugation of Souls*… We know this is possible."

"But that would mean they've succeeded in returning," objected Menara, her voice quivering. "The Titans managed to stop them the last two times, didn't they? Their ships were destroyed."

"Yes, but there was a new attempt a few weeks ago."

"No…" whispered Menara, bringing her hand to her mouth.

"The Titans intercepted them again," explained Menilmonea, "but the Council hasn't ruled out the possibility that a lone individual, sufficiently discreet, might have slipped through the cracks. It was still a hypothesis until tonight, but given the precision and violence of the attack, we are now convinced."

Aboren turned pale. "But if we're all potential suspects… What can we do? How can we trust each other?"

"We don't know how their mind control works, or whether the person being controlled is even aware of what they're doing," admitted Menilmonea. "And besides, this is still just a theory. The perpetrator could also be physically hiding within the city. After all, it was they who built it. They know every nook and cranny. There are bound to be secret passages we haven't discovered yet."

No one said a word.

Menilmonea spoke up again, taking on a commanding tone to break the silence, "Here's what we're going to do. At dawn, all the orators will lead expeditions with the apprentices and novices. Take them far away from here. Help the villages, explore the distant towers—whatever you need to do—but evacuate the Academy. We cannot afford to lose another student. Ask all the Keepers of Knowledge present in the city to go with you. Anyone who refuses to leave must be considered a suspect. This will allow us to start narrowing down the search. The impostor will do everything in their power to remain here."

The orators nodded solemnly. It was the wisest decision.

"I have also asked Captain Ofstaten to double the number of guards."

"What if the guilty party is a guardian of peace?" Aboren asked.

"That's one possibility, indeed," Menilmonea acknowledged. "Either way, we can't be certain at this point. But that's about to change. The Council is sending us help. Arabinoki is on his way."

A murmur of astonishment rippled through the gathering. The spider Titan rarely left his tower and his village.

"He'll be here in a few days. His ability to sense the flux is unmatched. He'll be able to help us detect if a mind has been… corrupted, or if a hostile presence lurks within our walls."

A wave of relief swept through the room. The direct assistance of a

Titan was the only defense they felt would be strong enough against this unknown threat.

"Until he arrives," Menilmonea concluded, "we'll have to stick together and be especially vigilant. I don't like this climate of suspicion, believe me, but we have no other choice if we are to survive."

XXVI

The Academy of the Keepers of Knowledge / Present Day

The return to the Residence was a surreal nightmare for Valianara and Evarine. Chaos reigned supreme. Squads of guardians cordoned off the entrances, sending novices and apprentices back to their quarters with sharply barked orders. The rumor had already caused a stir. There was talk of an explosion, of a monster that had escaped from the Library, of an attack by the Arkandians.

Once in their room, a wave of despair washed over the two friends. Valianara sat on her bed, her trembling hands resting on her knees, unable to banish the image of Alister's body from her mind.

A few moments later, there was a soft but insistent knock. Evarine opened the door. Kamartel was waiting, his face expressionless. He was ashen, his eyes darting frantically from one to the other. He slipped inside before they had a chance to invite him in.

"Tell me it's not true," he whispered, his voice choked with emotion. "I heard people saying… People are saying that Alister is…"

He couldn't finish his sentence.

Valianara looked up. She had to tell him. She had to make it real.

"He's dead, Kamartel. They… They killed him."

Kamartel's face contorted. He stumbled backward until he hit the wall, as if he'd just been dealt a blow. "But… we ate together at lunchtime. How is that even possible? Who could have wanted to do him harm? This is a bad dream."

Evarine burst into tears, collapsing into her chair. Valianara, in a hollow voice, recounted what she had seen. The alcove. The bodies of the orators. And Alister, destroyed. She spared them the gruesome details, but the reality was horrific enough without embellishment.

Kamartel slid down the wall and slumped to the floor, his head in his hands.

"Why him? He didn't bother anyone. He didn't hurt anyone. He just wanted… to be left alone."

A deafening silence settled over the room, broken only by Evarine's sniffles. It was the kind of silence born of incomprehension, of the brutal grief that strikes unannounced. The small squad, formed in joy and excitement just a few weeks earlier, had just been decimated.

"He didn't deserve this," Azymantias said softly. *"No one deserves this."*

Later, long after night had descended on a city that still hadn't gone to sleep, there was another knock at the door.

Menara and Aboren entered. They looked worn out: their features drawn, but their eyes keen and watchful. They looked at the devastated trio with maternal concern.

"We know how hard this is," Menara began in a soothing voice. "Losing a friend, a fellow human being. It's the worst kind of pain there is."

Aboren stepped forward. Her face, usually so stony, softened almost imperceptibly. Her presence, while not imposing, brought a measure of calm.

"Take tonight to grieve," she counseled in a deep, steady voice. "Hold nothing back. Mourning is the price of affection, and there is no shame in paying it. Know that all the orators share your grief. We are a family, and we are here to help you carry this burden. You are not alone in your loss."

She paused, letting her words ease the tension a little, before continuing, her natural pragmatism taking over, "At dawn tomorrow, you will leave the Academy."

She unfolded a parchment on Valianara's small desk.

"The three of you will be in the group I am leading to the villages in the northwest. A series of mudslides hit the region after the recent storms, causing considerable damage.”

She looked up at them. “We’re not going on a sightseeing trip. We’ll be assisting the Keepers of Knowledge in the field. This will be an opportunity to test your budding mastery of telekinesis in real-world conditions as you help with the relief efforts. Unfortunately, given the number of casualties, it will also be a brutal—but necessary—introduction to the healing applications of the flux. It will give you a purpose and remind you why we’re all here.”

Valianara, her throat choked with emotion, then asked the question burning on her lips, “What about Alister? Aren’t we staying for… for the funeral?”

“No,” Menara replied gently. “His body will be transported to Goaka tonight. He will be returned to his family to be laid to rest in his homeland. The same will be true for the two poor guardians of peace. Your duty, for now, is to stay alive and help those in need. The High Orator and Orator Aureal will be staying here to secure the Academy and find the murderer. You would only be targets if you stayed.”

A wave of conflicting emotions surged through Valianara. Sadness at letting Alister go on this final journey without her. Concern for Menilmonea and Aureal, who would remain in the lion’s den. But also—and she berated herself for feeling it—an immense sense of relief coupled with a feeling of purpose. She wasn’t merely fleeing; she was going to help.

“We’ll be ready,” she stated.

Aboren nodded, impressed by their resilience. “Try to get some sleep. Tomorrow will be a long day.”

The door closed behind the orators as they left.

Kamartel struggled to his feet, as if his legs could barely bear his weight. “I’m going to go. I need to pack my bag.”

He paused in the doorway, his hand gripping the doorknob, then glanced down the empty hallway leading to his now-silent room. “It’s going to be a strange night… being all alone out there.”

He walked off without waiting for a reply, leaving behind a feeling of oppressive gloom. Evarine, her eyes red, began gathering her belongings slowly and methodically. Valianara was about to follow suit when Azymantias's voice rang out, calm and calculating, *"We should stay. I could probably help."*

Valianara closed her eyes for a moment, refusing to be tempted by his proposal, however appealing it might be.

"We must obey orders, Azymantias. If the High Orator thinks she needs us, she'll send someone to fetch us. For now, our place is elsewhere."

"Certainly," the mage conceded, a hint of skepticism in his voice. *"Let's hope they can manage on their own. I'm not so sure they truly grasp what they're up against…"*

XXVII

The Academy of the Keepers of Knowledge / Present Day

In the depths of the night, as the city seemed to hold its breath, Kamartel opened his eyes.

There was no gradual awakening, no blinking to shake off sleep, no yawn. He went from a state of unconsciousness to icy lucidity in a fraction of a second. He sat up in an almost effortless motion. His face had turned into an impassive mask, stripped of the sadness that had weighed him down just a few hours earlier.

He dressed in the dim light with precise, unhurried, silent movements. Not a rustle of fabric, not a creak of a joint in his body. The young man walked over to his wardrobe, opened it with a soft click, and reached inside. He retrieved three items and slipped them into his pocket: a flint, a handful of dry tinder, and a small, twisted piece of metal.

Finally, he left the room. The hallway of the Residence was deserted, but he took no chances. He didn't walk; he glided along the walls, blending into the shadows cast by the blue glow of the city. He froze in front of the main entrance, where he could make out the silhouettes of two guardians of peace on duty. Their lanterns were set on the ground as they conversed in hushed tones. Passing through there would be impossible without alerting the entire Residence.

Kamartel felt neither frustration nor fear. He pivoted on his heels and slipped into the service corridor below the staircase. At the far end, a narrow window, situated more than two meters above the ground, had been left ajar.

Yesterday's Kamartel would have sought out a stepladder or abandoned the idea. Tonight's Kamartel didn't even slow down. With a sudden burst of energy, he sprang forward, propelled by a massive surge of flux. His fingers clung to the stone ledge with supernatural strength. He hoisted himself up in absolute silence, contorting his body with impossible flexibility to squeeze through the narrow opening, and let himself fall to the other side. He landed in the bushes, crouching, cushioning the impact with perfect precision. Ten yards away, the guardians didn't even turn their heads, hearing nothing more than the rustling of leaves.

Outside, the air was crisp. Security had been tripled. Patrolling guardians of peace crossed at every intersection, the sound of their boots pounding the cobblestones illuminated by their lanterns.

The Kamartel of yesterday—the cheerful, somewhat awkward young man—would have been spotted before he even moved. But not the one moving tonight. He was the shadow of shadows, anticipating patrols with unnatural foresight.

He froze, holding his breath for interminable minutes as a group of guardians passed less than a yard away from his hiding spot; his heart beat in a slow, steady rhythm, entirely controlled by the iron will flowing through him. With feline agility, he then scaled a low wall, his fingers finding invisible footholds in the stone, his body defying gravity. He crossed the upper quarters like a specter, invisible to the guardians' eyes. He felt neither fear, nor doubt, nor the cold. He was merely an instrument, pure will executing an intricate score.

He finally reached the foot of the monumental staircase of the Temple of the Mother. Four guardians of peace barred the entrance. Kamartel did not attempt to distract them. He circled the structure to the rear, where the slope was steep and the rock bare. He climbed, gripping the roots protruding from the temple's foundation, inching himself toward the open sanctuary.

He slipped between two alabaster columns, entering the sacred precinct.

The temple was shrouded in silence, bathed in the gentle light of the colossal tree that stood at its center. Kamartel stepped forward. There was no hesitation in his stride, no reverence for the majesty of the place. He crossed the nave and stopped at the foot of the towering trunk, where roots intertwined to form the heart of the structure.

He plunged his hand into his pocket and pulled out the flint, the piece of metal, and the tinder. His face remained eerily neutral.

He placed the tinder in the hollow of the oldest roots, striking the flint with the metal in a sharp, precise blow. A spark flew, catching the dry material, which burst into flames instantly. But for Kamartel, it wasn't enough. He channeled his flux, breathing it onto the nascent flame to feed it with pure energy, seeking to transform this small fire into a devouring inferno capable of consuming the very heart of the city.

The fire roared, shifting in color, licking the ancient bark with an unnatural hunger.

Contrary to his expectations, the tree did not burn. The bark didn't even blacken. The flames slid over the sacred wood like water over stone, powerless against the strange vitality pulsing through its fibers.

A faint rustling, barely a whisper on the cobblestones, echoed behind him.

Kamartel spun around in one swift motion. A strange fox stood behind him. It stood perfectly still, its three tails sweeping the air with a hypnotic slowness, its golden eyes locked on the impostor with a terrifying impassivity.

An inhuman growl escaped from the young man's throat. He threw himself forward, fingers curled into claws, ready to tear apart anything that stood in his path.

He didn't even have time to take two steps. The marble floor shattered. Brambles as thick as arms and twisting vines burst from the ground with terrifying speed. The sharp crack of their unfurling split the air, piercing Kamartel's eardrums. In a split second, they wrapped themselves around his legs, his torso, his left arm, stopping him in his tracks. His free arm reached out toward the Primal. Kamartel tapped into his reserves, draining his flux to the point of agony and shaping it into a wave of pure energy, a tidal wave meant to annihilate everything.

"Die!" he screamed, his voice warped with hatred.

The fox didn't move. He simply closed his eyes.

The wave of destruction swept in… And evaporated. With a muffled, incongruous puff, the deadly flux turned into a cloud of multicolored petals. They floated gently through the air, harmless, before settling on the Primal's snout or the stone floor.

Blinded by rage at this display of power, Kamartel focused all that remained of his flux to increase his physical strength tenfold, his muscles straining to breaking point as he attempted to break his bonds. But nature responded instantly. The brambles tripled in volume, tightening mercilessly, turning him into a statue of flesh and wood.

Yet he continued to incant, to spit out curses, fighting against the inevitable.

With a simple nod of his chin, the fox tightened his grip. Immediately, the vines grew heavier, crushing Kamartel to the ground, pinning him against the cold slabs with tremendous pressure. Just as he opened his mouth to hurl another insult, small, thin, and tenacious roots sprouted from the thick brambles. They crept between his lips, filling his mouth and forming a botanical gag that stifled his screams.

Completely bound within his green cocoon, Kamartel remained conscious, his eyes rolling in their sockets, wild with rage.

The fox approached and watched him. He did nothing else. He stood there, motionless, holding the young man's gaze with his golden eyes for several long minutes. Time seemed to stretch out.

Little by little, without understanding why, Kamartel's inner turmoil began to subside. The red rage that clouded his vision dissipated, replaced by a hazy confusion. His muscles, stiffened by excessive tension, ceased to struggle against the bonds. His body, battered by these unnatural efforts, finally surrendered to exhaustion. His will to fight left him, drained by the Primal's silent presence.

His eyelids fluttered, heavy as lead, and he eventually sank into unconsciousness.

A figure emerged from the shadows of the colonnades, walking

quickly but silently. Menilmonea's face was serious, her features tense with the strain of this endless night.

"*So, it's true?*" she whispered in the song to the motionless fox. "*Thank you for calling me.*"

She looked down at the figure bound like a mummy in the brambles. Her eyes widened in astonishment. "*Kamartel? But how...*"

"*It was not truly him. His soul was trapped inside a prison of twisted magic. The same tainted essence that seals the towers.*"

"*He was being controlled,*" murmured Menilmonea, her throat tightening.

"*That's right, completely under another's control. This little creature possesses astonishing resilience; he managed to outwit your guardians, make it this far, and launch several attacks of impressive power. It seems his master wanted to reduce the tree to ashes.*" The Primal turned its snout toward the intertwined roots beneath them. "*To reach the orb, I imagine.*"

"*Of course,*" Menilmonea said bitterly. "*They know full well that the sphere of negation is there.*"

She knelt beside the young man, studying his face, now relaxed in sleep, which contrasted starkly with the violence of his earlier actions. "*How is Kamartel?*"

"*I broke the mental prison that was locking his mind away. The mechanism was... uncomfortably familiar. Remarkably close to what the Titans endured.*"

"*The Arkandians call it subjugation.*"

"*What a perversion.*"

"*Is he all right?*" the High Orator asked with concern, placing a hand on the novice's forehead.

"*He will live. I am certain he will remember nothing. His soul was profoundly asleep when I untangled the bonds of control. For him, this night will be nothing but a black hole.*"

Menilmonea straightened up and gave the fox a grateful nod. "*Thank you so much. Without you, this night might have marked the end of our city.*"

"*Good luck with your hunt, Menilmonea. Find whoever is behind *this."*

With those final words, the fox's form seemed to lose its substance. It dissipated like mist in the sun, its contours melting into the tree's roots until it returned to the nothingness from which it had come.

Once alone, Menilmonea stepped to the edge of the terrace and signaled to the guardians of peace waiting anxiously at the bottom of the steps.

"Come up! And bring a stretcher!"

Kamartel was taken back to the Residence in heavy silence. The corridors were deserted; the curfew strictly observed. When they arrived at the boy's room, Menilmonea ordered the guardians to lay the novice in his bed gently.

But the moment his back touched the mattress, Kamartel's eyes flew open. He blinked, disoriented, his gaze darting frantically from the familiar ceiling to the two armored guardians, and finally to the High Orator herself. He sat up with a start, panicked, staring at his own dust-covered clothes. "But... why am I fully dressed? What's going on? What are you doing here?"

His eyes met those of the High Orator, inscrutable, and he turned pale instantly. He let himself fall back, his head in his hands. "Oh, by the grace of the Mother... It's because of my father's Briar, isn't it?"

Surprised by this unexpected turn of events, Menilmonea hesitated. She discreetly signaled the guardians to step back, then approached the bed. "What can you tell me about this, young novice?"

"I don't want to be banished, High Orator!" he cried, tears in his eyes. "I only did it to help him!"

"Let us pretend, for the moment, that I do not know the details," she replied calmly. "I want to hear your side of the story."

Kamartel took a deep, trembling breath. "My father used up all his Briar a few moons ago. He lost everything gambling at our village tavern. After that, he got into a fight and forced one of the other players to donate several grams. A great many grams. Except our Titan found out. He punished my father. He has to come every morning to sell the vegetables he must grow himself, until he pays back twice what he stole."

He sniffed, wiping his nose with the back of his sleeve. "He knows he made a mistake. He wants to make amends. But it's hard without help. Every morning, all alone, carrying his crates and then setting up his stall… I just wanted to ease his burden a little."

"And what exactly did you do?" asked Menilmonea, suddenly understanding the numerous reports about the boy's morning tardiness.

"I gave him almost all of my Briar," Kamartel admitted, bashfully, showing his bare wrist. "I don't need it here; everything is provided. I leave it in my closet so it can grow back slowly."

"And that's it?"

"And… And I was going to take his place in the morning before classes so that he could rest a little. I shouldn't have; I know the guilty party must carry out the punishment. But he's my father!"

Menilmonea struggled not to smile. The justice of the Titans was absolute, and as High Orator, she could not allow her heart to interfere with the law, even though she respected this young man's courage and loyalty to his father.

"Either way, you won't be able to help him anymore," she announced softly. "Since you're leaving on an expedition tomorrow with the others."

Relieved to see that divine wrath had not fallen upon him, Kamartel let the tension subside and burst into tears. "Oh, thank you, High Orator. Thank you so much!"

As his adrenaline began to ebb, another sensation took hold. He winced, bringing his hand to his ribs and arms. He then looked up, confused, at Menilmonea and the guardians. "But… wait. Why talk to me about this in the middle of the night? With the guardians?"

"That wasn't why I was here," Menilmonea admitted, "but I'm glad you told me the truth. It'll stay between us."

Kamartel looked at her, feeling quite sheepish. "But if that's the case… Why are you here? And why am I dressed?"

"You… You had a strange bout of sleepwalking. The guardians found you wandering near the temple. Don't you remember anything?"

"Oh no… No, I… I don't remember a thing!"

"I'm not surprised. I've seen cases like this before; it's… a reaction to stress and flux. Go see the healers tomorrow morning before you leave so they can examine you."

"That's probably why I feel so sore…" Kamartel murmured, rubbing his shoulder.

"Probably."

She dismissed the guardians and then left the room, leaving Kamartel alone with his aches and confusion.

"No one enters, and he doesn't leave," she ordered in a low voice once in the hallway. "And please make sure he actually goes to see the healers tomorrow."

Menilmonea prepared to leave; exhaustion suddenly weighed heavily on her shoulders. As she passed the girls' door, she stopped, hesitantly placing her hand on the cold wood. She knew Valianara was sleeping inside, no doubt tormented by Alister's death and the secret she carried.

She turned to one of the guards after pulling her hand back. "One last thing, please. Tomorrow morning, before the expeditions depart, ask Valianara to come and see me."

The guard nodded, and the High Orator walked away into the shadows of the corridor.

XXVIII

The Academy of the Keepers of Knowledge / Present Day

Outside, the deep blue of the night was slowly giving way to the subtle orangish hue of the coming dawn. The bell hadn't rung yet, but in the High Orator's quarters, the day had already begun.

Menilmonea stood at Aureal's bedside, a look of relief softening her drawn features. Aureal stirred, grimacing as she tried to sit up against her pillows.

"My head still hurts badly, but I'm clearly starting to improve. We should congratulate those who focused their power on healing me. They did an outstanding job."

"We were all so worried," Menilmonea sighed, adjusting the blanket around her.

She turned to Gideon, who was seated on a stool. His face was still pale, but his expression remained alert. "And what about you? How are you? Shouldn't you be in bed resting? You took quite a beating, too."

"I feel much better. And besides… I wanted to know how Aureal was doing. If she remembered anything."

Aureal gave him a faint smile. "That's sweet. But no, not much. We were walking, we came upon poor Alister, and then… nothing. I came to on the stretcher. I don't remember anything except the excruciating pain. I'm extremely glad Grumf wasn't there. If he'd been hurt or worse, I would never have forgiven myself."

There was a quiet knock at the front door downstairs.

"I'll leave you to it," said Menilmonea, rising to her feet. "I'll be right back."

"Yes, Mama," Aureal teased softly.

Menilmonea smiled despite herself and went downstairs to answer the door. It was Valianara, her travel bag slung over her shoulder, looking uneasy.

"High Orator, I was asked to come and see you before I leave."

"Yes, thank you so much for coming so quickly. Please come in. Would you like some tea?"

"Oh, yes, thank you," Valianara replied, rubbing her stomach. "I'm starving."

"I think I may even have some honey cakes somewhere. Go on, make yourself comfortable." Menilmonea pointed to the large table made of rough wood in the center of the room. Valianara sat down and paused to look around. She knew the High Orator loved nature, but she hadn't expected anything like this.

It looked as though a forest had decided to move in. Thick moss, wildflowers, and tangled roots covered nearly every wall, transforming the cold stone into a lush vertical garden. Small luminescent mushrooms sprouted here and there, and it was hard even to see the flagstone floor beneath the carpet of vegetation. The stair rail had become a long cascade of multicolored flowers. Only the kitchen area, with its utensils and countertop, was spared.

"It's almost certain that this metal plate can heat food," Menilmonea commented as she busied herself, "but we still don't know how to turn it on. So, I set up a little oven right here."

She slid a kettle over a small stone hearth where tongues of flame danced. Once the water was boiling, she served the novice.

Holding a steaming cup and a cake in her hands, Valianara asked the question that had been nagging at her. "What can I do for you, High Orator?"

Menilmonea turned toward her. She opened her eyes wide and discreetly pointed her index finger toward the ceiling, in the direction of the room where Aureal and Gideon were. "For now? Nothing. But I may need you."

She reinforced her statement with a meaningful wink. The message was clear: she needed Azymantias, but she couldn't say so aloud.

Valianara understood immediately. "Oh, right… I see. Would you like me to split from my expedition group?"

"I'm not ordering you to," Menilmonea replied carefully. "But if you wish to stay—while fully understanding the risks involved in the current situation—your 'sensitivity to the song' could prove especially useful in the investigations to come. You've already proven your resistance to Arkandian attacks."

"I see…"

"Clever," commented Azymantias. *"I suppose not many of you can hear this song?"*

"The only people I know of are the High Orator and myself," the young woman confirmed. *"It's the perfect cover."*

Valianara accepted the offer with a resolute nod. Menilmonea, looking satisfied, motioned for her to follow her upstairs. "Let's go talk to Orators Aureal and Gideon, then."

They climbed the flower-lined staircase. As she entered, Valianara's eyes were immediately drawn to a corner of the room. There, sitting majestically in a terracotta pot, stood the enormous red and gold tropical flower. The very same one from which the Primal had emerged during their first meeting.

"Oh, the flower from…" she began without thinking.

A cold flash of realization struck her. She bit her tongue so hard that tears welled up in her eyes.

"In the name of the Core…" Azymantias whispered, his voice tinged with panic.

Menilmonea turned to her, raising an eyebrow. "Excuse me?"

"You're going to have to improvise! Talk about all these flowers! Anything!" the Arkandian ordered.

"No, nothing…" babbled Valianara, her heart hammering. "I just think… that this house is incredible with all these flowers. It's so beautiful."

"Oh, thank you! This is where I feel most at peace."

"Well done," Azymantias congratulated her. *"But we have a bigger problem."*

"Yes, I agree."

Aureal, sitting up on her pillows, spotted her. "Hello, Valianara! I heard about your gift. What a story!"

Gideon turned his head toward her. His eyes seemed to scrutinize the novice with a newfound intensity. "Gift?"

"Yes. Valianara can hear the song," Menilmonea explained matter-of-factly. "She can't project herself into it quite like I can, but this gift could prove very useful when Arabinoki arrives to investigate."

"Oh…" Gideon simply said.

"He's looking at us in a strange way, isn't he?" the mage pointed out.

"I… I don't know. I don't feel comfortable."

She forced a smile. "I'm glad you're feeling better… Both of you."

"Thank you," replied Aureal. "Are you sure you want to stay? It could be dangerous if the attacker feels cornered. He seems immensely powerful."

"Well, now I see why Gideon wasn't killed in the attack," Azymantias observed coldly. *"But Aureal… How did she survive that level of force?"*

"She, too, is sensitive to the song. Not the Mother's, but the song of animals."

"By the four legions! That's incredible… So, there are several songs? How could we have missed all this for millennia?"

"Do you want an honest answer?"

"No, thank you. I already know it."

Valianara turned her attention back to Aureal. "Yes, I'm sure. If my abilities, whatever form they take, can help, I wouldn't want to be anywhere else."

"Do you think he understood?" she asked, casting a furtive glance at Gideon.

"I don't know. But stay on your guard. He's a master of manipulation."

Suddenly, Gideon stood up, staggering a little. "I may have misjudged my strength… I think I'll go home to bed."

"Of course, silly!" Aureal exclaimed affectionately. "I'll still be here if you need me later. Get some rest."

"I'll ask a guardian to accompany you," Menilmonea offered, heading toward the window.

"Yes, do that! Please!" Valianara screamed inwardly.

"No, thank you," Gideon declined with a wave of his hand. "I'm not far, and there are already enough patrols on the streets. No need to bother anyone on my behalf. I know the way."

Menilmonea hesitated for a split second, then nodded. "As you wish. Take care."

"He's strong," Azymantias remarked with a hint of admiration.

Valianara counted the seconds as Gideon said his goodbyes, descending the stairs with agonizing slowness. Finally, the front door closed behind him.

As soon as the latch clicked, Aureal, who had been watching him, furrowed her brow. "Valianara? Are you all right? You're shaking."

Valianara spun around to face the two women, her eyes wide with urgency. "I know who the impostor is!"

Her elders exchanged disbelieving glances.

"What are you saying?" asked the High Orator, her voice losing its usual authority.

"Can you confirm that, other than the two of you and the Council of Titans, no one else knows about the Primal?"

"Yes, and the spirit in the Chamber of Memory," affirmed Menilmonea. "It is the Academy's best-kept secret."

Valianara took a deep breath to steady the tremor in her hands. "Well, when I first entered the room and saw the flower in the corner, over there… I was going to say that it was the Primal's flower. I almost said it."

She paused, planting her gaze firmly in Menilmonea's. "I really was going to say it. I stopped myself just in time. What I mean is, I didn't feel any resistance. Nothing physically prevented me from uttering those words in front of Orator Gideon."

The blood drained from Menilmonea's face. She covered her mouth with her hand, horror-stricken. "By all the Titans! I taught you about the Primal's existence using the Secret Sentinel. If the magic didn't block you…"

"Oh, no!" Aureal whispered, feeling tears well up in her eyes. "That means…"

"That Gideon already knew," Menilmonea finished.

A heavy silence fell over the flower-filled room. Betrayal now had a familiar face.

"How dreadful!" Aureal exclaimed. "But couldn't he simply be under their magic's control? What does Azymantias think?"

Valianara closed her eyes for a moment to listen to her host's explanation before replying, "Azymantias says that the Secret Sentinel should have blocked what I wanted to say. The host soul, even when subjugated, remains the target of the protection. If Gideon didn't know, I wouldn't have been able to speak. The only explanation is that Gideon *himself* knows of the Primal's existence. He is an Arkandian."

Aureal seemed to crumble, devastated by this revelation. Menilmonea took the opportunity to add a piece of information she hadn't yet had time to share. "You should know that the Primal had to intervene personally last night. Kamartel, who was under the influence of a mind-control spell, tried to burn the Mother Tree at the heart of the temple."

"What?" Valianara exclaimed. "How? Why?"

"He was under a spell," Menilmonea explained. "Most likely cast by Gideon. The Primal managed to free him from the mental hold. That tree prevents the Arkandians from using their magic to get back here."

Valianara was stunned.

"He freed him?" Azymantias asked in surprise, a hint of awe piercing his usual haughtiness. *"That's impossible… Well, it's unheard of, at any rate. A subjugation is normally permanent or fatal once broken."*

"It seems you've finally met your match," Valianara remarked.

"Indeed. How exciting. Well, if the situation were less tense, of course."

"Of course."

Valianara turned to the orators. "And is he all right?"

"Yes, don't worry," Menilmonea replied. "He doesn't remember a thing. As we speak, he's probably on his way out of the city. He'll be safe away from here."

Aureal, still lost in the haze of her grief, shook her head. "Why kill Alister? Why attack? It doesn't make sense. And why hurt me? Something's not right. I've known Gideon for years. No one can keep up an act for that long! And why draw our attention to him now? It's impossible—he can't be an Arkandian."

Menilmonea nodded thoughtfully. None of it made sense.

"There's another possibility," Azymantias interjected. *"A much more logical one."*

"I have a feeling I'm not going to like this."

"You're right. What if Gideon has only just recently become the impostor?"

"But you said he can't be possessed—that it's him who's doing it!"

"Yes. Now. But the more I think about it, the more I believe the impostor can't always have been Gideon."

"I don't understand."

"I think that, for a very long time, the impostor was Alister."

"What? What are you talking about? That doesn't add up!"

"Alas, my dear, I'm afraid that, on the contrary, that's exactly what makes the most sense. He must have arrived via the coast and performed something few mages can do without significant assistance: a body transfer."

"And that would be?"

Her throat went dry despite the fact that she wasn't even speaking aloud.

"A profoundly violent act. The mage literally rips himself from his own body to inhabit another's, obliterating the original soul in the process. It is an absolute spiritual violation. Only a specific class of mages has mastered the technique, and even then, their success rate is extremely limited."

"You mean that this mage… sacrificed his body to project his soul into Alister's body?"

"That's right. In fact, that spell was banned, except for the Bloodhounds."

"The Bloodhounds?"

"Yes, a caste of mage hunters trained from birth to carry out the Magisterium's most dangerous tasks. They're essentially their elite warriors."

"And so… you think Alister has always been an impostor, ever since I've known him?"

"That's the most logical explanation, my dear. It was the perfect way to get into the Academy and roam around without arousing suspicion—at least until he could put his plan of attack into motion. Who would suspect a shy novice?"

"How awful! But I was so fond of him. I… I had feelings for him."

"The Bloodhounds are extremely intelligent. They are trained in both the arts of war and manipulation. You can't blame yourself."

Noticing the change in the young novice's complexion, Menilmonea grew concerned. "Valianara, what's wrong?"

"Nothing, I… I'm just shocked. Azymantias just laid out a terrifying theory for me."

"A theory? Can you share it with us?" Aureal encouraged her.

Valianara put her pride aside, took a deep breath, and recounted the hypothetical body transfer idea, the Bloodhounds, and Alister's deception.

"By Tunka's shell, that's unbelievable," Menilmonea whispered. "It would explain the pearls and the destruction of the jar. He's been with us for weeks…"

"Since the novices first arrived," Aureal realized. "So, he really did manage to get past the Primal's barrier."

Noticing the disbelief on Valianara's face, Menilmonea quickly told her about the various Arkandian attacks, Goaka's discovery of the boat and the body, and the boat's subsequent destruction.

Aureal continued, "But that means… Last night's attack… In the name of the Mother!"

"It was Alister who attacked you," Menilmonea concluded, her face dark. "He must have tried to kill you in order to transfer to Gideon, who is a much better host for moving around the Academy. He must be ready to take his plan to the final stage. And with his attack on the Mother's Tree having failed, who knows what he'll try next?"

Valianara nodded. "Azymantias confirms this theory. He likely didn't expect Aureal to resist through her song, though. And… And that's also why poor Alister's body was so ravaged. The transfer requires such tremendous power that it often reduces the body to shreds." She froze for a moment, her eyes blank. "Oh, no…"

"What is it?" exclaimed Menilmonea.

"That also explains why he never had his Briar! It must have vanished when the real Alister died."

Tears streamed down Aureal's cheeks as she was only beginning to accept the reality of the situation. "But then… Gideon… *My* Gideon, I mean… is dead? We can't save him?"

Valianara felt a lump tighten in her throat. She stepped forward slowly, letting her own eyes fill with tears.

"Alas," she murmured in a broken voice. "He likely did not survive the initial attack, since he was not sensitive to the song… This is what made the transfer easier for the impostor. Azymantias calls him a Bloodhound. He says it's a specialized class of mages trained for this kind of suicide mission."

Menilmonea stood up abruptly. "We have to stop Gideon, or whatever his name is. I'm going to speak with the captain of the guard."

"Azymantias strongly advises against confronting him without being properly prepared," Valianara warned. "He is immensely powerful."

"We can't leave him wandering around the city! Is he even back home yet?"

"Let me ask my spies," Aureal said, closing her eyes.

She stood motionless for a few moments, her face focused, then opened her eyes again, looking solemn. "He's not home. He's heading toward the transport ring."

"What's he planning to do there?" Menilmonea asked anxiously. "Can he reactivate it?"

"No," Valianara replied. "Not without an orb. But Azymantias says there's something else there: the nursery. That's where they used to create major power orbs. It was also where the dryads were imprisoned. It's a place protected by powerful magic. We've probably never even discovered it."

"Could he be producing orbs?" Aureal asked, frightened.

Valianara gave Azymantias time to explain the situation to her.

"He won't be able to produce a major orb because he only has access to a single pyramid. But he will be able to create one powerful enough to reconnect the city's ring to Arkandis."

The High Orator's eyes widened. "Are there more pyramids?"

"Yes. One per continent. Four in total. They channel the flux and send it to Arkandis."

After a pause, she continued, "To cast the spell that creates the orb, he would need four or five pearls and, crucially, dryad's blood. Azymantias doesn't think he would have been able to bring the pearls, because they would have been destroyed the moment they came into contact with seawater during the shipwreck."

"But there are plenty of them in the basin in the Pearl Room, and they're submerged!" Aureal exclaimed in astonishment.

"It's not water," Valianara corrected, relaying the mage's words. "It's an alchemical preserving fluid. It prevents them from germinating."

"Germinate?!" Menilmonea gasped. "Well… Never mind. We'll deal with that later. We've got enough on our hands already. If he didn't bring his pearls, how did he…?"

"Azymantias thinks he stole the ones from the Pearl Room."

"What? Is he the one who drained their power?"

"He didn't drain them; he replaced them with copies," Valianara explained. "It's not that they've lost their power—it's that they're fake!"

Suddenly, the truth dawned on her. It had been staring her in the face the whole time. "The pebbles! Alister spent his time rubbing round pebbles until they were polished. He said it was because it reminded him of his dead father—"

"His parents are still alive," Menilmonea noted dryly. "I had to write to them last night to inform them of what happened to their son."

"Why am I not surprised… Azymantias thinks it's entirely possible to infuse a little flux into pebbles that are smooth enough to give the illusion of a magical aura for a few days."

"How would he have made the switch?" Menilmonea wondered. "Guardians protect the room, and Aureal's friends would have detected any nocturnal presence."

"Except when we visited the room!" Valianara exclaimed. "He could very well have swapped them out then. Orator Gideon—the real one—let us handle them at will. Alister had his hands full of pearls; he kept picking them up and putting them back!

"He's lucky no one else handled them after you," Aureal remarked.

"He's not relying on luck," said Valianara, unable to hide her admiration for the impostor's cunning. "He deliberately arranged for us to go last… He made poor Kamartel sick on purpose so the other squads would go before us…"

She stared into space for a moment, appalled by the extent of the manipulation.

"So, he has everything except the blood?" Aureal summarized.

Valianara listened for a moment to the deep voice in her mind before answering. "Indeed. Azymantias freed the dryads just before his fall. He hopes they didn't manage to recapture some of them before they reached the safety of the forest."

Menilmonea's eyes widened in horror. "What are you saying? That those poor creatures might still be there, locked away in darkness for centuries?"

"Azymantias doesn't know," the novice admitted in a somber tone. "But he's certain: without the blood, the Bloodhound won't be able to fuse the pearls to create the orb. It's the catalyst. If he's heading to the nursery, it's because he thinks he can find what he needs there."

"And this nursery," Menilmonea asked, "how is it that we haven't found it?"

Valianara waited for the mage to explain the technical details.

"A high-level illusion seal hides the entrance. Without the right artifact to break it, the passage remains closed, appearing as an ordinary stone wall. You could walk past it a thousand times without seeing it. He likely has that artifact; likely an object called the Core disc. Incidentally, he must already have used it to access Azymantias's jar."

Aureal, despite her weakness, was struck by a flash of understanding. "That's why he needed Gideon's body! So, the guardians would let him enter the transport ring hall without arousing suspicion. A novice wouldn't have been allowed in. He could probably have forced his way in, but it must take time to create the orb, right?"

"Yes. Azymantias says it takes at least two full hours to produce an orb capable of powering the ring to open the passage to Arkandis."

Menilmonea stood up, a cold determination hardening her features. "I'm going to capture him. Now. The song will protect me from his magic."

"You can't go alone!" Aureal cried out, trying to sit up. "He's a trained killer! I'm coming with you."

No sooner had she tried to set foot on the floor than violent nausea seized her. She staggered, her face ashen, and had to sit back down heavily on the bed to avoid collapsing. Menilmonea rushed to support her, gently pushing her back against the pillows.

"You can't, Aureal. You're not in any condition. Your mind needs to heal. Remember, you nearly died!" She straightened up and smoothed her tunic, her gaze darting between Valianara and the corner of the room. "Don't worry, I'm not going alone."

As she spoke, the large tropical flower that stood in the corner of the room began to glow. The red and gold petals swirled, the stem thickened, and in an instant, the majestic form of the three-tailed fox materialized, its golden eyes locked on the High Orator.

Its mental voice resonated with a calm, protective power, *"That's right. I'm coming with you."*

XXIX

The Academy of the Keepers of Knowledge / Present Day

The Primal turned his golden eyes toward the window and signaled that he would go directly to the entrance of the hall to avoid drawing attention. *"So as not to arouse suspicion, I'll meet you right at the entrance to the hall."*

Menilmonea nodded, her face focused on the battle ahead. She then turned to Valianara. "You stay here. Aureal is too weak to protect herself should the situation turn against us. Watch over her and barricade the door."

Valianara nodded, ready to obey, but a familiar voice stopped her in her tracks. *"I'm not sure this is a good idea for the Primal."*

The young girl froze. *"What? You mean going to face the Bloodhound?"*

"No, entering the nursery."

"Why? Isn't that where he's hiding?"

"Because that room was built expressly to confine the dryads. Without knowing the song, Obinaelle knew instinctively that they had to be isolated from the flux, cut off from the outside world, prevented from communicating. She wanted to prevent them—rightly so, I now realize—from coming into contact with the Source."

"Meaning?"

"The room was originally built with a convergence of conductive rods."

"Azymantias… Hurry, they're about to leave!"

"Forgive me. It's quite simple: we found that certain metals, such as

iron, tin, or gold, distort the flux. The first version of the nursery was lined with metal tubes. On the inside, these tubes pointed toward the center to force each spell back inward, while the opposite arrangement on the outer wall created a protective shield. The result? A dead zone."

Menilmonea already had her hand on the doorknob. The Primal was already beginning to dissipate when Valianara cried out, "Wait, please! Azymantias believes there may be a problem. Allow me a moment, and I'll explain everything."

The High Orator paused, her fingers clenched around the cold metal of the latch. She turned slowly, her face marked with restrained impatience, yet her eyes betraying absolute trust in the novice. She knew Valianara wouldn't interrupt them over something trivial.

The Primal, meanwhile, instantly reversed his dematerialization process as soon as Menilmonea spoke. The mist that had begun to form solidified again in a fraction of a second, restoring his fur to its flamboyant, physical form. He turned to look at Valianara, awaiting an explanation with silent, attentive intensity.

"Did it work?" Valianara asked, her voice tinged with urgency.

"All too well, alas. From what I understand, the dryads were dying. So they removed the outer bars to let the flux in, but not out. As a result, the room exploded under pressure from the magic."

"By all the Titans…"

"Obinaelle, however, found a solution: the walls, ceiling, and floor were covered with downward-pointing rods made of an iron-tin alloy. Not content with merely directing the flux, these rods could also disrupt its coherence. If you cast a spell that leaves the room, it is destabilized, drawn to the ground, and drained into the foundations. Pure magic can therefore enter and exit, but no message truly escapes. No complex magic holds if it leaves the room."

Valianara immediately understood the danger. She observed the fox, a creature made of pure natural magic, of flux made flesh.

"I have concerns about the Primal," concluded Azymantias. *"He can shape this creature at will and likely project his consciousness into it. It is highly possible, then, that such a structure is a deadly trap for him. He could be drained, or… erased."*

Valianara took a moment to gather her thoughts then explained, "Azymantias says the Primal shouldn't go in there! It's possibly a trap."

She turned to the creature, wearing a serious expression on her face. "The nursery is designed to scramble and drain the flux toward the ground. There are metal rods, a special alloy… If you go in there, your essence could be drained by the very structure of the room. That's what was preventing the dryads from calling for help."

A deathly silence greeted her statement. The fox and the High Orator exchanged a meaningful glance. They were clearly deliberating on the matter.

Menilmonea broke the silence, "If what Azymantias says is true, we must not take any chances."

"I will remain outside to prevent any escape and secure the area. But you cannot face the Bloodhound alone, Menilmonea. His magic is vicious, designed to shatter human minds." He turned his golden gaze toward the novice. *"Take Valianara."*

"What?" exclaimed Menilmonea. *"That's out of the question! She's a novice, not a soldier!"*

"She is sensitive to the song," the Primal insisted calmly. *"That's what enabled her to resist the mind attack near the Library. And Azymantias's knowledge is a valuable asset."*

In Valianara's mind, the Arkandian's voice rang out, *"I wouldn't be as optimistic as our furred friend, but he has a point. Still, against a Bloodhound… Valianara, perhaps, if you let me take control, I could bring down even the strongest opponent using your sensitivity to the song."*

Valianara hesitated for a split second. It was a tempting offer. But then the image of Alister shot through her mind like a cold blade. *"I… No. I'm sorry, Azymantias. I'm starting to really like you, but after what Alister did… I don't think I'm ready to trust anyone. At least, not enough to hand over control of my body."*

There was a brief silence, then the elder mage replied, *"I understand. Trust is a privilege we cannot afford to offer lightly. I will help you as best I can as a passenger, if that is acceptable."*

Unaware of this internal debate, Aureal added, "I agree with Menil. We can't send her in there. It's madness."

Valianara set her gaze upon the two women who were so desperately trying to erect a shield between her and whatever danger lay ahead. In their eyes, she saw not just concern, but a visceral, ancient terror. A gaze she knew all too well: it was the same one that had darkened her mother's eyes years earlier, when she had found her lying broken and covered in blood at the foot of the family home. The absolute fear of seeing those you love disappear.

She took a step forward, mustering all the courage she could find within herself. "I'm coming with you, High Orator."

"Valianara, I already told you that—"

"No, listen to me," the novice interrupted, her voice shaky. You told us, during the ceremony, that the Arkandians thought of us as cattle. That they had stolen our lives, our history, even our dead. You told us we could no longer stand by and suffer, that we had to rise." She clenched her fists, her nails digging into her palms. "He killed a novice. He killed the real Alister; he killed the real Gideon. He defiled our academy and our friends. If I stay here doing nothing, I'll never be able to look myself in the mirror again. We aren't victims. I'm not a victim. With Azymantias's help, I can help you stand up to this monster."

Menilmonea studied the girl. She no longer saw the uncertain novice who had arrived a few weeks earlier. She saw a Keeper of Knowledge.

She sighed, a mixture of resignation and pride. She saw again the two young villagers who, ten rotations ago, had likewise decided that it was necessary to take risks to save those they loved. "Very well. Get yourself prepared, Valianara. We're leaving immediately."

They ran through the city. The shadows were lengthening, and every dark corner seemed to hide a potential threat. Inside Valianara's mind, Azymantias was giving her a crash course in defense against mental attacks.

"The Bloodhound won't go down without a fight. As soon as he sees us, he'll try to kill us, likely with a mental attack technique similar to the one he used on Gideon near the Library. Keep in mind that when that happened, you only sustained a small portion of the initial attack."

"Can I counter this spell? Protect myself?"

"The song is the first level of protection, but we'll need more in the event of a head-on clash. You'll need to sense the surge coming. It will feel like a sudden pressure, a vibration in the air. At that very moment, you'll have to focus all your energy on repelling the attack."

"Is that it?"

"Well, yes, but while you are clearly talented, it won't be an easy task, because everything will happen so quickly. I can help you with a simple focusing technique often taught to novices in battle: cross your forearms in front of your face while visualizing an impenetrable shield of energy. Making this physical gesture instantly helps your mind focus. In cases like this, timing is key."

Valianara practiced the gesture in her mind, clenching her teeth.

They finally arrived at the entrance to the transport ring. It was an imposing circular building, dotted with multiple arches through which a warm glimmer of light could be seen. Four guardians of peace in full armor were stationed at the main entrance.

Menilmonea didn't slow down. "Soldier! Is Orator Gideon inside?"

Surprised by her unannounced arrival, the guardian stood at attention. "Yes, High Orator. He entered a short while ago. But… he gave strict instructions. He asked not to be disturbed under any circumstances, as he was conducting a sensitive investigation."

She glared at him. The soldier gulped. "But of course he wasn't referring to you, High Orator."

Without another word, Menilmonea crossed the threshold, closely followed by Valianara.

The interior of the hall was monumental. At the heart of this vast, empty rotunda stood a titanic transport ring, three times the size of those in the towers. Its metallic structure glowed faintly with the city's reflection, but it was otherwise inactive. The transport fluid was frozen, inert, and as solid as amber glass.

Silence reigned, broken only by the echo of their footsteps on the stone slabs.

Valianara pointed to the back wall, behind the giant ring. A wide door led to a staircase descending into the darkness. "Azymantias tells me that this is indeed the door leading down to the nursery."

Menilmonea noticed that where there should have been only smooth stone, a dark, gaping rectangular opening had now appeared in the wall. "Why would he leave the passage open for us?"

"He says the room is a prison. Access to it can only be controlled from the outside."

They approached the gaping hole. Just before they set foot on the first step of the staircase, the marble floor cracked open in front of them with a sharp crack.

A sturdy stem burst from the stone and blossomed into a red and gold flower, instantly blocking the passage. This silent watchman pulsed with formidable energy.

"The Primal stays here," Menilmonea said, casting one last glance at the plant. "He'll stand guard."

The spiral staircase plunged into the bowels of the earth, descending at a dizzying pace. The black stone steps, barely illuminated by the distant glow from the hall above, stretched on endlessly.

Valianara rapidly lost track of time as she descended. The air grew heavier, thicker. It was charged with static electricity, making the hairs on her arms stand on end and her clothes crackle. With every turn of the spiral into the depths, the pressure increased. She felt as if she were sinking toward the very core of the planet, where the rock groaned under the weight of the world.

"Get ready," warned Azymantias. *"The structure of the flux is changing. We're getting close."*

Suddenly, the staircase opened into a vast expanse.

Valianara and Menilmonea froze on the threshold, breathless at the sight before them. It was not a mere hall: it was an inverted cathedral, a geometric sanctuary carved for giants, bathed in blinding blue light.

The ceiling, lost in the heights, formed a forbidding forest of suspended hexagonal pillars. Thousands of dark metal columns, pressed tightly together like the cells of a colossal beehive, pointed downward, poised to crush any intruders. The floor echoed this strict geometry, dotted with clusters of hexagons stretching into the shadows of the aisles.

But it was the storm raging at the exact center of the nursery that caught their eye immediately.

Gideon—or rather, the one who bore his face—stood there, arms outstretched, a minuscule figure against the overwhelming power he unleashed.

He did not sing, did not move. He was a pure conduit. Arcs of a violent electric blue surged from the floor and the stalactites, converging on him with a deafening crash. The air screamed, torn apart by the raw power of Arkandian magic.

At the heart of this maelstrom of energy, just in front of the Bloodhound, a shape began to materialize. An orb. It was a fusion of shadow and light, a tear in reality that pulsed like an unholy heart, voraciously absorbing the lightning bolts that struck it.

"By the Pact…" Azymantias whispered. *"He's managed to find dryad blood. He is definitely creating a major power orb."*

XXX

The Academy of the Keepers of Knowledge / Present Day

Gideon didn't appear to hear them. He remained rooted in his trance, his eyes locked on the molten core of the nascent orb, deaf to the crackling static electricity that filled the air.

"He's channeling the flux to accelerate the formation," Azymantias observed. *"We have to stop him immediately and bring the orb down. The vessel below is an artifact that allows the initial elements to clump together by utilizing the convergence produced by the pyramid's structure. If the orb is separated from it, the process will come to a halt."*

Valianara turned to the High Orator, shouting to drown out the surrounding humming, "We need to distract him and take down the orb!"

Menilmonea nodded curtly, her fingers already brushing against her medallion.

"Well, well…" Gideon's voice, amplified by the room's acoustics, abruptly cut them off. He hadn't turned around, but his tone was terrifyingly calm. "Visitors are already. I'm impressed. I really wasn't expecting you this soon."

He turned around slowly while maintaining the stream of flux. His gaze swept across the room, pausing briefly at the entrance. "You came without the fox? That's interesting. I witnessed his abilities yesterday. I wouldn't stand a chance against him in a direct duel."

"Don't take us for fools!" Valianara shouted. "We know full well he couldn't survive here."

Gideon raised an eyebrow. "You're a very interesting young woman. Almost suspiciously gifted, too."

He paused, his voice growing more reasonable, "I mean you no harm. Go back to your villages; forget this city. You aren't bad people. We are only interested in the pyramid. No one will have to suffer."

"And of course," retorted Menilmonea, "you won't be coming to steal our bodies when you need them, I suppose?"

"You don't have to believe me, but I swear to you it's true. Once we regain control of the pyramid and the link with Arkandis is restored, we will no longer need your… resources. We will leave you to live in peace. You have my word."

"That's impossible," Azymantias interjected. *"The Magisterium will never leave you in peace. Not without a heavy price, not without submission. All they understand is force."*

Valianara's anger, cold and fierce, rose to the surface. "You don't wish us harm? How dare you say that! You killed poor Alister! You killed Orator Gideon! You are monstrous!"

The Bloodhound's face hardened. "I am a soldier, my child. You are young and still full of hope. I like that about you. I was being sincere when we spoke yesterday in the garden, but you don't understand the world you live in." He gave a vague nod. "Nevertheless, I offer my sincere apologies to those two people. It was a tactical necessity. However, take this as a warning. We will do whatever it takes to reclaim this place. You must understand that your… utopia here cannot last. Reality will eventually reassert itself. If you refuse to leave, we will crush you."

"Don't let him buy time," Azymantias warned. *"He's still charging the orb even as he speaks. We need to act."*

"He's stalling for time!" Valianara shouted.

"Understood!"

At those words, Menilmonea's necklace began to glow an intense green, and she thrust both arms forward. The steps beneath her shook and shattered. Gigantic, gnarled roots, swift as snakes, burst from the ground and lunged at Gideon. At the same time, dozens of small, grayish mushrooms sprouted in a circle around him.

Their opponent reacted with superhuman speed. Continuing to channel with his right hand, he abruptly waved his left. A shield of faceted energy materialized around him and the orb.

He quickly discovered, however, that his defensive spell could not block the magic of the song.

The roots pierced through the energy shield as if it were made of nothing but mist, much to Gideon's shock. Caught off guard, he was forced to pull his second arm close to his body to bolster his physical defenses and repel the plants' assault, thereby breaking his connection to the orb.

Menilmonea screamed, "Now!"

At her command, the fungi she had grown exploded in a myriad of simultaneous blasts. The ground shook, leaving numerous craters in its wake. The shockwave struck Gideon head-on. Swept away by the blast, the Bloodhound was thrown backward several yards before rolling across the dusty ground.

Immediately, the roots seized the opportunity presented by his fall. They rushed toward his legs, wrapping themselves around his ankles and thighs to pin him down. Other vines, thinner and more agile, lunged at the orb, which, without Gideon's magical assistance, was falling heavily toward its base.

The enemy was dazed. Even so, that did not stop him from trying to free himself from the plants' tightening grip. He brought his free hands together in front of his chest, fingers intertwined in a complex, precise gesture, like an unholy prayer.

"He's going to turn his shield into a zone of repulsion!" Azymantias shouted. *"Quick, tell Menilmonea to retract the roots!"*

Valianara's cry was cut short in her throat. The spell had already been cast.

A zone of repulsion materialized instantly around Gideon. In a fraction of a second, the roots and vines within the spell's radius froze, turned gray and brittle, before crumbling to powder, neatly severed at the boundary of the spell.

Menilmonea gasped, clutching her chest.

Gideon stood up, brushing the dust off his tunic with a newfound calm. He took a few steps back, making sure his zone of repulsion encompassed not only himself but also the orb and its stand. No song magic could reach him now.

"You are an interesting opponent, High Orator," he conceded, still breathing a little heavily. "Your magic is indeed strange. I haven't seen anything like it since our battle against the Primals. It's just as well that our repulsion magic works on it."

"He has to stay focused to maintain the zone of repulsion," noted Azymantias. *"He can't channel the orb at the same time! That's something, at least."*

Gideon, who seemed to have anticipated their thoughts, smiled coldly. "You're only delaying the inevitable. The orb has been initiated. It will be completed even if I'm not actively channeling it. It'll just take a little longer. And I have all the time in the world."

Menilmonea turned to Valianara, her face marked with anxiety. "How much time do we have left?"

Valianara listened to the mage's reply. "An hour, at best."

Gideon's eyes turned to the novice, narrowed with intense suspicion. "By what sorcery do you know this? Such an estimate requires a deep understanding of Arkandian thaumaturgy."

He stepped toward the edge of his protective bubble, confusion written on his face. "Who are you really, young woman?"

Gideon paused, his eyes shifting from the forming orb to the two women blocking his path. Finally, a shadow of regret crossed his face, and he shook his head. "There are too many unknowns here. You leave me no choice. Know, however, that I will take no pleasure in killing you."

With those words, he slowly raised his right arm, palm open toward them. The air around his hand began to vibrate, warping under the heat of a massive accumulation of energy.

"He's going to cast an expulsion spell!" Azymantias shouted. *"Protect yourselves!"*

Valianara reacted instinctively. She raised her forearms in front of her face, desperately trying to visualize the shield of energy that

Azymantias had earlier described to her.

Menilmonea understood instantly and opened herself fully to the song. She planted her feet wide to steady herself, anchoring them to the ground like age-old roots.

Gideon raised his eyebrows, taken aback by their swift reaction, then spread his fingers wide.

The world turned blue.

A dense, howling wave of flux surged from his palm. A torrent of pure, destructive energy swept through the room with the force of a landslide. The light was blinding; the sound, a continuous roar that shook their bones.

With her stomach knotted in terror, her mind retreated. The image of the shield wavered and collapsed before it could fully take shape. She was lifted off the ground like a wisp of straw and hurled violently against the stone wall. Her mind seemed to expand beyond her body, held in place only by the song, as she slid to the floor, breathless. Her vision dotted with black stars.

A few feet away, Menilmonea stood firm, her eyes half-closed. She let the song wash over her. The wave of Arkandian flux hit her, but instead of crushing her, it wrapped around her like the tide around a rock. The wall behind her shook under the residual shockwave; the stones cracked, but the High Orator remained untouched, standing in the eye of the storm.

As soon as the flux subsided, she rushed toward her ward. "Valianara! Are you okay?"

She helped her sit gently. The novice blinked, fighting off nausea, still feeling numb.

"Yes… Yes, I'll be fine," she croaked. "I couldn't raise a shield. It happened too fast."

"Apparently, the song still managed to protect you fairly well," Menilmonea noted with relief. "An attack like that could have killed you instantly."

"Yes, I could feel my soul breaking apart… but all I have now is a monstrous headache and more bruises than I can count."

She slowly got to her feet, leaning on her elder's arm.

"Unbelievable," commented Gideon, who hadn't moved from his protective bubble. "That song is truly a mystery. It's a shame we weren't able to investigate this phenomenon more closely when we fought the Primals."

He lowered his arm, realizing a new attack would be pointless if he had to keep his own defenses up.

"Stalemate," he noted. "We'll just wait patiently for the orb to charge. Then I'll be able to create a zone of repulsion wide enough to protect me all the way to the transport ring."

With a nod, he gestured toward the doorway leading back up to the city. "You can clearly see there's nothing you can do. So leave while you still can."

Valianara ignored his suggestion and turned to her inner world. *"Are you all right? Azymantias?"*

Receiving no answer, she mentally made her way to the great wall that contained the mage's mind. The wooden and iron door was securely closed.

At least one of us knows how to protect himself, she thought.

She opened the door again.

"Thank you, young lady."

"You didn't trust me. And not without reason, either."

"That's not it, my dear. I knew you wouldn't be able to summon the shield in time. And your song... We don't know if it protects me as well."

"That's right."

"Surprisingly, I'm not particularly curious about that. Are you going to hold out? I can feel your heart is pounding."

"I'm in pain all over, but I'll survive."

"Remember that he couldn't use his full strength because he had to maintain the zone of repulsion around the orb. He would have torn your soul out otherwise. I know of a few Bloodhounds capable of such mastery."

"Do you know who he is?"

"It's possible, actually..."

Unaware of this internal debate, Menilmonea asked Valianara, "Any ideas?"

Valianara immediately relayed the mage's strategy. "We have to keep attacking him. Keep your roots as close as possible to his shield. At the slightest lapse in concentration, the zone of repulsion could collapse, and you'll have to… What? By all the Titans! You'll have to kill him on the spot. You'll also have to knock the orb to the ground to halt the process."

Menilmonea closed her eyes for a second, then her face hardened. "I'm ready to defend us, even if the outcome goes against my convictions."

"I respect that, High Orator," said Gideon, who had been listening to their words intently. "On the other hand… Why are you letting your novice dictate your actions?"

"That's none of your concern. If you let us subdue you, I promise to share our secrets."

Gideon gave a cold smile. "I'm not that curious."

The roots summoned by Menilmonea grew, encircling the protective bubble. They began circling Gideon like sharks made of wood and sap, searching for a weak spot, skimming the deadly zone without actually touching it.

"It's pointless, my dear," Gideon sighed, his eyes still fixed on her shifting orb. "Why keep trying? You're only delaying the inevitable."

"You don't know everything, despite your magic! You were so arrogant, so sure of your superiority when you left, and yet here we are, controlling your beloved pyramid. Never would you have imagined that mere villagers could defeat your guardian or traitor. You have no idea what we're capable of."

Gideon fell silent.

Valianara, though, felt like she had no choice. She knew what had to be done. Still, she let Azymantias make the first move.

"We can't win, Valianara. Not like this, anyway. He's far too powerful, and your High Orator is exhausting herself trying to keep up the pressure, while he has access to the flux of an entire continent because of the pyramid. The time has come to resort to more radical measures."

"I know," she replied, her heart heavy. *"I realize that. I think I've known it ever since we left Menilmonea's house. I can see that this is the only solution."*

A respectful silence hung for a moment within their mental bond.

"I am an Arkandian," the mage continued with solemn gravity, *"but I reject their practices. I have grown older and changed, seeing the consequences of our actions. I no longer recognize their way of life. I honestly want to help you."*

"In any case, we have no choice," Valianara declared. *"I must trust you."*

"I promise you won't regret it."

"May the Mother hear you. Tell me what to do."

Time seemed to stand still as Azymantias explained the process to her: the release of the barriers, the voluntary surrender, the invitation to let another will move her limbs. It was counterintuitive, terrifying, but it was necessary.

"Ready?"

"Yes."

With those words, she let go, and her body collapsed to the ground like a puppet whose strings had been cut.

"Valianara!" cried Menilmonea.

Forgetting Gideon for a moment, she rushed toward her student to help her up, but Valianara's hand rose, in a sharp, precise gesture, signaling her to wait.

"You took the full brunt of my spell, young lady," Gideon remarked. "Even with your song, you must be shaken. Why continue to endure this? You must rest!"

But the young woman now standing up was somewhat different. Her movements were more fluid, more confident. She brushed the dust off her tunic with an elegance that was uncharacteristic of her.

Finally, she looked up at the High Orator and gave her a knowing wink with a sly smile. A smile that bore no resemblance to the innocence of a novice.

Menilmonea froze, understanding instantly. She took a step back, her gaze locking with that of her student, which suddenly seemed ancient.

"Oh…" she whispered. "In the name of the Mother, do not make her regret her choice. She does not deserve to suffer."

"I know that well," Valianara replied, though with a more authoritative tone. "You can trust me."

"Let's hope so."

Gideon, who had witnessed the interaction, narrowed his eyes cautiously. Something had shifted in the air, a subtle vibration he couldn't quite put his finger on. He said nothing, but his hands twitched. Without knowing why, he was starting to feel nervous.

"Take this opportunity to learn from what I'm doing," Azymantias counseled in Valianara's mind. *"It'll be worth months of theoretical training."*

"Understood," she replied, fighting the wave of existential nausea washing over her. *"Although right now, I'm mostly just trying not to go insane watching my own body move without my consent."*

"Yes, I admit it's an unpleasant experience."

Without warning, Azymantias raised Valianara's two hands, palms open and facing Gideon. He didn't merely draw from the ambient flux; he sucked it in with terrifying voracity, blending it with the flux Valianara naturally carried within her from the song.

"By the Core…" marveled the older mage. *"The song alters the flux. It's denser, more vivid. It feels as if I were channeling through several pearls at once. How marvelous."*

Gideon, noting the maneuver, let out a small, contemptuous laugh. "Amusing. Are you trying to mimic my attack? You're going to end up hurting yourself, little one."

Without hesitation, Azymantias unleashed the accumulated power.

Menilmonea witnessed the creation of a controlled cataclysm: a beam of white light, crackling with raw energy, shot from the girl's hands. The air tore apart with a piercing screech. The ground before her didn't just shatter; it was pulverized, carving a smoldering furrow as the beam hurtled toward its target. It was an attack of a magnitude far greater than that of the Bloodhound.

Sharpened by centuries of practice and his hunting skills, Gideon's instinct overrode his conscious mind. In a split second, he crossed his arms, materializing a diamond-hard, arc-shaped shield before him.

The impact was apocalyptic.

Under the violence of the shock, Gideon could not maintain his concentration on the zone of repulsion. The bubble burst. But the thermal and magical shockwave was such that Menilmonea's vines, which had crept too close, were instantly vaporized. The High Orator let out a cry of pain, gasping as if she had been burned.

Despite his impenetrable protection, Gideon was knocked back; his boots scraped the ground, carving two deep gouges into the earth.

Azymantias's beam, deflected by the shield, struck the back wall. The stone burst into a shower of debris, leaving a smoking crater several feet deep. The entire cavern shook, even dislodging dust from the hexagonal stalactites.

Gasping for breath, Gideon straightened in his singed clothes, covered in sweat and dust. Though shaken, his composure returned. With a swift gesture, he re-summoned the zone of repulsion around himself and the orb before Menilmonea could react.

"I offer my apologies," Azymantias said to the High Orator. "The song merged with my attack, multiplying its power tenfold. I didn't think it would affect your roots."

"I understand. I'll be careful." Menilmonea grimaced, her face pale. "Because of that, I couldn't grab Gideon or the sphere of negation when the zone of repulsion fell."

"We may not need them," Valianara's mouth replied with icy assurance. "The power the song gives me is such that I should be able to crush his defense."

Gideon stared at them with a renewed intensity. The glint of contempt had vanished, replaced by stunned conviction. "Azymantias? It's you, isn't it?"

He shook his head as if to dispel a hallucination. "It's the only logical explanation: you've found a way to survive your jar. In truth, I'm only half surprised, you old scoundrel."

Valianara—or rather, Azymantias—let out a laugh that sounded strangely deep in the young girl's throat.

"You're quite brilliant, my dear… Oberron. I'm not mistaken either, am I? I know of only one Bloodhound capable of enduring what I just threw at you. I still remember our duels during the Feast of the Pact."

"Ha, ha! Well done! So, you've been putting on an act all this time? You missed your calling as a Bloodhound."

"Well, no, it's more complicated than that," Azymantias retorted. "We're dealing with a case of dual association. The likes of which have never been seen."

Menilmonea cleared her throat loudly, reminding them of her presence and the urgent nature of the situation.

"Yes, sorry. This isn't the time," Azymantias apologized.

He took a step toward their opponent, Valianara's hands open in a gesture of appeasement.

"Oberron, my friend, you need not continue. You can see for yourself that they have succeeded where the Magisterium failed! Look at what they have built upon the ashes of our civilization. Their magic truly comes from the Source, but unlike us, it is not a threat to them—it sustains them. That song they speak of is its signature! Stop defending our dying empire. Here, we might help them build the world the original Pact was meant to create. A world without castes, without oppression. We would no longer fear the Source. She would be our partner!"

"Perhaps you are right. But you know as well as I do that I cannot. I am a Bloodhound. I must finish my hunt. So, step aside! Let me re-connect the pyramid, and I promise I'll plead this people's case before the Core." He let out a short, dry laugh. "And I'm sure High Magistrix Avamar will be receptive to my request."

Azymantias blinked, the perfect control he exercised over Valianara's face slipping for a second. "Avamar? High Magistrix?"

"That's right. She survived. Together with High Magistrix Nabuanor, she helped Obinaelle cast the teleportation spell before the island was swallowed up. They make up the new Triumvirate. Don't you want to see her again? To understand what she went through to keep our people alive… Because of you?"

A heavy silence settled in. Azymantias seemed to consider the offer, or possibly the full weight of his guilt. Finally, he shook his head with a smile. "I don't think that's such a good idea. Not for now, anyway.

As you say, she went through hell because of me. I doubt her feelings toward me have been left unscathed. Your assassination attempt is proof of that. She doesn't want to see me again. She wants to erase me."

Around them, the roots and vines summoned by Menilmonea had regenerated and continued to circle the Bloodhound, waiting for an opening in his defenses.

"You're going to have to kill me," Oberron concluded.

"It would seem so."

Azymantias cast a glance at Menilmonea, silently signaling her to retreat. The High Orator pulled back her plants to keep them out of reach of the coming cataclysm. The mage raised his hands again. This time, he sought no element of surprise. He drew upon the song, summoning a quantity of flux that made the surrounding air groan.

Oberron reacted instantly. He prepared to let go of the zone of repulsion to focus all his energy on his personal shield. He anchored his feet to the ground, arms crossed, ready to absorb the impact.

The attack struck. Unlike the first, it was not a simple explosion. Azymantias unleashed a continuous river of screaming white light, a torrent of pure energy that gushed from the young novice's palms to crash against the defenses the Bloodhound had just erected.

The shield flared, shifting from blue to deep purple under the tremendous pressure. This time, to his great astonishment, the Bloodhound's protection began to give way. Cracks appeared on the surface of the magical disc, creaking like glass about to shatter. The flux of the song was wild and dense. And Oberron was losing his footing.

"I have him!" Azymantias exclaimed. "The structure is collapsing. One more push and it will be pulverized!"

His face contorted with effort, one knee buckling under the strain, the Bloodhound realized he would be defeated if he didn't make one last desperate move. He intensified his efforts, for under the torrent of flux pinning him in place, the slightest movement became a monumental feat. And so, while holding up his shield, he fought fiercely against the magical pull of gravity to move his right arm. His whole body trembling, he felt several teeth snap under the strain of his jaw. He managed, however, to slip a clenched hand inside his jacket, from which he pulled out a small, round object that glowed faintly.

"He's grabbed something. It looks like a pearl!" Valianara exclaimed. *"He didn't use them all for the orb!"*

Oberron clenched his fist around the artifact.

"That's what makes the Bloodhounds so powerful. They're trained always to have a solution. He isn't trying to create an orb of optimal power," Azymantias analyzed. *"He doesn't care about restoring the zone of repulsion over the pyramid, for example. He needs enough power to stabilize the bridge and reestablish the link with Arkandis. With his technical mastery and this new reservoir of pure flux… I fear he might be able to stand up to us."*

An azure shockwave pulsed from Oberron's fist. The pearl flared, injecting a surge of raw energy into his faltering shield.

The cracks in the shield closed almost instantly. The barrier, which had threatened to fade just a second earlier, thickened and grew brighter, repelling Azymantias's white torrent with renewed vigor. Oberron appeared serene amidst this deluge of pure power.

"This is a test of endurance," Azymantias explained. *"Do you understand what that means?"*

"I… I understand. It will come down to whoever falls first."

"Exactly. And he is very strong. Much stronger than I am in this borrowed body that doesn't quite fit me. But we have the song. So we must hope that he falters first."

"What if we give out before he does? What will happen?"

"If you channel too much flux for too long, the body can't hold out. You'll eventually exhaust your life force, and the energy will tear you apart. Physically."

"By all the Titans! I see. Well, know this: I… I believe in us!"

Azymantias intensified the flux. The beam became blinding, illuminating the nursery with a harsh light that dispelled the shadows. The noise was deafening; a continuous crackling, as if the universe itself were tearing apart.

Menilmonea could no longer hide her anxiety. "Will you be all right, Azymantias?"

Struggling to find the words, the mage nodded. The High Orator, though frustrated, resigned herself to holding back. She had tried to extend her roots toward the Bloodhound, but this maelstrom of destructive magic completely engulfed him.

Valianara, meanwhile, felt her muscles stiffen, and her bones vibrate under the power coursing through her. She was nothing more than a conduit, a channel of flesh for a nearly divine power. Facing her, Oberron grimaced, blood trickling from the corner of his lips and sweat streaming down his forehead. His boots began to slide backward inch by inch. Yet his shield held firm, splitting the river of magic flowing all around him, scorching the walls of the hall.

It was a duel of pure will.

Menilmonea, her eyes wide with horror as she watched the novice's skin begin to smoke, screamed through the din, "You're going to kill Valianara! Her body won't withstand it!"

"Let me focus!" Azymantias roared, his usual voice distorted by the supreme effort. "If she dies, I will go with her. And I don't plan on dying today!"

Menilmonea clenched her teeth.

For what seemed like an endless stretch of time, pushed to the breaking point, Valianara watched her own body convert the flux and the song into pure destruction. Desperate, she felt her life unraveling, consumed by the flow of energy too great for her to handle.

"He isn't moving."

"I can see that!" grunted Azymantias. *"The Bloodhounds are trained from birth for this kind of combat. Their regenerative and control abilities are beyond human. And I think that's also why he chose Gideon's body. Gideon must possess heightened sensitivity to the flux."*

Valianara felt the intensity of the attack gradually diminish. The river of light was thinning. Oberron was going to win. It was only a matter of minutes.

Her gaze, through the wall of heat, fell upon Menilmonea. The High Orator had trusted them, had placed the future of her world in the hands of a novice and a ghost. A wave of infinite sadness engulfed her. She thought of her family. Her village. Her father. Her mother. Her friend Batany. They would become slaves again, mere cattle for an arrogant group of mages in search of immortality. She imagined the wars that would come, the blood of the defeated Titans. All because they couldn't break the defense of a single man. They were so small in the face of the Arkandians' millennia-old power. So insignificant.

If only the Primal were here, she thought bitterly.

She looked at the hundreds of metal rods on the ceiling and cursed this architecture—the product of the pride of a people who had been willing to build a prison to enslave other children of the Mother—a room designed to trap life itself.

That was when she felt a cold shiver race down her spine.

"What was that?" Azymantias asked abruptly, his concentration wavering for a moment.

A connection had just been formed. *"I think I have an idea."*

"I'm all ears, my friend!"

With a flash of insight, Valianara laid out her plan to him, then asked, *"Do you think you have the strength to do it?"*

"It's quite possible. But if it doesn't work, we'll have nothing left."

"I'm aware of that."

"In that case…!"

With that, Azymantias separated Valianara's hands. He focused the torrent of white light onto his right hand, maintaining pressure on Oberron's shield while narrowing the beam's width. Under such an intense concentration on a single limb, Valianara's skin instantly began to redden.

Menilmonea, standing back, watched the scene with unease. She had to trust this unlikely pair.

Oberron smirked with satisfaction behind his shield as the difference began to take effect. He planted his feet firmly, ready to seize victory. It was then that, in one fluid motion, Azymantias raised Valianara's left hand and targeted the metal rods hanging above the Bloodhound's head. In a sudden shift in pace, he cut off the flow from his right hand and channeled, in a single blow, the full power of the song and his own magic into his left arm.

A blinding flash struck the metal stalactites.

As Valianara had predicted, the iron-tin alloy captured this massive influx and acted as a reverse lightning rod. The rods channeled the energy and, true to their design, forcefully returned it to the ground, seeking the shortest path to the foundations.

That path was Oberron.

The Bloodhound, still fixed on the shield that was now of no use to him, failed to anticipate the blow.

The column of energy struck him head-on; a divine spear falling from above. There was no scream, no struggle. The raw magic coursed through his body, overloading every nerve, every cell, before rushing into the ground. In an instant, Oberron's essence was scattered into the fabric of stone and earth beneath the city, swept away like dust in the wind. His empty body crashed heavily to the ground.

Silence fell over the nursery, marred only by the smell of ozone and burned stone.

Azymantias fell to his knees, gasping for breath. He stared at his trembling hands, scorched and smoldering. Valianara's body was reduced to a mass of agony, but they were alive!

Menilmonea wasted no time. As her roots shot out to wrap around Gideon's lifeless body, binding him as a precaution, other vines surged from behind the orb's receptacle and collided with it, causing it to topple. It ceased pulsing instantaneously, reverting to a simple silver sphere.

"Rest assured, he is indeed dead," Azymantias whispered.

Menilmonea stepped forward, her face marked by exhaustion, though her eyes shone with relief. She helped him to his feet. "Thank you, Azymantias. Without you—"

"Thank Valianara," he cut her off. "It was her idea."

"Well," the High Orator resumed, her tone hardening imperceptibly. "It seems to me this would be the right moment to give her back control of her body."

Azymantias did not answer. He did not move. He stared intently at Gideon's lifeless body, which the roots had dragged back to the foot of the stairs. He observed it with a calculating intensity that sent a shiver down Menilmonea's spine.

The ground trembled. With an ominous crack, several roots burst through the paving stones around Azymantias. The air grew heavy with a strong scent of moss and sap, while a multitude of vines and brambles began crawling toward the mage. At his feet, myriads of gray mushrooms proliferated at a frenzied pace with damp, almost mocking snaps.

"Azymantias?" Menilmonea insisted. "You're going to give her back her body, aren't you?"

XXXI

Nursery / Present Day

Menilmonea's roots pulsed, ready to immobilize the novice if her passenger made one wrong move. But Azymantias remained motionless, meeting the High Orator's gaze with a disconcerting calm.

"Of course I'll give her back her body," he declared. "Just give me a few moments to propose an idea to you."

"Don't play with my patience, mage. What does Valianara say about this 'idea' of yours? Have you spoken to her about it?"

"No. I sealed her off the moment Oberron died. For her, time stopped the instant we won. She knows nothing of this conversation."

Menilmonea's eyes widened with rage at this violation, but Azymantias raised a hand to stop her. "I needed to speak with you as one adult to another. I guarantee I will return her body to her. But listen to me first."

"I'm listening. But make it quick."

Azymantias turned his head toward Gideon. "This body will die in less than an hour. Without a mind to sustain vital functions, the vessel cannot live for long. If you allow me to go back up and retrieve the Mind Focalizer, I could enter this body and free Valianara at the same time."

Menilmonea let out a mirthless laugh. "I see. You had it all planned. You never intended to help us for nothing or be confined to a necklace. You were waiting for the chance to steal yourself a new skin."

"It wasn't planned at all! I'm merely adapting to the situation; that's what has allowed me to survive for millennia. I need a body, and this one is no longer of use to anyone. It would be a waste to let it rot."

"You're vile. Have you thought about his family? His loved ones? Aureal? Can you imagine how it would feel for her to see the man she loved walking around, possessed by someone else? By the soul of an Arkandian?"

"I understand that: the pain, the grief, the distress. But I ask you to be pragmatic, High Orator. Put your feelings to one side for a moment and give it some thought." He stepped forward, ignoring the roots brushing against his throat. "Think of the tactical advantage I could provide you if I were in full control of my powers, in a body capable of channeling the flux. I could tip the scales. I could teach you all the secrets of Arkandian magic, decipher your Library, and train your students. You would be prepared for their return."

He pointed a finger toward the ceiling, toward the outside world. "As you can imagine, the Magisterium won't stop here. They want the pyramid. They didn't send their best Bloodhound on a mere whim. They will be back, Menilmonea. More of them, and stronger. You will lose without me."

Menilmonea remained silent, the weight of responsibility crushing her shoulders. Azymantias's cold logic was unrelenting.

"What's to stop you from fleeing?" she finally asked him. "Or worse, that you won't go back to your own people and hand the pyramid to them on a silver platter?"

"Nothing—nothing but my word and my circumstances. I can't go back to the Magisterium. They'd torture me for centuries for what I did. I'm the man who destroyed their world. You saw what they tried to do with my jar." He held her gaze. "I was being truthful when I tried to convince Oberron. I honestly believe that here you have the first stirrings of a society that could function according to the terms of the Pact—a society where magic would serve life rather than consume it. I would love to see that. I wish to be a part of it."

Menilmonea looked at her friend's lifeless body, then at the possessed young novice standing before her. She thought of Aureal, of the pain she was about to inflict on her. She also thought of the Arkandian fleets that might already be preparing to descend upon them. She had experienced what a single one of their soldiers was capable of.

And above all, she thought of all the villages, of all the lives she was bound to protect.

Slowly, the roots that threatened Azymantias returned to the earth.

"There is no perfect decision when you are in command, High Orator," the mage commented softly. "Power is a matter of choosing the lesser of several evils."

Menilmonea remained silent for a moment.

"You Arkandians—you taint everything you touch," she then whispered.

The last of the mushrooms disappeared.

"My people are cursed, but that's something I intend to change. You won't regret placing your trust in me."

"I have just one condition," Menilmonea interrupted, raising a finger to curb his enthusiasm. "I will first discuss this with Aureal. I will not desecrate Gideon's body without her explicit consent."

Azymantias bowed his head respectfully. "So be it. Let's go see her." He took a step to follow her, but once again, roots sprang up to block his path.

"No," ordered the High Orator. "Wait for me here. I will speak to her, plead your case, and explain the necessity of this choice. If she agrees to your request—and only if she does—I will return with the Mind Focalizer. The Primal will remain at the top of the stairs, in case you are tempted to take flight."

Azymantias froze, then slowly backed away. "I understand. Thank you. Sincerely."

Menilmonea turned her back on him and began climbing the long black stone steps, leaving behind the amber light of the nursery.

As soon as her figure disappeared up the stairs, Azymantias gathered his concentration. He visualized the heavy door of the mental fortress and, with an effort of will, forced it open.

Valianara regained consciousness. The change in context was jarring. *"But… What happened? Where is the High Orator?"*

Azymantias's voice echoed, tinged with a slight hesitation—unusual for the once-mighty mage. *"I… I locked you up in a silo. I needed to speak with her alone. I offer my apologies."*

"What? You've got some nerve! With all due respect… Please don't do that again without telling me!"

Azymantias gave her time to collect herself. After a brief moment, she continued, *"It's really very strange, this temporal rupture. It feels like we blinked, but the world moved on without us. Where is the High Orator?"*

"She's gone back to the surface. I was trying to convince her to let me use Gideon's body."

"Azymantias! Really? Is that why you won't give me back control?"

"Yes. And I know what you're going to say. But I'm thinking tactically. I would be far more useful with a body capable of channeling the flux than stuck in a necklace."

"And of course, you're doing this purely out of the goodness of your heart? For the greater good?"

"No, obviously not; I want a body. I want to live, to touch, to feel again. And I understand all the moral implications of this, Valianara. I'm not a monster, despite what my past might suggest."

The novice sighed. *"And what did the High Orator say?"*

"She wants to discuss it with Aureal. She'll have the final say."

"Yes, that makes sense. It's the least she can do."

"If she refuses, I'll return control to you immediately."

Valianara analyzed the proposal from another, more technical angle. Alister's fate came back to her. *"Let's say you can do it… I thought that body-to-body transfer irreparably destroyed the original host? Look at what was left of Alister's body."*

"If it's done without a tool, by brute force, yes. It's a violent tearing apart. But with the Mind Focalizer, it should be done without causing you any harm. The artifact is designed for a clean extraction."

"'Should'?"

"Yes… That's why I freed you," Azymantias admitted. *"Initially, I wanted to do it without even telling you. I wanted to take advantage of your absence to carry out the procedure as soon as Menilmonea returned.*

But I realize that by acting in such a way, I would be behaving like a true Arkandian." He paused, as if to gather his courage. *"So here we are. I'm being completely honest. I think I can pull it off; after all, I devised the theories behind this contraption, but there is a risk. For you as well as for me. Do you still want to try?"*

Valianara considered the question very quickly. *"Wouldn't it be simpler to use an intermediary object? From me to a necklace, then from the necklace to Gideon's body? That would protect my body from the final transfer."*

"The risk remains the same. The part I'm unsure about is the initial extraction. It's the moment when I have to separate myself from your mind without taking a piece of it with me, or without leaving irreversible damage. I was looking for the right moment to tell you about it, but circumstances prevented me."

Valianara would have liked to sit down. *"So, if Aureal agrees… I'm putting my life in your hands and those of a device that's over a thousand years old?"*

"That's exactly right. But look! You trusted me with Oberron, and you were right to do so!"

The young novice didn't know how to respond. They remained silent for a long time, enveloped in the charged silence of the nursery.

The tension was finally broken by the sound of hurried footsteps on the stairs. Menilmonea emerged from the shadows, the Mind Focalizer clutched to her chest.

The face, controlled by Azymantias, lit up with a broad, triumphant smile. He held out his hands to take the artifact, but the High Orator did not move. She kept it out of reach, her gaze hardened by a promise she intended to keep.

"Aureal has agreed. However, she wants to ensure that nothing remains of Gideon. That you will not be able to access his memories, his feelings… Everything he once was to her."

"I guarantee it," Azymantias assured her with absolute seriousness. "I could have accessed his residual memory if I had proceeded as Oberron did—that is, transferring myself immediately upon the host's death, taking advantage of the soul's still-vivid resonance. But as things stand, there is no memory in the brain of that body. Everything has vanished. It is an empty shell."

Menilmonea maintained eye contact for a few seconds, searching for the slightest trace of a lie, then her shoulders slumped slightly.

Azymantias seized the moment. "I freed Valianara. She's with us, and she knows what I mean to do."

"Is she in agreement?"

"She trusts me."

"*Well, that's a somewhat hasty summary,*" the young woman noted.

"*Don't you trust me?*" Azymantias asked.

"*I have no choice, for one thing. You're not going to stay in my head for the rest of my life.*"

The High Orator still seemed hesitant. With a sigh, she handed the Focalizer to Azymantias.

As soon as the object was in his hands, his movements became surgical, marked by a millennia-old familiarity. Valianara's slender fingers slid the bronze and silver gears along their axes, realigning the internal mechanisms with satisfying clicks. Azymantias adjusted the articulated mount of the cylindrical body, checking the positioning of the facets of the large amber gem against the two lower sapphires. He delicately turned a small dial near the eyepiece, his face bent over the object like a watchmaker over his masterpiece.

After a few moments of meticulous tuning, he sat down on the cold floor.

"Lay Gideon's body down next to me," he asked. "Head to toe, please."

With a gesture from Menilmonea, roots emerged from the broken slabs, lifting the orator's lifeless body with infinite gentleness and placing it exactly where he had indicated. Azymantias then set the Focalizer between them, directing the garnet toward Valianara's face.

He looked up at the High Orator. "I'm going to need your help. I can't operate the machine and be extracted at the same time."

He gestured toward the large amber gem.

"When I cast the spell, you'll see the garnet change color. It will turn dark orange, then blood red. That will be the sign that it is

drawing out my essence. At that moment, Valianara's body will start convulsing. Don't worry—that's normal. But don't you dare touch her. If you break contact at any point during this process, I will be scattered into the ether."

Menilmonea nodded, her hands pressed together to hide her trembling.

"After a few moments," the mage continued, "the garnet will return to its present color. That will mean I have been stored within its matrix. You will then need to rotate the focuser on its axis and point the tube toward Gideon's head. And finally…"

He guided Menilmonea's hand toward a small silver-encrusted dial on the side of the device. "You must turn this piece. Not the other one, under any circumstances. This one, specifically, is a quarter-turn to the right. It will release the flux to the new vessel. Is that clear?"

"Perfectly clear," Menilmonea agreed, her throat tightening.

"Then, let's begin."

Azymantias closed his eyes for a moment, then his voice echoed one last time inside the novice's skull. *I thank you for your trust and your hospitality, my child. It was… an interesting coexistence. We'll meet again soon.*

"See you in a moment!" replied Valianara, her voice quivering with fear. *"If I could, I'd cross my fingers for both of us."*

"You should be able to do that very soon."

Then he cast the transfer spell and released his grip on the girl's body.

XXXII

Nursery / Present Day

Azymantias stood amid the rubble, on the steps of the nursery. He raised his hands, which had once belonged to Gideon. He brought them up to his face, turned them over and over, watching the light play on the skin. He clenched his fists, then opened them again, testing the tendons, the nerves' response. With a deep inhalation, he savored the ozone-laden air filling his broad, deep lungs. He felt... aligned. At last.

The experience of coexisting within Valianara's slight frame had been... disorienting. Beyond the cramped confines of a shared skull, it was the very biology of the young girl that had troubled him. His mind, shaped by millennia of existence in a male body, had struggled to accept the reality of his host. The center of gravity was different, the distribution of muscle mass disconcerting, the internal chemistry unfamiliar. Every movement he had initiated as a temporary pilot had felt like wearing a badly tailored garment, too tight in some places and loose in others. Here, in the reanimated shell of the orator, he found a familiar structure: the mechanics of the shoulders, the weight of the bones, even the line of sight. Everything fit together with the precision of a well-oiled machine. He was back in a home that felt like his own.

A few steps away, a faint moan sounded. Valianara stirred. Menilmonea, who had not left her makeshift bedside, helped her sit up. The novice brought a hand to her temple, rubbing her eyes to dispel the last traces of the transfer.

"How do you feel?" the High Orator asked her.

Valianara took a moment to take stock of herself inwardly. Everything seemed to be in its place: nothing but the soothing silence of her own thoughts and the distant murmur of the song.

"I'm fine!" she whispered, a smile of pure relief lighting up her pale face. "Although every part of my body aches in one way or another."

She turned her head toward the figure standing upright beside her. It was Gideon's face, but the posture and the aura of authority emanating from him did not belong to the man she remembered.

"Thank you for keeping your word, Azymantias," she said with sincerity.

The Arkandian bowed slightly, a graceful little bow that sat oddly with the orator's build. "You proved to be a worthy host, my dear. The very least I could do was not to destroy what you so graciously lent me!"

Menilmonea straightened up, not taking her eyes off the old mage, still searching for a sign of deceit. "And you? How do you feel?"

Azymantias cracked his neck, producing a sharp sound that echoed through the empty room. "Better. Infinitely better. This body is far closer to what I'm used to."

He shot a sidelong glance at the novice. "No disrespect intended. But let's say your… form… wasn't quite tailored to my mind."

Valianara, despite her exhaustion and the strange nature of the situation, couldn't help but smile. "I'm not offended. I'm delighted to have gotten my 'form' back."

Azymantias let his eyes wander over the metallic stalactites hanging above their heads, then to the dark alcoves lining the immense room. A shadow passed over Gideon's face, an expression of ancient melancholy that clashed with the orator's familiar features.

"The last time I was here," he murmured, as if speaking to himself, "there were seven dryads imprisoned in this room. They were treated like cattle. The poor creatures were scarcely alive…"

Valianara shuddered, picturing the scene. The memory of the unfinished orb came back to her, and a logical question arose. "Speaking of which… How did he find the blood? Did he bring it with him?”

Azymantias folded his arms, deep in thought. “That’s one possibility. However, I highly doubt the Magisterium recaptured any dryads—or even dared to do so. If I were them, I’d keep a low profile for a few millennia before risking the Source’s wrath again.”

While they were talking, Menilmonea was inspecting the perimeter of the room. Her attention was caught by a disruption in the perfect symmetry of the northern wall, far behind where the mage had been standing.

“And that, over there… What is it?” she asked, pointing to a massive door, almost invisible in the dim light, set into the black stone.

Azymantias narrowed his eyes.

“I don’t know,” he confessed. “I’ve only been here a handful of times, to tell the truth. This used to be Obinaelle’s domain.”

Valianara stared at the door. A terrible realization was forming in her mind.

“Could it be…?” she began, her voice catching in her throat.

She left the question hanging, but the ensuing silence spoke louder than any words. Everyone realized what she meant.

Menilmonea turned pale. “Let’s take a look.”

They crossed the vast hall to join the far end of the room. Once they reached the dark doorway, they lifted the latch and pushed the heavy door. It swung open, exposing a darkness that carried the stench of stagnant water and decay. The soft orange light from the nursery seeped through the opening, bathing the damp brick walls. The sight that met their eyes made them recoil in disgust. It was a dungeon. Water trickled down the walls, feeding a thick, slimy moss that had invaded the cracks between the stones. Rusty iron chains swung from the wall.

But it was the sight of what lay on the floor, strewn with fallen leaves, that made their blood run cold.

A creature. Or rather, the sketch of a living thing, carved from wood and pain.

It was curled up into a ball, its knees drawn up to its chest, its gnarled arms wrapped around its legs as if to protect itself from its hostile surroundings. Its skin was made of bark, its muscles of intertwined vines. Two large plant-like wings protruded from its shoulder blades, folded heavily across its sides like a cloak of despair. Woven from thin branches and ivy, they dragged pitifully through the mud. A mane of withered foliage and brittle twigs crowned a face set in rigid lines that stared back at them with unbearable melancholy. Small white flowers, pale and fragile, grew like a last desperate attempt by life to reassert itself in the midst of this emptiness.

Moss and dampness had coated it so thoroughly that it seemed to have merged with the surroundings. However, very slight movements indicated that it was alive. Just barely.

Valianara raised a hand to her mouth to suppress a gasp. Azymantias stood frozen in the doorway, unable to take another step.

Menilmonea, however, walked forward.

The High Orator closed her eyes for a moment, inhaling deeply to calm the pounding of her heart. She opened herself to the song. Usually, she would have heard a vibrant symphony. But in this prison cell, it was smothered, broken, like a violin whose strings had been loosened.

She continued advancing.

The creature reacted instantly.

The movement was sudden, terrifying, considering how close to death the being appeared to be. The dryad drew in on herself violently, clenching her limbs against her body with desperate force. She turned her wooden face toward the wall, hiding her eyes, her entire body quivering like a leaf in a storm. She expected to be struck. She anticipated pain. She assumed that they had come to take the few drops of sap she had left.

Menilmonea stopped abruptly, her heart breaking at such palpable terror. She gently crouched down to bring herself to the creature's level, her hands open, palms facing the sky as a sign of peace.

She did not speak with her voice. She projected her thoughts into the song, reaching out blindly for the dryad's mind in the darkness that surrounded her. She finally found an echo. Faint. Distant. A spark buried beneath layers of trauma.

With infinite gentleness, she touched that consciousness. *"Don't be afraid…"*

The dryad flinched, her bark-like fingers clawing at the stone floor.

Menilmonea urged her, pouring all the warmth and kindness she could into the mental channel. *"We are friends. Those who hurt you have gone. They will not return. We are here to save you."*

She waited for a response. A word. An image. A sign of understanding. There was nothing.

Instead, a wave engulfed her. It wasn't a coherent thought. It was a lament. Slow. Heavy. Suffocating.

Menilmonea surrendered to the feeling. There was a taste of cold ash and stagnant water in this ode. She was struck head-on by a despair so black, so deep, that she nearly lost her balance. She felt shame—the shame of having survived when her sisters had died. She felt the unfathomable abyss of hundreds of years of solitude, in the dark, without sun, without earth, without the whisper of trees. She felt the urge to end it all, to let herself go, held back only by her physical inability to take her own life.

When Menilmonea opened her eyes again, tears beaded on her cheeks.

She intensified the mental connection, projecting images of blue skies and a lush canopy to counter the darkness.

"I'm going to set you free," she whispered. *"I'm going to take you up there, into the open air, far from this black stone and this foul water. I'm going to introduce you to someone… Someone who can take care of you."*

The shell of terror cracked ever so slightly. The dryad stopped trembling. Her vine-like muscles slowly relaxed, abandoning their defensive posture. She didn't push away Menilmonea's hand when it brushed her shoulder.

With infinite tenderness, the High Orator slipped an arm under the creature's shoulders to help her to her feet. She pulled gently, encouraging her to move. But the dryad's legs gave way beneath her. She was as heavy and inert as waterlogged deadwood. She fell back, a small, dry crackling sound escaping her throat.

"Don't strain yourself," whispered Menilmonea, catching her as she

fell. *"We'll have to do this another way."*

She summoned her medallion. The stone floor immediately split open. Supple roots emerged from the mud, slipping beneath her to form a verdant cradle that lifted her with the delicacy of a mother carrying her child.

As she left the ground, a feverish, skeletal finger rose to point at the medallion, which pulsed with an emerald glow against Menilmonea's throat.

The orator heard a thought in her mind. *"The Father-Tree!"*

Menilmonea took the medallion in her hand. *"It's a half-heartseed. It was given to me by a powerful friend. It is he who awaits you up there."*

In the song, the funeral dirge subtly shifted in tone. The dissonance of despair faded, giving way to a new sound. Menilmonea wasn't sure, for the change was subtle, but she was convinced that it was something approaching hope.

She turned to Valianara and Azymantias, who were still waiting in the background.

"I'm going to introduce her to the Primal," she announced matter-of-factly.

The other two nodded and stepped aside to clear the way.

Menilmonea set off toward the exit. Behind her, the party formed a silent, graceful procession. The roots did not drag the dryad; they took turns carrying her. A root would push forward, lift the fragile body, move her a few feet, then gently place her in the arms of a new root that had just sprung up further along, before returning to the ground. It looked like a bark-covered centipede, a fluid wave of vegetation carrying the poor creature across the length of the hall, then toward the steps of the black staircase, faithfully following in the footsteps of Menilmonea, who led the way toward the light.

Once they reached the hall, the roots set the dryad down with infinite care before the tropical flower. The creature did not move, curled up on the cold marble, her broken wings spread like dead leaves around her. Menilmonea stood next to her, motionless. She said not a word, but the air around her vibrated with an intense concentration. She was in the midst of a conversation with the Primal.

Standing back, Valianara watched the scene, her heart tight in her chest. "I hope the Primal can save her. She must have endured hell all these years."

Azymantias's reply was slow in coming. "I hope so too. But… if they managed to capture her, that doesn't bode well for the others."

Valianara frowned. "What do you mean?"

"Her sisters wouldn't have abandoned her. They must have been slaughtered while trying to help her escape. Sadly, I could only give them a few minutes' head start." He paused. "I imagine the troops dispatched in pursuit must have had strict orders: strike fast and hard. They couldn't be allowed any time to communicate with the Source… with the Mother, I mean. Either they managed to overpower them, or they were doomed."

Azymantias's gaze fell upon the plant-like figure lying prostrate on the ground. "This poor soul must have been more susceptible to our controlling magic than the others. That's what saved her life—if enduring centuries of torture in the dark can even be called life."

Finally, Menilmonea broke her concentration and turned to her companions, just as a low rumble caused the very structure of the hall to shake.

Above them, the building's roof seemed to liquefy. Gigantic roots, as thick as columns, pierced through the stone as if it were mere mist. They descended majestically, wrapping themselves with maternal tenderness around the dryad's delicate body. In a few moments, she was lifted, cradled in a cocoon of living wood, and raised high into the air before disappearing into the shadows of the ceiling.

Menilmonea joined them, her face weary with exhaustion, but her eyes shining with a fresh emotion.

"The Primal is taking care of her," she explained. "She quieted down instantly in his presence. She calls him the Father-Tree and seems to recognize him as if he were a long-lost relative. Yet the Primal told me he'd never seen a dryad in his life before today. We'll certainly learn more once she's back on her feet—which may take a while, given her condition."

Azymantias, his arms crossed over his chest, stared at the spot where the creature had vanished.

"This could give us a major advantage," he remarked thoughtfully.

Valianara couldn't help but smile inwardly at the use of "us."

Menilmonea, for her part, frowned. "Why?"

"It seems clear that dryads possess a means of communicating directly with the Mother. Look at what happened to Arkandis after they attempted to flee. The Source's reaction was immediate and devastating."

He turned his gaze toward the High Orator, a calculating twinkle in his eyes. "Reading between the lines, I gather that even the Primal is incapable of it. Otherwise, he would have invoked her already, wouldn't he?"

"No, you're right. He says she is too distant, too vast for direct conversation."

"Well, it would seem these little creatures have the goddess's ear," concluded Azymantias with a satisfied smirk. "If we manage to gain her trust… Having a divine entity as an ally could significantly reduce our problems with the Magisterium."

Menilmonea fell silent for what seemed like an eternity, studying the face of the man who now bore the features of her friend Gideon.

"For you, it's all strategy, isn't it?" she finally blurted out, a hint of bitterness in her voice.

Azymantias shrugged, a smooth movement that already seemed natural to his new body. "Essentially. I'm afraid I'm still too Arkandian. It's an old survival instinct. But don't take it the wrong way, High Orator. I only want what's best for your… for our world."

Valianara, standing back, listened to the exchanged words in silence. She felt oddly torn. On one hand, Azymantias's calculating coldness sent a cold shiver down her spine; a reminder of the callous cruelty with which the Arkandians had disposed of their lives. On the other hand, she had to admit that without this capacity to see the world as a chessboard, they would all be doomed sooner or later. She was surprised to find herself agreeing with both sides; an uneasy position that perhaps marked the end of her innocence.

"We're all going to need some time to adjust, that's for sure,"

Menilmonea sighed, rubbing her temples. "But I do appreciate your willingness to help us. And while we await confirmation that our new guest can actually contact the Mother, we're going to need your skills to prepare for whatever the Arkandians have in store for us."

She cast a worried glance toward the staircase leading down to the nursery. "Do you think Oberron succeeded? Was he able to send a signal?"

"No, I doubt it. Communications over long distances require massive infrastructure. Only this ring can reach Arkandis."

His gaze lingered on the giant metal structure that sat, silent and unlit, in the center of the hall. His eyes crinkled—his mind already working at full speed. He had just figured out how to move a new piece on the grand global chessboard. "Maybe we could…"

"Yes?" Menilmonea encouraged him.

The old mage turned to her, a daring glint in his eye. "I have an idea that, as outlandish as it may sound, could buy us valuable time. A lot of valuable time."

"I'm listening."

Azymantias swept his arm toward the giant ring.

"Let's offer them a trade."

Thank you for reading Valianara's story!

If you enjoyed this book, please don't hesitate to post your thoughts online. A few words, even a review—it doesn't have to take long but can prove tremendous in helping this book reach more readers.

Thanks in advance for your support!

And if you're interested in what happens next, or receiving digital wallpapers, please don't hesitate to subscribe to my newsletter:

https://list.deltakosh.link